consolation

CORINNE MICHAELS

Editor: Lisa Christman,
Adept Edits

Interior design and formatting: Christine Borgford
Perfectly Publishable

Cover design: Okay Creations
Cover photo © Perrywinkle Photography

To Crystal, there are few women who can endure the life you do. You're strong, beautiful, and no one's consolation prize.

I hope you never lose your sparkle.

prologue

natalie

"OH, CHLOE, IF you'd like to come out, please wait until your Daddy gets back," I insist, holding my belly as another Braxton Hicks contraction hits. I grip the dresser and try to breathe through it. It seems like they're coming more frequently.

Once it passes, I try to finish what I came in here for. Aaron is away, but I want the nursery done so we can enjoy the next few weeks once he returns. I walk around what will be her room, putting a few more of the pretty pink dresses in the drawers. Aaron and I have fought about the vast array of pink things that are now strewn around the house—he hates it, I love it.

He insisted we paint her room in camouflage. Brown, green, and black camouflage for a girl? No. I almost sent myself into labor with that argument. I got home and he and Mark were drawing it out on the walls. I launched various household items at Mark while throwing him out of the house. My husband found out shortly after how much he could suffer by my hands. I may not be a SEAL, but you don't mess with me either. In the end, I won with purple walls and the sheer netting around her white crib.

"Daddy's going to love this room, Chloe. I can't wait to see his face when he sees the pretty butterflies." Needing to take another break, I sit in the rocking chair and rub my stomach. It soothes me knowing she's in there. I can protect her—it's my job. I love being pregnant and it's a miracle we were able to conceive her. I've already told Aaron I want to try for another one as soon as she's born. I close my eyes and sink, allowing the world to fade away.

I imagine holding her in my arms, sitting here in this chair, soothing and kissing her. I picture Aaron with her asleep on his chest as she gets to hear his heartbeat. She'll own his world and have him wrapped around her finger.

Knock, knock, knock.

I hear the door, but it takes me a few seconds to get out of the chair.

KNOCK, KNOCK, KNOCK.

They bang louder this time.

"Coming!" I yell at the door. Jeez, give me a second.

Waddling to the door takes me a minute since I'm the size of a whale.

I open the door and see Mark Dixon, Aaron's boss and close friend. He works at Cole Security Forces with Aaron and served with him for years. His head is hanging low and when he looks up, his eyes are full of sorrow.

"What's wrong?"

"Lee," he chokes on the one syllable of my name. The one Aaron uses. Something is definitely not right.

"What happened?" I ask again as I begin to shake.

Tears fill his eyes and I know. I know my life is never going to be the same. I know everything I've ever feared is about to come true because Mark doesn't cry. Mark wouldn't be at my door if something weren't really, really wrong. "It's Aaron."

My heart stops beating and the world I live in ceases to exist. "Don't," I beg with tears blurring my vision and my breath accelerating.

This can't be happening.

"Please, don't, Mark. Please," I beg him again, because once he says it . . . but I know it's futile. It doesn't matter because he can't stop it. It's already happened.

"Natalie, I'm so sorry."

The dreaded words that every military wife fears. Only I wasn't supposed to have to worry about this anymore. We were done. We got out. I wasn't supposed to ever fear this again.

Please, God, don't take him from me. Please!

"But, I'm p-pregnant. I'm having a baby," I stammer as if that will somehow make none of this real. "He said he'd be back. He said he . . ." I trail off as it becomes difficult to breathe. My hand flies to my mouth to stifle the scream about to escape. Everything goes colorless.

"It was an IED. I'm sorry," Mark says as his eyes glimmer with unshed tears.

I fall.

But he's there, cradling me in his arms. "I'm so fucking sorry."

"No. No. No." Mark holds me as I sob clutching my stomach. "You're lying," I hiss, tearing myself out of his embrace.

"I wish I were," he says as I struggle to get up.

"It was a mistake. He's having a baby. He said it was a simple in and out!" I scream and throw my hands against his chest. "You're lying!" I scream, even knowing it's not a lie.

"I'm sorry."

"Stop saying you're sorry!" My sorrow turns to hatred. I hate him. I hate everyone in this moment. I hate Aaron and everyone who was there. I hate this house and everything in it. I hate the air that he no longer breathes. Hate consumes me. Hate smothers me. "Get out!" I yell and push against his chest. "Get the fuck out of my house! Aaron will be back in a few days and then we're going to get ready for our daughter to be born."

"Please," Mark beseeches and I refuse to look at him.

This isn't happening because Aaron's alive.

He's not dead. How dare Mark lie to me.

"He'll be back. He wouldn't leave me. He promised." Aaron wouldn't lie to me. He never does. When he left for missions, he would always say goodbye like it could be our last. But this time he kissed the tip of my nose and said, "Now don't have that baby until I get back."

"Can I call someone? Your mom?"

"No, you can't call anyone because he's not dead! Go get him, Mark! Go get my husband and bring him home." I step back pointing my finger at him. "You all promised. He promised." I clutch my stomach as a sharp pain radiates, but it's nothing compared to the agony sitting on my chest. Tears flow relentlessly as I struggle against his hold. "He promised."

"I know he did," Mark says as he holds my head against his chest.

"He lied."

My life is gone.

My heart is dead.

I'm a widow at twenty-seven.

chapter

one

~three months later ~

"AARON GILCHER WAS a man who left this Earth too soon. He was a loving husband, father to his unborn child, and friend," the priest speaks softly. "We are gathered today to say goodbye but not farewell. He will live in our hearts as long as we hold on to him." A sob escapes my chest. I can't hold it in. My stomach drops with the realization that he's gone. He's really gone and this solidifies it. The final piece of a puzzle that I was desperate to not put together.

I feel hands grasp my shoulders and squeeze. I don't need to look to know who they belong to. Jackson and Mark are at my back on either side. Protecting me when my husband no longer can. My mother grips my hand while my father holds Aarabelle. After she was born, I wanted to honor her father. I battled with the name we'd chosen versus something special. In the end, when I saw her, I knew. I wanted her to have part of her father for the rest of her life.

"Lord, please lift the hearts around us and grant them peace during this time. Help us to remember Aaron and give us a sense of calm knowing he's in your arms." He finishes the prayer and the part I've dreaded most is next.

"Lee, I'm right here," Mark whispers from behind me.

I nod because if I allow myself to speak, I know I won't be able to control the emotions threatening to escape. *Be strong, this will all be over soon.* I look down at my black dress and try to focus on anything but this. I tuck the long, blonde strands of hair that fall around my face back behind my ear. I begin to tremble and Mark's hand tightens.

The honor guard that had been standing off to the side rounds in front of me. I know the four of them. They were his friends, his brothers, and now they have to give me the last thing any wife wants to ever hold in her hands.

The emotions are shoved down deep, but I can see in his best friend's eyes how much pain he's in. Liam flew in from California to be here. He was Aaron's closest friend for the last eight years. They graduated SEAL training together. The bond forged from risking their lives was unbreakable. The news of Aaron's death rocked him and he'd vowed to be here.

Liam and Jeff pull the flag taut as I try to keep my eyes open, but I can't. I hear the slapping of the fabric being snapped tight. I inhale and focus on exhaling. The pain that emanates from my chest is unbearable. I'm being torn apart from the inside out.

I feel my mother squeeze my hand. I look up to see Aaron's former chief kneel before me. "Natalie, on behalf of the President of the United States and the Chief of Naval Operations, please accept this flag as a symbol of our appreciation for your loved one's service to this Country and a grateful Navy."

Tears fall uncontrollably as my heart falters. His hand extends and I know I need to take it. I have to . . . but I can't move my hands. I lift the one and it trembles as I nod. When he places the flag on my hand resting on my lap, I sob again. *This can't really be happening.* I mean, I've known for three months he was dead, but this . . . this flag is it. It's the finale I don't want to happen, proving this isn't a lie.

My hand drops. I look in his eyes as another tear splatters on my skin.

"I'm sorry, Natalie. Aaron was a great man."

"Thank you," I somehow manage to say.

I close my eyes and drop my head.

How is this my life? Why did this happen? How do I go on? All of these questions jolt through me and seethe, festering in my heart.

I hear the sounds of crying all around me, but none of it matters. No one can know the extreme agony I'm living right this moment. Losing the love of my life, the father of my child, eats me alive. My life was exactly as I wanted it. It tears through my body taking anything good and swallowing it whole.

Fuck life.

Fuck love and fuck everyone who told me they were sorry.

I look over at my baby sleeping in her grandfather's arms. I have Aarabelle. I have a beautiful girl who needs her mother.

The SEALs begin their ritual. I've watched and pitied wives who had to sit through it. I wasn't the one having to suffer during those moments, nevertheless here I am.

Senior Chief Wolfel moves forward and removes the trident from his chest. He steps toward the urn, where a wooden chest sits beside it. The wooden chest takes the place of a casket. There's no body to bury, just a piece of him. He was blown apart, just like me. Wolfel stands there for a moment before pressing it into the box and pounds it with his fist. The sound of the metal piercing the wood travels through my soul. It's as if it were penetrating me.

He turns to the urn and salutes.

One down, twenty more to go.

"I'm sorry for your loss, Aaron was a great man," another member of his former team says to me. I nod, unable to speak, knowing the imminent sound of another pin being pounded will breach the air in a moment. Over and over, the men approach me, offer their condolences, and then continue their ritual with their tridents.

I can't do this.

I start to shift, but Mark's hands hold tight. Before I can think, Liam steps forward. His crystal blue eyes are bloodshot as he tries to hold it together. It's obvious he's shaken. The bond between Aaron and Liam was unbreakable. "Lee, I . . ." He stops and swallows. I place my hand on his giving him a sign that I don't need his words. I know what he's feeling. The loss is evident in his eyes.

"I know," I say softly. His head bows forward and touches my hand. I place my other hand on the back of his head and I feel him shake.

"He was my brother," Liam says as another tear falls from my cheek.

"I-I . . ." The stuttering of my words are all I can get out while he looks at me.

He takes a second and draws a deep breath, stands, and walks over to the box. Initially, Liam refused to accept Aaron's death, since there was very little to identify him. He wanted to believe he was alive somewhere, but I knew. I felt it once I came to accept it.

I glance at my daughter once more. She lies cooing

in her grandfather's arms, completely unaware that she'll never have the comfort of a father. I'm fortunate to have the man who rocked me and held me when I was in pain hold her now. If I could go back in time and ask my daddy to hold me as his little girl and tell me it'll be okay, I would. She's safe and secure, while I feel open and exposed.

Gazing at the sailor who stands before the memorial, I close my eyes and try to dispel the thoughts that assault me. I've lost him after all this time. The years of worry and dread while he was active duty I'd endured. Only to have a false sense of security descend once he left the Navy. Now look where all that comfort landed me.

Finally the last pin enters the box and I look up to see Jackson with his head hanging. The guilt he carries for sending Aaron to his death is insurmountable, but I know Aaron wouldn't have had it any other way. He wanted to die with valor and honor. If it were Jackson or Mark who'd died, he would've wished it were him. But now my daughter and I pay the price for his choices.

Glancing around, I acknowledge the others who grieve the loss of this amazing man. I look at the crowd and see the faces of his friends and family. His mother who sobs uncontrollably next to his father. She's drowning in her anguish as she buries her only son. Former sailors who served beside him and friends from Cole Security Forces sit grief-stricken over his loss.

There are a few faces I don't recognize. A pretty blonde stands to the side, wiping her eyes. A brunette, who I assume is Catherine, mourns in Jackson's arms. There are so many people, so many uniforms. It's a black sea of mourning. Aaron was a loved man, so I'm not surprised, but no one loved him more than me.

Today is the last day I will allow myself to feel sorrow,

the last day I will shed tears, because tears don't change anything. I need to harvest whatever strength I have and hold it tight. I'm a mother who has an infant that needs me to be both mom and dad.

One day, they say. One day this will stop hurting.

Lies.

This will never be okay or stop hurting.

I'll never be the same. The woman I was before died the minute the knock on the door came. I'm a shell of the woman I was. The woman who was loving, open, and full of hope is gone. Hope is a weak bitch who couldn't give two fucks about what you want. So I rely on faith. Faith that I'll make it through this and find my heart again.

chapter

two

IME PASSES. HOURS become days, days turn to weeks, months pass in a blur, and I continue to live. But am I living? I breathe, I get up and get dressed, but I'm numb. Sure I smile and throw on a happy face, but it's all an illusion. Inside I'm lost in the abyss of grief.

It's been three months since Aaron's funeral. Same shit different day. My daughter is growing and I have no one to share it with. Thankfully she's sleeping through the night, so I'm not a complete mess. Those first few months were enough to put me over the edge, but at the same time, she kept me going.

Loneliness consumes me, but I don't let anyone know.

"No, Mom. I'm fine," I huff and put the phone to my shoulder, trying to assure her for the millionth time. If it's not her, it's Mark calling to check on me.

"Lee, you're not fine. You're barely functioning. I'm getting on a plane," she chides.

That's the last thing I want. She stayed with me for a month after Aarabelle was born, and I thought I was going to lose my mind. Her nagging and forcing me out of the house was enough to make me question my decision to let her come at all.

"Jesus, I'm fine. I'm living and Dad needs you at home.

Aarabelle and I are doing great even," I lie. I stopped letting anyone know what my life is like six months ago. Apparently there's a time limit on grieving before people start talking. My friends are still concerned that I haven't really done anything. I don't go out, and I refused to go back to my old job as a reporter. I don't want to be on the air and talking to families going through tragedy. I'm going through it now.

She gives a short laugh, "Liar."

"I'm not lying." I grab the baby monitor and head out on the deck. Which is the best thing about this house. When Aaron and I found this place, I fell in love. It backs to the Chesapeake Bay and the deck is where I spend most of my day. I feel close to him here. I can feel him in the wind—which is crazy, but when I close my eyes, it's like his hands are touching me. His breath glides across my neck, pushing the hair off my face. The sun warms me and I can pretend. I can allow myself the illusion that he's here. He's just out on a mission and will be home soon. I hold on to the feeling as long as I can because it's so much better to pretend than face the fact that my husband is dead.

"Right. You're always *fine*. You're a damn zombie," she scolds.

"I got a job," I blurt, hoping it'll throw her off.

"Doing what?" she asks skeptically.

"I'm going to work for Cole Security." I can almost hear the disapproval through the phone. Too bad I don't care what she thinks.

"Oh, that sounds like a great idea and a wonderful way to start moving on."

"Glad you agree," I reply, knowing damn well she's being sarcastic.

She doesn't understand. She and my father are still happily married. I lost my happily ever after. I want to be close to him, to feel something, to still have something to share with him. Cole Security Forces is the last place Aaron was alive. It's the place he spent his days in working for Jackson. He's in that office. He's in this house. I can't move on. I can barely breathe . . . but I do. For Aarabelle. Every day I get my ass out of bed, I get dressed, and I live in what small way I can. And all I want is a tiny piece of what I once had, so I'm going where I can feel him more strongly. It's starting to fade here. I can no longer see him in the bathroom shaving, or remember what he sounded like when he laughed. I try so hard to hold on to it. I want it, but each day I lose another part of my life with him. The pain remains, but my memory of Aaron is slipping away.

"Natalie?" she questions as I wait in silence. "I think you should come for a visit. Maybe if you get away for a little, it'll help you move on."

"I am moving on!" I yell and then draw a deep breath.

"How? Have you met with the insurance people? Have you taken care of any of the paperwork you needed to?" she pesters me.

I swear she's picking a fight just to get me to lose my temper. "I am. I'm done talking." I don't have an answer for her because the reality is . . . I'm stuck. I'm living in an endless cycle. Nothing changes. Nothing happens. I refuse to clear out his drawers or closets because then he's really not coming home. Of course, I can't tell anyone this. I need him. I want him so badly, but he left me that day. He kissed my nose and then my belly and told us he'd be home in a few days. He lied.

My eyes close and I can see his face. At least I still

have that. His deep, brown eyes with tiny flecks of gold flash through my mind. The way his hair was always kept in a buzz cut. Aaron. My world.

"Natalie . . ." My mother's soft voice breaks my daydream. "Please, let your father and I come get you and Aarabelle. We'd love to spend some time with you both."

"No. I love you, Mom, but I'm doing good." I see the monitor light up and Aara's voice breaks through. "The baby is waking, I gotta go. I love you."

"When you decide you're not fine, call me. I love you, baby girl."

I press the end key and put the phone away. Sitting here for a few minutes, trying to get a grip before I get my daughter. I love her so much, but she's a clone of her father. Every time I look at her, it takes every ounce of strength I have not to cry. She gazes at me with those innocent eyes so full of love and it breaks a piece of my heart apart. Why won't she ever get the chance to hold her father's hand? Make him a cake. Tell him how much she loves him or to just know the love of a father. She deserves that. She should have both of her parents to guide her, but instead she only has me . . . a broken woman.

Each time her "uncles" come around, I hate them a little more. I hate that they can see her, hold her, touch her, but the one man who created her never will. The anger boils in my soul like a black cloud. It covers the light I'm desperate to see. Making the hope die out before it has a chance—because he's dead. He took it away when he left this Earth. I want him back and not only in my dreams. I want to roll over and feel him next to me—instead I get cold sheets and an empty bed.

"Aaaaaa." I hear my beautiful, little girl call out and I struggle to pull myself together. She makes random sounds while lying in her crib as I sit here in misery.

Stifling the emotions that burn, I gather the strength I rely on from my paltry reserves and go get my daughter. "Hi, peanut," I coo as I enter her room. Just looking at her puts my life in focus. It's amazing to me how children can completely alter your world.

Aarabelle is on her back looking at me with the love I'm desperate to hold on to. To her, the world is perfect. She doesn't know pain, and in some ways she's lucky. At least Aara didn't fall in love with her father to have him stripped from her life. The things I worry about she'll never fear because she'll never have known it.

"Aaaaa!" she squeals as I look down at her. Her dark brown hair sticks out haphazardly and her brown eyes shine with adoration. She makes me want to get through this.

"Hi, baby." She kicks her legs and her arms flail uncontrollably as I bend to scoop her up.

I hear a knock on the door as I cradle Aara in my arms. Every single time it happens, my heart clenches and my stomach turns. It's been six months since that knock happened, and it still feels like the first time. For a while, I prayed it was Aaron going to show up and tell me this was all a giant misunderstanding. I place Aarabelle in her swing and draw a deep breath.

Unhurriedly, I move to the front door trying to quell the desires I conjure without permission. It'll be Mark again . . . I tell myself and focus on breathing. It's like having a mini panic attack each time.

I answer the door and a man is there with his back to me. His arms are thick and his shoulders broad. The tight shirt clings to every ridge on his body. I take in the walnut-colored hair that's short and trimmed. He seems familiar, yet it couldn't be because he's in California. "Liam?"

Slowly he turns, easing into a wide grin. His tall, hulking body blocks the sun behind him. My face falls as seeing him brings it all back. Liam Dempsey. If having Mark and Jackson around is what I consider difficult, then Liam is going to be agony.

He removes his aviators and there's a gleam in his eyes. "Hey, Lee. I was in the neighborhood. Wanted to come say hi." His crystal blue eyes shimmer in the sun and I secure my mask firmly in place. If we're going to talk about Aaron at all, I need it. I don't feel . . . I don't hurt.

"I didn't realize California and Virginia are now neighboring states. Last I heard you were still out west?" Even I can hear the monotone in my voice. There's no way these guys don't see it. I'm not fooling anyone, but I really don't care. I pull my long, blonde hair to the side and grip the door.

I take a second to look at him. He looks bigger, taller, or maybe I haven't been around enough people. But everything about Liam looks . . . different. His frame takes up more space than I remember and he's let the scruff grow out on his face. Yet it only helps define his strong jawline. I may be grieving, but there's no way to ignore how good-looking he is.

"Can I come in?" he asks sweetly.

He's Aaron's best friend, his swim buddy, his brother through and through. Liam has been a part of our life for a long time and seeing him makes me feel Aaron's loss even more. I nudge the door open and allow him to enter. *Just focus on breathing, Natalie . . . he'll leave soon.*

"I tried to call," he says while looking around.

"Oh, I never saw it." The lie slips out. He's taken this oath to Aaron far beyond my patience. I've started ignoring his calls because he wants to talk about the past. The stories of them in the field, or worse when he wants to reminisce about my wedding. Liam also has this uncanny way of seeing too much. He knows how to read people, but especially me.

He walks over and grins, his blue eyes shimmering with amusement. "Sure you didn't. We haven't really talked much since I went back to Cali."

Because I don't want to. I bite the words back and go for a softer response. "Not much has changed." Yet everything has.

"Aarabelle has gotten big and you look great," he says as he tosses his phone and keys on the table.

"Thanks."

Liam smiles and pulls me into a hug. "I'm not worried about you dodging my calls anymore," he says, letting me go.

"Why's that?"

"I'm living here now."

What?

Crap.

chapter

three

"**D**ON'T LOOK SO happy. I was in the area and wanted to come check on you since you were *missing* my calls." Liam's eyes divert to the flag encased on the mantel. It sits there, reminding me daily how that'll be the only thing I have of him. I want to throw it against the wall. Smash it until there's nothing left and burn it. I hate that flag because I'd rather have *him*. I want Aaron, not some token for his service.

"I *am* happy. I just didn't know you were up for orders," I say as I grab Aarabelle and pull her into my arms.

His eyes stay on the mantel. "Is it really that bad?" he asks.

"No, of course not," I say, wishing I had some way to pull his attention away from the awkward conversation we're having.

Liam turns and his eyes stay fixed on Aarabelle. "She's beautiful, Lee." His hand grazes the top of her head. "I have something for her."

I draw a deep breath and cradle Aarabelle close. "Really?"

He chuckles and removes a necklace out of his pocket, "I got this for Aarabelle before you had her. When I was overseas I thought it was something a little girl should have, but . . . well, I'm never having one." His lips twitch with amusement as he lifts the gift in the air.

Stepping closer, I look at the tiny, green jewel that hangs on the end of the chain. It's small, delicate, and yet breathtaking, surrounded by diamonds. "Liam, this is too much."

"Nah, like I said, not like I'll ever have kids. I'd have to find a girl who actually might like me." Liam snickers hoarsely and looks out the window.

"Yeah, I could see where that could be difficult for you," I joke and relax a little. "Thank you though, it's beautiful."

He smiles and places his hand on Aarabelle. "So is she."

She is. She's tiny and a handful, but to me she's perfect. Everything I've ever dreamed of is wrapped up in my arms. I hold her close and nuzzle her. "Yeah, I think so too."

Liam clears his throat, bringing my attention back to him, "I saw his car is still in the drive. Have you met with the Veterans' Affairs people yet?"

I nod and try not to look at him. I've put off doing the things I know I need to do. Closing out all of Aaron's accounts, his will, selling his car, maybe even this house, but I don't want to. "I've been busy."

He steps closer and his hand grips my shoulder gently. "I can help if you need me to."

Everyone always offers to help. That's the thing I've learned the most about death. People come out of the woodwork offering a hand. They cook for you, clean your home, fix the broken shutter, but it's all superficial. No one knows what to say, so they try to *do,* but after a week or a few months, the help no longer comes. You have no choice but to face life head-on and learn that people for-get—they move on. But I haven't. I live the hell that was forced upon me day in and day out.

"I'm fine." I give a fake smile. "I have Mark and Jackson if I need them, plus I'm sure you have plenty of other things you need to worry about. You just moved and I know checking in takes a lot of time."

"I took leave, plus I like bugging you anyway."

"Really, I can handle it."

"No one is saying you can't. I'm saying you don't have to. Lean on the people around you. He was my friend and you are too, so don't be too proud." His eyes pierce mine as he locks his gaze.

What is with these men and their inability to let me be?

"Okay, fine," I concede.

"Good. Not like you had much of a choice. I'm kinda relentless."

I snort, "I remember."

An awkward silence falls between us. Thankfully, Aarabelle stirs, bringing my attention to her.

"Have you heard from Patti?" Liam asks.

"No, she's pretty much disappeared since Aaron's death." My mother-in-law understandably didn't take the news well. She's cut off contact with all of us. She refuses to see Aarabelle and wants absolutely no part in my life. She claims if I loved him, I wouldn't have let him go. I would've demanded he stay. If she knew her son at all, she'd know that wouldn't have worked.

Liam takes a step toward the mantel and his hand reaches out to the flag. He stands there staring at my mini memorial. Aaron's photos line the shelf. His boot camp photo, our wedding, and one of the two of them all sit next to the flag. His trident sits in front. Liam's hands brace the stone wall and his head falls. I watch him as his fingers tighten and turn white from clutching the ledge. It's as if he's forgotten I'm here. Tears threaten to fill my eyes as I watch his closest friend silently mourn. It's a moment where I can almost feel the pain radiating off of him. I turn my back and give him some privacy.

"People handle shit differently I guess," Liam mutters quietly.

I turn back around as he grips his neck. "How are you handling it?" I question.

He turns and shakes his head. "I've called his number a few times. I was drunk, and I don't know, it was just instinct to call and tell him something stupid. The first time it went to his voicemail and . . ." Liam's eyes snap back to mine as he catches himself. "What about you?"

My façade shifts into place as I repeat the speech I've given so many times. "I'm living. It's hard, but I'm handling it."

Liam knows me. He's also an interrogator for the SEALs. He's one of the best, and for some reason I forgot who I was lying to. "Really?" he asks unbelieving.

His large frame moves forward as he assesses my reactions. I try to remember all the things Aaron practiced on me. How he would make me stand my ground, not shift or move my eyes, but Liam is a different ball game. "Yes," I say confidently.

"You know who I am, right?" His calloused hand grazes my wrist and my heart rate accelerates. I'm not afraid of him, but he's the first man to touch me intimately since Aaron's death. Even though we're just friends, my chest tightens. "You're lying to me," Liam says in his deep voice.

I suppress a shiver and try not to look into his eyes. I

don't want him to see what I'm hiding deep inside. He can read me, he's trained to see through my layers of bullshit, and I need to keep myself shielded from him.

"Natalie." He lifts my chin, but I keep my eyes closed. "You can tell me. I can't imagine if it were *you* that *he* lost that he'd be fine. He'd be a fucking mess, a lunatic with broken furniture all over the house. So you don't have to be okay. You can be angry or whatever else."

His words seep through my soul and I open my eyes. "I don't get to be whatever else. I have Aarabelle," I say as I look at the baby in my arms. "I have to be fine." The steel wall I hide behind is strong and solid. I'm safe there.

"That's not true. You're going to keep bottling this shit up and then explode."

I grit my teeth and let out a deep breath through my nose. "What's your deployment schedule look like? Will you be around?" There's no doubt in my mind he knows I'm diverting. I want out of this conversation.

"You know I can't tell you that, but I'm here for you. I'm going to do a few things and then we can figure out what else has to be done."

"I really don't need the help," I say even though I don't know what I need anymore. Aarabelle stirs and I rock her gently.

"Okay, well, I need to do something for the next month I'm on leave, so you're helping me."

"Now who's the liar?" I ask.

Liam rolls his sleeves and winks. "I never lie."

I laugh an honest laugh for the first time. He's lying about lying. Aarabelle begins to fuss, and as much as I want to argue with him, she needs to eat.

"Which SEAL team are you with?"

Please don't say four.

I don't know why it matters. The way he lets out a hesitant sigh, I brace for it. "Four," he steps closer and puts his hand on my shoulder. "He should be with me."

"No, he should be with *me*."

"Yeah, he should," Liam says and the sadness is apparent in his eyes.

This hurts us both. Liam and Aaron were brothers. If one died, they both died. Aaron once spoke of the brotherhood they shared in comparison with that of Jackson and Mark. While they were all close, he and Liam were almost blood thick. They carried each other through BUDs training, and when Liam's sister died, Aaron was by his side the entire time.

"I'm sorry, Demps," I say as I shift Aarabelle in my arms.

"Why the fuck are you sorry?" he asks, sounding affronted.

"You two were close. I know this isn't easy for you."

Liam pinches the bridge of his nose. "Is this what you do?"

My jaw falls slack as I try to figure out what he's asking me.

"You pretend." Liam's eyes soften as he studies me.

"I don't know what you all want," I say, exasperated. He smiles and I want to slap him. What the hell is he smiling about?

"Finally some emotion. I'll see you soon. I've got work to do around here."

"You're an ass."

"Yup. Go take care of Aarabelle. I've got the other shit." Liam kisses my cheek and then the top of Aara's head and leaves.

I stand here knowing I'm not going to get rid of him.

He's noble, honest, and when Liam made a vow to Aaron, he meant it. He will be here for me in whatever way I need.

Liam Dempsey is going to be my demise.

chapter

four

"*H*ELLO?" I HEAR my best friend, Reanell, call out from the kitchen.

"In here, Rea."

"There you are. I brought over a few meals the wives made this week. I put them in the freezer." Her generous heart causes a warm glow to flow through me. She's been my rock these last few months. Stopping over, bringing food, watching Aarabelle so I can nap.

"Thanks, but I'm doing good. I promise."

This used to be me. I was the one who headed the relief groups. Made sure that the wives of fallen SEALs had food, help, and friends. Funny how life works—now I'm the wife I used to pity.

"Never said you weren't. Now gimme that baby," she says with her hands extended as she takes Aara from me. "Hello, princess," Reanell coos and snuggles Aarabelle. She's impossible not to love. "So?" she questions me.

"So?"

"Who was the guy outside messing with Aaron's car?"

My eyes widen and I rush over to the window. "What?" I ask, pulling back the blinds. "Who the hell would be messing with the car? There's no one there. Why didn't you call the cops?" I look down the driveway, but I don't see anyone.

"He smiled and waved at me, so I didn't think much of it. Plus, he had the telltale signs, so I assumed maybe you were finally accepting some help," she remarks.

"What signs?"

She sighs and lifts Aara up and down, "G-shock watch, tribal tats, and the whole I'm-so-amazing-just-ask-me vibe. Typical SEAL."

"I'm going to check it out. Can you watch her?"

"Stupid question."

I open the door and stop short.

"Hey," Liam is standing there covered in grease.

"Hey, yourself." I clutch my chest and try to slow my racing heart.

He wipes his hand on the rag he's holding. "Sorry, I didn't mean to scare you. I knocked earlier but you didn't answer."

"I must've been with Aara. What are you doing?" I question.

Looking down at his clothes then back up, he raises his brow. "I've got his car running again."

"I see that. I mean, why are you working on his car?"

"I'm helping."

Letting out a deep breath, I count backwards from ten. I can do this. I need to sell his things and start putting my life in order. "Okay, I thought maybe I'd have a few days, but . . ."

"My leave is up in four weeks, I figured I'd get started right away."

Makes sense, but there's no part of me that's ready for this. In my head I know this is the right thing to do, get it over with. Start to move on, but it makes my new reality so final. But death is final, so why am I trying to fight it all?

"You're right. It's fine."

Liam takes a step closer and the look in his eyes sends a shiver down my spine. "One day that word is going to leave your vocabulary and you're going to realize lying to me is pointless."

Now I know why he's so damn good at his job.

"Yeah, okay." Trying to brush him off, I smile and tuck my hair behind my ear. He turns without another word and heads back to the driveway.

"Well, that was intense." I jump at the sound of Reanell behind me. I forgot she was here and always lurking.

I turn and see her with Aarabelle asleep in her arms. "He was Aaron's friend. He's stationed with SEAL Team Four and is helping around the house—apparently."

"He can help me when he's done here," she says as she looks out the window.

"I doubt your husband would approve," I chide and flop on the couch.

She laughs and sits in the rocking chair. "Mason isn't the jealous type," she jokes. Her husband is the commander of Team Four. Reanell might joke, but she would never do anything. However, she loves to irritate him and rile him up. "What team did you say he was with?"

I pull my legs up and giggle, "Four."

"Fuck."

"Dumbass," I reply laughing. Huh. I laughed again.

"Well, well. It seems someone is helping in more ways than one," Reanell marvels and then looks away.

"Why?"

"Because you're laughing."

"I laughed before," I retort.

"No, you fake laughed. This is the first laugh that didn't look like it physically hurt you. Sure, you've put on a great show. But I think this Liam guy is a miracle worker," she murmurs and walks out the room.

Maybe he is. Or maybe he's the first person to not put up with my shit.

chapter

five

"DO YOU HAVE any questions, Mrs. Gilcher?" Mr. Popa asks. He's the liaison sent by our insurance company who plans to guide me through the paperwork.

"I'm not sure," I mumble. In all honesty, I haven't heard a word that he's said.

"If she has any questions is there a number where she can reach you?" Liam asks from beside me.

He's been here almost every day, making sure I go through one more thing on my list. Hell, he even made the list. I don't look at it though. I get up and make sure everyone is fed. I can't worry about all this other crap because it doesn't matter. Well, I guess this part does. I'm not working yet and have no income coming in. I need to take care of everything, but I keep worrying about functioning. Then Liam comes in and makes me handle it all.

"Sure, here's my card. Mrs. Gilcher, once we get the forms signed, the sooner we can get the money moved over. It's imperative we get this process started. A lot of time has already lapsed." He hands me the card.

"Thank you, Mr. Popa. We'll be in touch." Liam shakes his hand and walks him to the door.

I feel him sit beside me and he pulls me against him. I take the comfort he offers and lean into him. "This will get easier, right?" I ask.

Of course no one knows. Even the wives who lost their husbands tell me it does and yet it doesn't. Amy lost her husband last year in a firefight and she said every day she wonders how she gets up and breathes. Jillian said the only way she finally felt human again was when she got rid of almost anything Parker touched, but I can't do that. Making it like he never existed wouldn't make my pain go away. But handling all the death paperwork and dealing with putting him to rest . . . this is what hurts.

"I'm not sure," Liam replies honestly. Thank God for that. He never lies to me or tells me what I want to hear. He gives it to me straight and yet is never hurtful. These last two weeks I've come to rely on him more than I ever thought possible. His friendship means the world to me.

"Yeah, me either."

"Why don't we get Aarabelle and go do something?" he suggests.

I gaze into his blue eyes and see the excitement. He's been here every day for the last two weeks and has done nothing but care for me in some form or another. Here is this single, very good-looking man who has put his life on hold for his best friend's widow.

"You don't have to babysit me. I'll be fine."

His mouth falls slightly slack. "Am I bothering you?"

"No!" I exclaim. "You're a single guy. You don't need to be spending your time with me."

"Shut up. You're loads of fun. I mean, where else could I get to meet a woman who's not trying to get in my pants?"

I burst out giggling. "Happens often, huh?"

Liam tilts in conspiratorially, "Well, I don't mean to brag, but I've been known to break a few hearts . . . and beds."

"Breaking beds because you're a fat ass doesn't count."

His face falls and he looks genuinely affronted. Next thing I know, he tears his shirt off and every ridge and ripple in his skin is on display. I've known him for years, seen him in a bathing suit more times than I can count, but there's something different in this moment, but I'll never let him know.

"Fat? Show me!" he challenges me.

I stand and poke his side. "What, you don't giggle like the doughboy when I poke you?"

Liam laughs, "I don't think you should joke about poking, Lee." He smiles and grabs his shirt.

"Why do you make everything dirty?"

"Because I'm a guy," Liam says like it should be obvious. "I'm going to go for a run and a couple hundred push-ups since you think I'm fat."

"Ohhh, don't cry . . . it happens to everyone when they hit that age," I joke and it feels foreign. I've forgotten this part of myself. I find myself laughing more and more, reminding me of the person I used to be.

Liam turns and eyes me cautiously. "Let's pretend you didn't call me old and fat in the same minute."

"Pretend away . . ." I trail off and saunter into the kitchen. Before I reach the door, I glance over my shoulder to see his reaction. He stands there stunned with his mouth agape. I grin and proceed forward, leaving him there.

"I'll show you fat," I hear him say under his breath as the door swings closed.

I stare at the countertops across the kitchen. The trace of a smile lingers on my lips when a part of me starts to hurt. The part that thinks it's too early to feel okay again.

Shouldn't I hurt and be sad? It's only been six months. Then there's the other side of me that says *It's been six months already . . . live.* Aaron wouldn't want me to be alone. He wouldn't want me to be sad all the time.

"You got any coffee?" Liam asks as he yawns, walking into the kitchen.

"Do you know who you're asking?" I say laughing. I get the things out and pour him a cup. "I'm a single mom. Coffee is my drug of choice."

"Thanks." He lifts the cup and practically chugs it. "I'm gonna head out and work on the car again. There are still a few things I need to fix before it'll sell."

Liam inclines back, not breaking his gaze. I look at him, really take a second to look. His eyes always have a gleam to them . . . a little sexy and a little mischief brew behind them. The three-day-old beard he always wears makes him appear rugged and tough. Of course his body screams danger, but he's not overly in your face about it. He knows he's sexy, but he's relaxed.

"Okay, I'm gonna take a walk down to the beach while she's still asleep." I walk over and place my hand on his shoulder and grab the baby monitor. "Thank you, Liam. I appreciate everything."

His hand covers mine. "Anything you need, I'm here." He pats my hand and I walk away with a soft smile, thinking about how it feels having him around.

I put away the coffee mug sitting on the counter. Opening the cabinet, I see Aaron's favorite cup. The one I gave him on our last anniversary, it says: No one loves you like me. The past hits me full force.

"Aaron, stop!" I giggle as he grabs my waist and throws me down in the sand in front of our house.

"Say 'uncle'." He tickles me as I squirm beneath him.

I giggle and try to get out from under him, even though I know it'll never happen. "If you love me, you'll stop."

Immediately his hands leave my sides and he places them beside my head. "No one will ever love you as much as I do."

My hand glides up his arm and I press it against his cheek. "No woman will ever love you as much as I do."

"No woman will ever get close."

"Better not."

He rolls to the side and pulls me against his chest. I rest here and relax into his embrace. "Do you ever think about what you'd do if I was gone?"

His question startles me. "Sometimes." It's been three years of him being in the teams and I'd be lying if I told him I didn't think about it. He's deployed almost every six months, and each time, they get harder and harder. I want my husband, but I understand his duty. It's difficult to love someone and know they might not come home, but the idea of not loving him is unimaginable. I was built for this life—not every woman can be a military wife, but even fewer can handle being a SEAL wife. You have to love deeper, stand stronger, but know that at any moment bonds can break. We fight like everyone else, but Aaron and I want this. We've seen so many friends go through infidelity and divorce, but we keep our love on course. He leaves in three days and I'm soaking up as much time with him as I can.

"I'd want you to love again, Lee," Aaron says as he kisses the top of my head. "Promise me that if something happens to me you'll find someone else."

I don't want to promise. I don't even want to think of the possibility, so I stay quiet.

Aaron bristles and forces me to sit up. Turning to look at him I see his eyes harden. He's not going to back down. "Promise me."

"Nothing's going to happen, so my promise isn't needed. Besides would you really want someone else sleeping in our bed? I don't."

"I need to know you'll be loved. I need to know if I'm gone, you'll have someone to protect you."

His words both warm me and infuriate me. "I don't need protection."

"Natalie," he says tenderly. "I know you're strong, babe. I know you don't need to be protected, but I need this. I need to know you'll find someone to be there."

"I really don't want to talk about this."

He pulls me back across his chest. "I know, but I don't want to leave without it."

"Then don't leave."

The laugh escapes his chest as we both know it's funny because it's not his choice and he surely would never skip out.

"Fine," I say reluctantly. "I promise." Hoping it's the one promise I can break.

A tear falls and the need to leave this house makes it impossible to breathe. I rush out of my chair and head out onto the deck. I wish I could forget it all. He would talk about valor and courage, he would tell me how he always hoped when he died it would be for something. It feels like it was all for nothing.

I start to walk down the beach as the water rushes up and covers my toes. The wind blows and I close my eyes and feel it wash over me. I stand in the wake of the waves and try to feel him.

"Aaron, I miss you," I whisper into the wind. "I hate

that you left me. I wish you could see what each day is like for me. Our daughter is growing so big. I need you. She needs you." More tears fall upon my cheek as I pray to my husband. "You made me make these promises. Promises I can't keep."

"Hey," a deep, thick voice calls gently from behind me. "Lee . . . you okay?"

I turn and Liam steps closer. "Yeah, I'm fine," I reply as I wipe under my eyes.

He walks closer, blocking the sun behind him. "I saw you run out and then you didn't answer me when I called out to you."

My guard is down and I'm vulnerable. I know he can see it all. "I'm fi—"

"Don't say 'fine.' You're not fine. You're crying and you've never been a liar so don't be one now. Come here," he says as he steps forward with arms open.

I walk toward him and slam into his chest as his arms wrap around me like a vise. The mix of emotions comes crashing around me and I sob in his arms. "Why did he have to go? Why couldn't he just stay home? I hate this. I'm so alone. I want him home," I cry out as my fingers grip his shirt and hold on. "I need him so much! I miss him so much it hurts to breathe!" I pull Liam close as I lose it. "God! It's not fair!"

"No, it's not," he says as he rubs his hand up and down my back.

"But he left and now I live every day wishing he didn't get on that damn plane. He was out! He wasn't supposed to die!" My legs start to crumble but Liam keeps me up.

"You're so strong, Lee." I look up and his eyes say so much. "Don't downplay how hard this is."

His words envelope me and I know it's true. I'm

strong, but there are parts of me that aren't. I never want to know pain like this again. I've built a fortress around myself because I have to protect my daughter and myself. I realize where I am, in his arms, crying in the ocean. "I'm a mess. I'm so sorry."

"Natalie, goddammit, stop saying you're fucking sorry. Have you cried at all since he died? Have you let yourself grieve at all?"

I step back and he grabs my wrist. My eyes stay downcast as I try to muster any strength I have left. "Yes, I grieved." I glance at him and draw in a deep cleansing breath. "What good does crying do? He's dead. He won't ever come home. I have a daughter, a house, a mortgage, and a shit ton of other things to worry about." The words rush out uncontrollably. "You get to go on your missions and escape the hell that slaps me in the face every day. I'm alone, Liam. He left and all I have is a folded up flag and a lifetime of heartache. So, yeah, I grieve."

Liam releases my arms and steps out of the waves. "You think missions are an escape? We all remember the men we've lost when we go out there. We look around and know the plane could be one body less. That it actually *is* a body less. I know the chances and I live for this. I hate that you have a flag on your mantel and would give anything to trade places with him. What the fuck do I leave behind?"

I take a step toward him and close my eyes. I know how they all feel about each other. They trust each other more than a husband and wife. To Aaron, his teammates were whether he lived or died. So many nights we spent talking about how he would take a bullet for any of them. I remember being so angry and yelling about how stupid he was. How he was willing to die for one of them and how that would affect me. He would kiss me and tell me it was the way it was.

"I think Aaron would've wanted it this way."

Liam looks up and our eyes lock. I see the man he is. The man who would've taken his place but can't, so he's here—for me. Every day, Liam is here. He helps me, makes me laugh and smile. Cares for us.

"He would've what?" he asks confused. His hands clench, and I step forward and give him some of the comfort he's given me.

"Wanted to die like this. To feel like it was for something or someone. If Mark or Jackson would've gone on that mission, he would've hated himself. Wishing he could've taken their place. He always wanted to go down in a blaze of glory. To die for a reason. I don't know what the damn reason is though."

"Me either. I would've gladly changed places with him. He had you and Aarabelle to live for." Liam's hand grabs mine and he pulls me close. "Are you gonna be okay?"

I do have Aarabelle and I have my entire life ahead of me. I deserve to be happy and it's time I started to live like it.

I look up and give a tiny nod, "I think I will be."

"I think you will too."

chapter

six

"KNOCK, KNOCK," I hear Reanell call as she opens my door.

"What's up, my love?" I ask, my voice radiating with delight.

"You're awful perky this morning," she looks at me skeptically.

I'm starting a new outlook from this day forward. I can continue to be sad and mopey or I can remember Aaron as the man he was. The husband, sailor, and hero, not the martyr I've made him. I go back to work in a few weeks, I have a great support system. It's time to start taking baby steps.

"Well, who wouldn't smile at your beautiful face?" I ask sweetly.

"Could it be the sex-on-a-stick outside shirtless fixing the shed?" She looks out the window as she moans. "God, men like him aren't real. They're sent to toy with us."

Looking behind her, I suppress a groan. She'll take that as something it's not. But seriously, holy shit. His back is taut and the muscles ripple as he lifts the two-by-four and then nails it into place. His arms flex and I gawk. He wipes his brow as the sweat trickles down his face and I fight the urge to keep looking. I turn my head but my eyes stay glued to him.

Reanell clears her throat and stares at me with her brow raised. "Well, well, well. What do we have here?"

"Nothing. What?" I pretend to sound confused at what she saw.

"Right. Nothing at all."

"Nope. Nothing to see here."

She looks back out the window. "There's plenty to see my friend. Plenty indeed."

I need to flip the attention. "Did anyone ever tell you you're a horny housewife who needs a job?"

"A few times. Mason appreciates that I can shop without buying."

I laugh and slap her arm. "Yeah, it's about the only thing you don't buy."

She looks away and snorts. "Accurate. I'm also not buying your diversion. I saw you eating him alive."

"No, I'm not even ready to go there. Let's change the subject, okay?"

"No, not until you admit he's hot."

"Why does it matter if I think he's hot?" I scoff.

Rea smiles and puts her hands on her hips. "Admit it."

"Fine, I won't deny it. He's hot."

"I knew you thought so," she smirks.

I roll my eyes and smother the desire to choke her.

"Besides, if you did deny it, I would be worried," she laughs. "How about while Aarabelle's sleeping, we can do some stuff around here?"

I look at the mantel and my heart falters. I can feel him everywhere and I'm not ready to lose that. Already I've lost so much. Just pulling into my drive without his car there will be one more reminder. Loss and anger are at war in me. I'm mad at everyone and everything, but then I have to go on day by day. I don't get to sulk and be sad because there's a tiny baby that we made together. I close my eyes and think of him.

"Sure," the word falls out.

We spend the next few hours cleaning papers and things around the house. I'm sweating and huffing from carrying all the boxes up and down the stairs. It's been a long day and I look like hell but feel a little lighter. We've got things organized, and as much as I want to stop, I also want to keep going. I worry the strength I've harnessed will be lost tomorrow.

Before I can tell Rea my plan to keep on, she looks over and frowns. "I need to get home. Mason wants dinner early and I want a new purse."

She's a mess. "How do those go hand in hand?"

"He likes to eat. I like Michael Kors. If I don't get a bag, he can starve," she winks and grabs her purse.

"Sounds perfectly reasonable," I reply with a huff. "I'm going to finish up. Thank you for today."

Reanell kisses my cheek. "I'm proud of you. I know this isn't easy, but it was time."

"Thanks, you know that it's been seven months today?"

"Since he died?"

"Yeah, crazy, right? Aarabelle is so small to me that I forget."

Reanell sits on the couch with her purse in her arms. "I think we all do. You were pregnant when he died and then Aara kind of shifted time. It's a good thing though. She's given you a way to keep moving."

"Maybe."

"And Liam being around making you do stuff helps

too, no?"

I think about what she says and try to come up with an argument. But it's true. Liam has forced me to handle everything in the last few weeks. In a short amount of time he's taken care of months' worth of things.

"He's helped a lot."

"I better bounce, but I'm glad you're doing well. You look better too."

"Thanks, I think."

"Don't do anything I wouldn't do," she winks.

I nod and she leaves. Aarabelle is taking her afternoon nap in her playpen. She ate and played for a little and now I have about an hour before she'll need to eat again. I decide to hang the curtains in the living room that have been sitting in the closet for months.

Getting all my tools out, I grab the ladder and mark the spots where the new rod will go. I can do this. Take that, Martha Stewart. Once everything is up, I get the screw and it won't go in. I try again and the screw falls and I fumble with the drill. "Damn it," I curse as it falls to the floor. Grabbing the drill, I hear a laugh behind me. "Am I amusing you, Dreamboat?" I ask as I try to align the screw. I know using his call sign pisses him off . . . which is why I said it. Aaron used to lose his shit when I called him Papa Smurf.

"I think you want to wound me."

"Never. I'm just . . ." I struggle with the stupid screw that refuses to go in. "Stupid damn drill is broken!"

"You have it set to reverse," Liam says chuckling and he climbs the ladder behind me.

"Get down!" I yell as his weight makes the ladder tilt a little.

"Push that button there," he says against my neck.

"You're not going to fall. I'll be the one who breaks their neck."

I suppress a shiver as he lifts my hand and pushes the back of the drill. "Fine, maybe I'll elbow you," I joke to try to keep my mind off how his body is pressed against mine. The body that I stared and marveled at. *He's only helping, Natalie.*

"I'll take you with me. Now, push hard and screw."

I lose my grip on the drill. "That sounded so bad!" My head falls forward and we both laugh hysterically. "Oh," I say as my stomach hurts.

"You made it dirty!"

"You told me to push hard and screw," and I start laughing again.

Liam rests against me and we both try to control our breathing. "Okay," he breathes again. "Now, make sure it's aligned in the hole."

"Oh, God. Get down. I can't do this." I giggle and snort.

"You snorted!" he says as he grips my hips and helps me off the ladder.

"You made me," I reply incredulously.

"Well, put it in the hole and screw."

"Stop!" I hold on to the ladder as tears fall from laughing so hard.

Liam keeps going. "If you don't know how to put it in, I can help."

We both laugh and I hear Aarabelle cry.

"Now you've done it," my voice is full of humor.

Liam grabs the drill, "You get Aara, I'll make sure you don't have to re-plaster the walls."

I clutch my chest and reply dramatically, "Oh, my hero."

He gives a mock salute with the drill and I leave him to his power tools. Maybe he really is a miracle worker.

After a little while, Liam has all the curtains hung and a few pictures I found during my cleaning. Aarabelle plays happily in her swing.

"A little to the left," I instruct Liam as he tries to align the photo.

"Here?"

"Ummm, maybe to the right? But just a smidge." I laugh to myself as his head drops, clearly frustrated.

"Lee, I'm going to nail this to the ground if you make me move it again," Liam grumbles as he moves it back to where it was originally.

I take a step back and try to keep from laughing because this is actually fun. "You know," I muse. "I think maybe I should put it in the hall." I bite my lip to keep from busting out.

He groans and puts the photo down. I hear him take a few deep breaths. When he turns, I bat my eyes innocently. "I'm going to let this sit here for a minute."

"Oh, but I want to hang it." I giggle and Liam bursts out with a loud guffaw.

"You're a giant pain in the ass."

"Yeah, but where else would you go for abuse?" I simper and shrug.

"Work."

"True. I mean, they probably won't call you fat or old . . . yeah, right, they totally will," I tease, reminding him of our previous discussion.

"Take it back."

I raise my brow. "Never."

"Do you really want to brawl?"

"You'll lose. I was trained."

He breaks out into a run straight for me and I sprint toward the kitchen laughing. He's going to kill me, but I can't back down. I lean against the door hoping I can keep him from coming in.

"Why are you running, oh trained one?" he asks from the other side of the kitchen door.

Shit. I'm trapped.

chapter

seven

"LIAM, I WANT to remind you that I'm in possession of many sharp objects here in the kitchen."

I hear him snicker once. "You forget, I'm trained in knife fighting."

"Ugh. Okay, can I just say uncle?"

"Maybe," he says but then nothing else.

After a few seconds of silence, I try to ask again, "Liam? Uncle."

No response. I wonder where the hell he went. I hear Aarabelle over the baby monitor and know I can't stay here forever. "Liam?" Again, no response. I have two choices. I can try to keep myself blockaded in here or I can grow some lady balls and face him. I can do this. I've given birth naturally, buried a husband, and still manage to function. Screw him.

Slowly I creep the door open and he's not there. Well, that wasn't what I was expecting. I take a step into the hallway and look around. These guys are stealthy and Aaron used to love to scare the crap out of me when I wasn't expecting it. He'd hide behind doors and in closets then jump out so I'd scream.

"Liam?" I ask, trying to sneak toward the living room. When I turn, I see him holding Aarabelle with a sly smile.

"Saved by the baby."

"I wasn't scared," I say confidently.

"Liar. But I'll let you have it."

I laugh and extend my arms. Liam hands me Aarabelle and I pull her close.

"I like that sound," he says almost as an afterthought.

"Huh?"

Liam steps forward and brushes my hair back. "Your laugh. It took a while to get it to come back more."

My jaw falls and I stare into his eyes. He's brought me back . . . almost. Given me back my smile and I hadn't even known it. Liam's been here and managed to help the old me come out. "I . . ." I trail off unsure of what to say.

"I gotta get going, but I wanted to give you this. I found something in Aaron's glove box."

"What?"

Liam pulls an envelope out of his back pocket and his eyes tell me what it is. The *If you're reading this* letter. When I didn't receive one after he died, I assumed he shredded it when he got out of the Navy. Considering it's usually left with your closest friend, and neither Mark nor Jackson had given it to me, I presumed. Then with Liam being around, I thought for sure Aaron threw it out, not thinking we'd need it. But here it is.

I extend my hand and take it.

"Was there anything else?"

The one thing I wanted was our wedding ring. After the explosion, no personal belongings were sent back. Maybe he left it too?

Liam looks at the other letters in his hand, and I hate the pain I see. "A letter for Jackson, Mark, and one for me were in there as well."

"I don't know if I can read this," I reply honestly.

"You'll read it when you're ready. I've got some things I need to get done," Liam says and grabs his coat. He kisses the top of my head.

I nod and gaze at the letter in my hand. I want to read it, but I can't right now. Not with Aarabelle awake. I have no idea how I'm going to handle this. I place it on the table and decide I'll read it later.

The night passes and I get Aarabelle to bed. I'm exhausted and worn as I flop on the couch and turn on the fireplace. The letter sits there and the need to read his words is too much to fight. I miss him and maybe this will help me feel close again.

My throat is dry as my finger tears through the seal. My heart beats rapidly in my ears as dread begins to claw its way through my body. Can I read my husband's final message? Inhaling through my nose, I count backwards as my hands shake.

The wind blows and I know he's here with me.

Biting my lip, I think about Aaron and what he'd say to me right now. He'd tell me to "man up" and read it. I smile to myself as I hear his voice in my head. Tears blur my vision, but I wipe them away and read my husband's last words to me.

Lee,

If you're reading this, I'm no longer here. I've broken my promise to come home to you, even though it was a promise I knew I couldn't really make. Know that I didn't go willingly. I wanted a life with you—forever. There's not a single part of me that ever wanted you to read this. First, because I'm not good at this crap. Second, because I've failed you on some level. I always told you I am a SEAL—the best, elite, and untouchable. I believe that.

There's a reason why we're trained like we are—we do the shit that no one else could. So, somehow I fucked up. I got in a situation and my training failed. I'm sorry.

My life was never the same after we met in Ms. Cook's class. You sat next to me and I knew I was a goner. Then I saw you before the homecoming game and you had that damn skirt on. I almost fucked up the game thinking about how to get you to go on a date with me. After weeks of telling you how awesome I am, you finally caved. I felt like I'd won the lottery. You were the best prize. Hell, you are the best prize. We went to that awful restaurant but you smiled the whole time. When I walked you to the door and you kissed me before I could have done some stupid awkward shit, I knew one day I'd marry you. I knew you'd be the woman I'd spend every night next to. Because you're my fucking world, Lee. You're the sun, the stars, and the everything in between.

Everyone says in these letters we give these great speeches about random things. I've probably rewritten this damn thing twelve times. I can only tell you this: I love you. I've always loved you and I'll love you far past my death.

I can't tell you what to do because, well, I'm gone and you wouldn't listen anyway. But, you made promises. You deserve to have the life you wanted . . . one with a man who loves you more than his own life. A man who will give you a family and the love that you need. If we have kids, I hope you give them a father. They'll need that. Someone to teach them to throw a ball, how to ask a girl out, how to keep the stupid boys who only want one thing away. If we have a girl she's never allowed to date . . . ever. Make sure that no boy puts his dipstick anywhere near my daughter. Tell them about us. Tell them about how much I would've loved them. If they ask why, tell them I was protecting them. I'm not a proud man, but I'm proud of the life we've had. You've stood by me, pushed me, and made me a better man.

I've made mistakes in my life, but you were the best thing that ever happened to me. You loved me when I probably didn't deserve it. Know that when I close my eyes at night I always see you. And when I draw my last breath at the end, it'll be your name I say last. Without you, there would be no me.

Love me when I'm gone.

Aaron

The tears fall and I clutch the letter to my chest. "I'll love you forever," I whisper and hope somewhere, somehow, he hears me.

CHAPTER EIGHT

LIAM

"**F**UCK!" I YELL out and punch the tree. My knuckles scream out in pain.

I pick up my pace and start to run again. I need to work out and be ready for the team. I can't be sitting around and then not be in peak physical condition, but every damn day I'm at her house. I can't stay away or stop myself from checking on her. It's like a drug. So I run . . . I run and try to stop my mind from drifting to her and Aarabelle. I think about the way she laughs, how her smile lights up the room, and how much I like being the one to put it there. This shit needs to stop.

The music blares in my ears as I sprint. I count and breathe, focusing only on that. I can't think about her blonde hair. I won't worry about whether she's read the letter. I refuse to worry about whether she remembered to call the mortgage company. Because I'm not her fucking anything. I'm the dickhead who won't leave her alone because of a promise. At least that's what I keep telling myself. I'm nothing to her and I can never be. I shouldn't even be thinking about this.

I run faster and stop to do some push-ups. I'll show

her fat and old.

My phone rings and it's a California number.

"Hello?"

"Dreamboat, it's Jackson."

"Hey, Muffin. What's up?" I ask as I try to catch my breath. I've met Jackson Cole a bunch of times. Aaron worked for him when he left the Navy and our teams were both deployed together at the same time to Africa. We weren't really close but drank together a few times.

"Not much. Wanted to check on Natalie and see if she needs anything."

Natalie told me about how he took Aaron's death hard. He felt like he was responsible. He got himself shot when he went over to investigate and bring Aaron's remains home. Not that there were many remains left. "She's putting on a good show. She's stubborn as all hell but finally taking care of some things."

He sighs and I wonder what he was expecting. It's only been about seven months since he died. No one would be ready for much more than she is.

"She starts working for me this week. I wanted to make sure everything is okay."

I forgot about that. Shit. "Yeah, I'm sure she'll be good. My leave is over this week and who knows what the deployment schedule is like."

"Ahhh, I heard. Four, huh?"

"Yeah, man." I lean against the tree since this is going to be another few minutes. "How's Cali?"

He laughs and pauses, "I'm adjusting."

"She worth it?"

"You have no idea."

"Thank God," I say. This is no life for a woman. The home-again-then-gone-again life. How the hell any of these guys are dumb enough to marry someone I'll never know. It's unfair and I don't need anyone clouding my judgment when I'm on a mission.

Jackson laughs as if he knows something I don't. "One day. One day everything you thought, you'll forget—for her."

My mind flashes to Natalie and Aarabelle. The grin comes without any thought. Fuck. I'm not supposed to feel anything for her. Goddammit. This isn't allowed.

"Or not."

I push it down because I'm sure it's not anything.

"One day," Jackson repeats.

It's because I'm spending so much time there. Helping her hang pictures, mowing the lawn, and taking care of the things that need to be done. Yeah. That's it. Nothing more. I'll lock that shit down before it becomes anything else because she's my friend. She's my best friend's wife.

"One day. I gotta run. Literally," I say to Jackson and stretch so I can get back to running. I need to get this crap out of my head.

"Take care. I'll be back east soon and maybe we can grab a beer."

"Sounds good, Muff." I disconnect the call and blare some Jay Z hoping I can get lost in the bass.

Trying to focus on the trees passing by and how bad my muscles are going to hate me later, I end up thinking about the letter sitting in my car. Why the fuck did he write to all of us? My letter sits in my rifle case and it goes to my mom, not any of the guys. I start to think of Natalie and how she's doing. Did she read the letter? Did he tell her something that is going to cause her pain or will it put her at ease? I turn and head back on the trail, running faster than I did before.

Once I reach my car, I throw my phone on the dash. I can't go back there. I'm not her boyfriend and I never will be. I need to get laid. I grab my phone and call my buddy who's stationed here.

Quinn answers on the first ring. "What up, dirtbag?"

"Hey, fuckstick. I need to go out tonight. You game?"

"Hot Tuna? Lots of willing pussy."

Sounds perfect. I need to get balls deep in some girl and get the other one out of my head. "Meet you there around ten."

I disconnect the phone and lean back in my seat. My legs are screaming after the run I just did. Every time I would start to zone out, I'd start thinking about Lee and Aarabelle, wondering what they are doing. You can't not love that kid. She looks like Aaron, only cuter. What the fuck have I gotten myself into? And where in the last few weeks did this shift at all? She's Lee for Chrissake. She's the messy hair, sweat pants, and no bra girl I've known for eight years. I've seen her practically naked and even though any man would have to be blind not to look twice at her, I've never had anything more than friendship towards her. So what the hell is different?

Enough thinking.

Time to get wasted and laid.

"HEY, FUCKER! WASN'T sure you were going to show," Quinn sits back with a beer in his hand.

"Passed out after my run," I state.

Quinn and I have been friends for a few years. We both went to the same training site in Nevada and kept in touch. When I found out I was heading to SEAL Team Four, I was glad I at least knew a few guys.

"Been a while since you worked out, huh?"

"I've been busy," I say and signal for a beer to the bartender.

He looks at me and smirks. "Busy . . . right."

"That's what I said."

Quinn nods and looks at the game on TV as I look around the bar. He's right. This place is crawling with women looking for some attention. They're not even subtle. Fine by me.

"So, what's been going on? I haven't heard from you."

"I've been helping Natalie get stuff done. Since Aaron wasn't active, the Navy is no help."

"Yeah, I heard about that. Aaron was a good guy. Sucks about how he died." Quinn taps my beer and we both take a gulp.

"It's fucking weird. The whole thing."

"What do you mean? The IED in Afghanistan?" He looks at me as if I sprouted another head. "Tell me where the weird part is."

My training tells me there's more to that explosion. "Why the fuck was he there? Why was his caravan hit? I know these assholes don't give a shit, but Jackson's company isn't stupid. They know that region. Then the fact that Cole was shot when he went to the site doesn't add up. Why and who is targeting Cole's company?"

The thing about Quinn is he's an easy read. Which is why he's a sniper on our team and not intelligence. "Don't start trying to look for shit that's not there. He was killed by an IED and you said it yourself—they don't care. So they killed him because they could. Plain and simple. As to why Jackson was shot, again they're American— enough said."

"Sure," I reply to placate him. I don't think it's plain

and simple, but Quinn is too stupid or self-absorbed to give a shit. He's simple and follows orders, never thinking about it again. I, on the hand, don't do either well.

"Hi there," I hear from behind me. Quinn's eyes widen as he takes in the company we have.

I shift and see the two women. One has black hair cut right above her clearly fake tits. The other has blonde hair pulled to one side. She's fucking hot.

"Hi, ladies."

"Is that seat taken?" the blonde asks, biting her lip. I'm fucked . . . and hopefully she will be soon too.

"What's your poison?"

She smiles and sits on the stool next to me and crouches down, showing me her rack. Her fingertip traces the wood right by my arm and my cock stirs. "What's your name?"

"Liam," I reply and lean closer.

"Well, Liam . . . I'm Brit. How about you buy me a shot of whiskey and we'll find out what else is my poison?"

On a normal day, this type of shit would piss me off, but today, Brit seems to be just what I need.

The hours pass and we drink and spend the evening with Brit and her friend, Claire. They're both practically begging to go home with us. I'll never understand what these bitches think. Why would any man want to take you home to Mom if I was able to fuck you the first night we met? That's not the kind of girl I want to have a life with. That's the girl I'm going to fuck and forget.

"I'm probably too drunk to drive," Brit whispers in my ear.

"Want me to give you a ride?" I ask, and her lip is back between her teeth.

She nods and her tongue darts out and licks the red

marks. I'm going to lose my shit.

"Let's go then," I sweep my arm forward and Brit stumbles into my arms.

"Yes. Let's."

chapter

nine

natalie

"SHHH, IT'S OKAY, Aarabelle." I'm starting to get nervous. It's been almost two hours straight of her screaming. Tears fall and nothing is soothing her. It's almost two o'clock in the morning and I don't know what's wrong. I gave her medicine when she felt warm before, but she's still not calming.

She wails over and over and I can't get her to take a break. She still feels hot to me, so I grab the thermometer, and my heart races when I see her temperature.

Throwing things in the diaper bag, I need to get her to the hospital. She's running a 105.2-degree fever. I grab my phone and toss it in the bag. When I turn to get her, I see her eyes roll back and she begins twitching on the floor.

"Oh my God!" I scream and run over to her.

Her body convulses and I turn her to her side. Aarabelle's limbs flail and panic grips me. I hold her as she shakes and tears stream down my face. It only lasts a minute, but my heart is in my throat.

"Aarabelle!" I burst out as she starts to cry again and I rummage through my bag for my phone. I dial 9–1-1. I lift her in my arms and hold her tight.

The dispatcher's calm voice comes through, "9–1-1, state your emergency."

"My daughter. She's had a seizure I think. I don't know. Her fever . . . it's high . . . and I don't know what to do!" I blurt trying to gather my wits. I'm frazzled and frayed. Aarabelle cries loudly as I rock her back and forth in my arms.

"Is she conscious, ma'am?"

"Yes, she's crying and has a high fever. I put her down to get ready to go to the hospital and then she began shaking," I cry and every part of me feels weak. My heart is racing as I watch her, hoping it doesn't happen again.

"Okay, what's your address? I'm sending an ambulance."

I give the dispatcher the information and she stays on the line as we wait for help to arrive. In minutes, the EMTs arrive and they instruct me to grab her car seat as they take her vitals. I throw my phone back in my bag, grab my stuff, and climb in the ambulance.

"Okay, Aara. Mommy's got you," I say soothingly as I buckle her in her seat. "We'll be at the hospital in a few minutes."

She cries and I fight the tears threatening to come again. I've never been this scared in my life. Watching her shake uncontrollably was terrifying. I couldn't survive if something happened to my baby.

The lights and sirens blaze as we rush to the emergency room at the children's hospital.

"Her fever is still high, but we should be at Children's

Hospital of Kings' Daughters in a few minutes, ma'am," the young EMT says.

I'm not sure if I even acknowledge him because I'm so focused on Aarabelle. She's finally stopped crying, but I'm not sure if it's a good thing or not.

Once the ambulance stops, they rush us into a room where the nurses are waiting.

"Hi, Mrs. Gilcher. I'm Dr. Hewat," she walks in quickly and heads over to Aara. "What's going on with Aarabelle?"

I explain what she's been like during the night and how she's been extremely fussy. She examines her and explains the course they're going to take to get her fever down immediately. They need to get an IV started and then they're going to run some tests.

The nurse comes in and gets the IV hooked up. She makes sure Aarabelle's monitors and fluids are working and lets me know how to call for help. Once Aara settles a little, the nurse takes her temperature and vitals again. She's finally fallen asleep from exhaustion and I have a second to think.

"Any changes?" I ask hesitantly.

"Not yet, but the medicine can take a bit," she says and heads out of the room with a sympathetic smile.

I grab my phone to send a text to Reanell, letting her know where we are and to call me when she wakes. No point in worrying her.

"Sir," I hear outside the curtain before it flies open.

"There you are!" Liam exclaims and looks panicked.

"Liam?" I stand and he looks at Aarabelle.

"I heard you talking about the hospital. Why didn't you call me?"

I look at him, his face is ashen and his eyes are wide.

The nurse pushes him back, "Ma'am, do you want me to call security?"

"No, he's fine." I step forward and Liam looks at Aara again. "What are you doing here?"

"I heard my phone ring and I saw you calling. You never call me, so I figured something was wrong. I heard you talking about a hospital, but you wouldn't answer me. I had to drop someone off and then I came running. I didn't know if she was okay." Liam barely gets the words out and my heart falters. He looks so concerned.

"I'm sorry. I didn't realize I called you."

"Why the hell didn't you?"

My jaw falls and I see how hurt he is. "Why would I? I can take care of myself and my daughter."

He closes his eyes and lets out a deep breath, "I never said you couldn't, but why the hell should you do this alone? I'm your friend, aren't I? I told you I want to be here for you. I thought . . ." He trails off.

"Thought what?"

I see it in his eyes. He's holding something back.

"I thought you would've called."

"I'm sorry, I didn't want to bother you." I don't know what else to say. I honestly never thought of calling him. Liam's been so much help, but I don't want to rely on him.

"What's wrong with her?" he questions.

I look at Aarabelle sleeping and I brush her hair back. "I don't know. She started running a high fever and then she had convulsions. I called emergency services and they rushed us here. They're running some blood tests and they're waiting to see what comes back."

Liam comes around the side of her bed and puts his hand on mine as I begin to cry silently. I pray it's nothing serious. I can't handle anything more. Between Aaron's letter the other day and now Aarabelle, I'm going to lose my mind.

Dr. Hewat enters and looks over the papers. "Hi, Mr. Gilcher, I presume?"

My eyes shift to Liam.

"No, just a friend," he says with an easy grin.

"Sorry, my mistake."

"Is she okay?" I ask, needing answers.

She looks to me and then her eyes move to Aarabelle. "Right now I'm ruling out a few things but I need to run an additional scan. With her fever still not coming back to normal, I need to be sure. Her counts are elevated indicating an infection. They'll be here in a few minutes to take her for the test."

"What are you testing for?"

"Let's rule out a few things and then we'll know the best course of action," Dr. Hewat replies and walks out.

Liam is by my side in a heartbeat. "It'll be fine."

"Right. Like Aaron would be right back."

"Lee," he chides and then stops.

I wish I had the confidence he does. It must be nice to be the one who doesn't have to sit around and worry. They go and do. They fight and live off the high while the families sit around and wonder. We don't know if they're okay. We just suffer through it. Now, I sit here months after my last tragedy and wonder if my daughter is going to be okay.

He sits beside me and I lean on his shoulder. I'm exhausted both physically and emotionally. What the fuck else is life going to throw at me? Once again, I have to be strong though.

Aarabelle rests and I close my eyes. Liam's strong arm wraps around me and I take the comfort he offers. I inhale his sandalwood and musk scent, and it calms me. I love the smell of a man. I miss the smell of a man. Especially this kind of man—one that exudes strength, confidence, and dominance. They command the space around them.

I focus on how secure I feel in this moment. The way I used to feel when Aaron would hold me. I think of the letter he wrote urging me to love again. Could I give another man a chance to hold me like this? Right now . . . I don't know. But being in Liam's embrace makes me want to be open to the idea.

Something shakes me gently and I open my eyes. The hospital smell hits me first and I realize I must've drifted off to sleep. Rubbing my eyes, I sit up and Liam stretches. His shirt lifts and I see the ripples of his abdomen. *Look away, Natalie.*

"Mrs. Gilcher?"

I nod and head over toward the nurse. "Yes."

"We're going to take Aarabelle for her scan. She'll be about forty minutes. You can wait here or you can come up and wait outside. It's totally up to you."

"I'll come with," I say matter-of-factly. There's no way in hell you're keeping me away from her.

Liam places his hand on my shoulder. "I'm going to run and get some coffee. Need anything?"

My heart swells at his concern. "No, I'm good. Thank you for being here."

"I'll always be here for you, Lee."

"I know. You promised him."

His thumb grips my chin and he forces me to look at him. Blue eyes shimmer with some unnamed emotion. I want to look away, break the connection, because I feel it. I feel something and I don't want to. I'm not ready. It's way too soon, but it's there, starting to make its way through me, and I'm terrified he'll see it. The need to close my eyes becomes intense, but I can't, or maybe I really don't want to. Maybe I want him to see it, but God, if I'm not scared. "Go with Aarabelle," he says as his hand drops.

My cheeks paint red and I close my eyes finally. Shit. I was wrong. Maybe he doesn't feel anything for me.

"Ma'am?" The nurse calls to me as she unlocks the wheels on Aarabelle's crib.

"Ready," I say, knowing I feel anything but. This is all too much and my feelings couldn't have come at a worse time. I need to focus on my baby and then I can worry about myself and my stupid feelings.

chapter

ten

WAITING IS AGONY. Waiting sucks. Waiting is all we seem to be doing.

"You should head home," I grumble as I snuggle into Liam's chest. I want him to want to leave. Which is stupid because he's my pillow right now, but if he wants to go, this nagging, festering feeling inside might leave me alone.

Liam sags in the chair so I have a more comfortable position, and the rumble of his laughter vibrates through his chest. It's now 5 A.M. and no one but Aarabelle is sleeping. "I'll leave right now if that's what you really want."

Butterflies stir in my belly. What do I want? I wish I knew.

"Nah," my reluctant reply falls out. "I need my pillow. I'm going to keep using you for now."

"You can use me anytime, Lee."

I can reply or choose to pretend. I'm going with pretending. The nursing staff has the world's worst or best timing, depending on how I want to look at this, because she strides in to check on Aara. My head rises and I head over to be close to her.

"We're just checking her fever again," she explains and begins to assess her vitals.

Standing next to my daughter while they check her again, the fear gnaws its way up. Wondering whether the fever has come down any lower, and if not, what's the next step? She looks at the thermometer and shakes her head no. She's still running around 101, but at least we're out of the danger zone.

"Are the test results back from her scan?" I ask.

"I'll check on it, but the doctor will be in as soon as we know anything." She smiles and grips my hand. "It's a good thing the fever isn't rising."

I close my eyes and nod. I guess it's good. I wish she wasn't sick at all, but I'm happy Liam is here. The waiting has been agony and I can't imagine not having his support. I look over at him as he rests in the recliner and fight the urge to giggle. This six-foot, bulky man is spilling over this tiny chair. His legs almost touch the crib Aarabelle is asleep in and his arms practically touch the ground. It's comical. His hair is a mess and his three-day-old beard only makes him look more adorable. He was always handsome, but the more I look at him, I see the small things. The crinkle around his eyes and the scar on his forearm that add to his appeal. He's going to make some woman very happy.

"Are you done staring?" he grumbles with one eye open.

Shit.

"I wasn't staring. I was trying to figure out if you were dead since you weren't moving," I lie and turn so he doesn't see my cheeks redden.

"Sure you were . . ." He gives a low chuckle.

"Whatever, you're old and fat." I wave my hand at him.

Liam's large frame rises and casts a shadow over me.

He takes a step toward me with a smirk on his face. My eyes stay locked with his. He's out of his mind if he thinks I'm going to back down.

With a measured step he comes closer. Neither of us breaks our gaze.

I read the hesitation behind his eyes. He's as unsure as I am, but we're both too stubborn to give in.

"Aaaaaa," Aarabelle cries out, and I break and look at her.

"Hi, baby girl," I say softly and lift her carefully so I don't disconnect anything. She still feels warm and begins to fuss. Why isn't the fever breaking?

Liam's firm hand squeezes my shoulder as if he can read my distress. "I'll call the nurse," he declares and goes to press the button.

Before he can, Dr. Hewat walks in, lifting papers in the chart. "Okay, we got the results back from the scan and her blood screen." She looks at us both with empathy swimming in her eyes. "She has a urinary tract infection that spread to her kidneys, which is what caused the fever. We need to treat her with antibiotics and make sure her kidneys are functioning properly. Also, I want to watch the fever since she did have the convulsions. But she should be fine. I'm going to order the medicine now."

I release a breath with relief. She's going to be okay. Thank God.

"Will the fever come down?" I question.

"It should. Can you place her on the bed for me?"

I lay her down and the doctor comes around the other side. She begins to listen to her heart and abdomen. "She's doing well, and I think once we get the antibiotics working, the fever will break and she'll be back to normal," Dr. Hewat explains and pats my hand. "In the meantime, we need to keep her hydrated and watch her closely."

"Okay," I nod and Aarabelle lifts her arms for me to pick her up.

Scooping my baby in my arms, I pull her close and say a silent prayer of thanks that this was not anything serious. She's my world and I don't think I could survive burying my husband and my child in the same year. I can't even allow my mind to drift there.

Liam's eyes gleam as he rubs the side of her face with adoration in his eyes. He's a good man and he cares about Aarabelle and me. He could've been at a bar or doing whatever else he wants, but he came to us. I'm grateful that he's here. I place my hand over his and a charge runs from my fingers to my shoulder. We both look at each other and my body locks. I see the catch in his breath as he feels it too.

Moving my hand away quickly, I take a few seconds to calm my racing heart and walk to the other side of Aarabelle's crib. Distance . . . I need to keep my distance. I don't understand what's happening. Liam is my friend, he's Aaron's friend . . . it's wrong to even think about him.

"Lee?" Liam breaks me out of my thoughts. He begins to step around, but I put my hand up to stop him.

"I'm fine. I think I'm overwhelmed, but I'll be fine."

"Back to 'fine' again. Got it."

Screw him. I am fine. "What does that mean?"

"I'm tired. You're tired. Tomorrow if you're feeling up to a sparring match, I'm game." Liam yawns and flops in the chair behind him. He pulls his beanie over his eyes and smirks.

Bastard.

chapter

eleven

"OKAY, MISS AARABELLE, ready to head home?" the nurse coos as I buckle Aarabelle into her seat. The IV of antibiotics finally got the infection under control, which brought her fever down. After two sleepless days and nights, I'm more than excited to be heading home.

"I'd say we are, right, baby girl?" I ask rhetorically as I nestle the blanket around her. I can't wait for the day when she'll talk. Then I won't feel so silly having full-blown one-sided conversations.

"Well, good thing that hunk of a man came here, huh?" she asks me, looking around the corner.

I try to hide my amusement and giggle silently. "Yeah, he's a good friend."

"Oh, you're not dating?" her eyes grow and she bites her lip.

"No," I say slowly and I realize she's fishing. A pang of jealousy stirs in my chest. He's not mine by any stretch, but he sure as hell isn't hers. "Well, not officially," I add on and mentally slap myself for it.

There's no reason I should be cockblocking him, but something inside of me doesn't want her to have him. Or have a chance at him. I'm going to hell.

"Hang on tight to that one, because that beanie and

that smile . . ." She slaps her hand over her mouth, clearly embarrassed at what she's said. "I'm sorry. I don't know what got into me."

Placing my hand on her arm, I giggle. "It's okay. He's easy on the eyes."

She gives a short laugh. "Yeah, you could say that."

Before I can respond, Liam walks in and gives a knowing look. He heard us. Great, this should be fun.

"You girls ready to hit the road?" he asks with an underhanded chuckle.

I shake my head and bite my tongue.

"I could leave the room, if you want to keep talking about my hotness," Liam offers and flops in the chair he slept in two nights in a row. He refused to leave Aarabelle's side.

I walk over and rip the beanie off. "Arrogance doesn't suit you, Dempsey." The giggle escapes me at the way his hair sticks out in various directions. "No one thinks you're hot right now, buddy."

He stands and walks toward me slowly. His warm breath bathes my neck as he leans in so only I can hear, "I think we both know that's not true." Liam's finger glides against my arm and I shiver. "We can pretend though." Slowly his finger reaches my hand and my heart is racing. I enjoy the feel of his hands on me more than I should. I can't explain what's happening between us because it's never been like this. It's always been friendship. He shifts back and snatches his hat from my hand.

I look over and try to get my breathing under control. Liam tries to pretend, but I see the desire pooled in his eyes. He's not as unaffected as he's feigning, but Liam is trained to restrain his emotions. Fine, I can play the game too.

I pull my hair over my shoulder and lean down a little, giving him a tiny glimpse of skin. "It's not pretending when one of us doesn't feel that way." I grab the diaper bag . . . *real sexy, Natalie* . . . and try to maintain my alluring look.

Liam isn't buying it and he lets out a deep, loud laugh. "Nice try, babe. Let's go." He grabs the diaper bag off my shoulder and heads out of the room.

"Looks like Mommy's lost her touch," I say to Aarabelle as I grab the car seat and head out.

"YOU MEAN HE stayed the whole time you were in the hospital?" Reanell asks suspiciously.

"Yes, he wouldn't leave." I grab my coffee mug and curl up on the sofa. We've been home for a few days and Liam hasn't stopped by. He texted me yesterday to wish me luck on my first day of work, but I haven't replied.

"Hmmm," Rea says as she taps her lip. We've been trying to analyze everything, because there's a part of me that wonders if I'm making this all up. "I mean, he was Aaron's best friend."

"I know. I think it's just his duty to him. It would explain why he kinda disappeared after he dropped us off."

She looks at me trying to see through me. "Do you want him to stop by?"

"Reanell, please. It's not even been a year. There's no way in hell I want another man. I love my husband."

Grabbing her drink, she comes over to the couch and sits next to me. "I know you do, but you're a woman. Liam is a good man. A man who seems to care about you and Aara very much. Would it be such a bad thing?"

I think I've entered into another dimension. My friend who told me if her husband died she'd join the convent because it would be too hard is urging me to entertain this. "Yes, it would be bad. First off, Liam has never had a serious girlfriend, let alone taking on a widow and a baby. Second, he's a SEAL!" I yell out and then recover. "Fuck . . . he's a SEAL. Deployments, possible death. I couldn't." I start to panic.

"Hey," Reanell grips my hand. "I'm not saying it's good or bad. I'm just saying sometimes the heart wants what the head says no to. I don't know if your heart or head want anything."

"Sleep. They want sleep."

She laughs and releases my hand. "That's why I'm here. Go take a nap. No more talk of boys. I'm glad he came to the hospital and took care of you. You needed someone and he was there."

"Yeah, he was. Okay, I'm going to rest. Thank you for coming over and watching her for me. I can't keep my eyes open." Reanell is a godsend. She called and I filled her in on everything, and without saying another word, I heard her car start to head to my house. It's a sisterhood, being a military spouse. Even though Aaron wasn't active anymore, we're still family. When one needs us, we're there, especially in the special ops community.

"Any time, my friend. Now go get some beauty sleep."

I kiss her cheek and head to bed. Once I'm stripped down to my shorts and tank, I lie on my back and stare at the ceiling.

Rolling over, I grab Aaron's letter and read it again. His words give me hope for the future and yet at the same time break me further apart. All I wanted was a life with him. I read about how he felt when we met. If only he knew. "You didn't have to work so hard to get me," I say aloud, relying on my faith that he can hear me. "I loved you from the moment I met you. I was yours before you even spoke a word. God, you were so handsome," I sigh and close my eyes.

"I remember the first time I saw you . . . you had that stupid hat on backwards and were wearing your football jersey. You nodded your head to me like I should fawn at your feet. Idiot," I laugh softly. He was so cocky and full of himself. There was no way I was going to let him know how much I already wanted him. "Now I'm here without you." Tears stream down my face. He's gone and I'm in pain.

"Why, Aaron?" I roll and face where he would be if he were in our bed. My hand grazes his pillow and another tear falls. "You say to move on, but how? You didn't tell me how to do that. I can't love anyone else. I don't know how. You were my first love, my only love, the first man in my heart and in my body. Hell, you are my heart and I don't know how to let go of that. If I let someone else in, then I'll lose you forever." I continue to speak to myself, praying for an answer, because I don't know how to give him up. "You have to show me, or give me a sign." I clutch his pillow and sob relentlessly until I fall asleep, wishing I were in his arms. Safe and happy in the arms of my husband.

chapter

twelve

"HER FOOD IS labeled and I wrote down all the times she needs to eat," I instruct the nanny I hired. She's a friend of Reanell's and came highly recommended.

"We'll be just fine." Paige bounces Aarabelle on her lap as she giggles.

"Okay, I'm sure I'll call only around a hundred times."

Paige smiles reassuringly. "I expect no less. First days are scary, but Aarabelle and I have a busy day of fun planned."

I secretly love that she's paying more attention to Aarabelle than me and my neurotic-ness. First day of working at Cole Security and I no longer think this is a good idea. Leaving Aarabelle and then stepping foot into the building where Aaron worked is daunting. I thought maybe I could feel closer to him, now I'm not so sure if this is the right move.

"I'll have my phone on me and the number to the office is on the paper by the fridge." I'm clearly stalling. I don't know how to spend the entire day away from Aarabelle.

Paige brings Aara over to me. "It'll be fine. If we need you, I'll call. I promise."

Nodding and drawing a deep breath, I kiss my daughter and turn to head to work.

I can do this.

Once I reach my car, I notice the note and flower on the windshield. I open the note and my lip turns up.

Hey Lee,

Sorry I've been MIA but I'm back at work and my schedule is jacked up. Have a good first day. Be sure to give the guys hell.

Liam

Sitting in the car, I try to wipe the smile off my face but I can't help it. It's the sweetest, most thoughtful thing anyone's done for me in months.

Starting the car, the phone connects to the bluetooth and I decide to call him.

"Hey," he answers on the first ring.

"Hi," I say, still smiling. "I got your card and flower. Thank you."

"I was jogging and wanted to let you know I didn't forget about you. I've been busy getting checked in and caught up to speed." Liam's voice is thick and restrained. There's a part of me that doesn't fully believe him.

"Right. No, it's fine. I've been busy too," I lie.

Liam chuckles, "I got a call on Aaron's quad if you're still wanting to sell it."

Another part of Aaron that I'll lose. "Sure."

"Lee?" Liam utters my name reluctantly.

"Yeah?"

He pauses and clears his throat. "How's Aara?"

That wasn't what I was expecting based on the tone of his voice. Not that I had any idea what he was going to say, but Aarabelle isn't a touchy subject. "Good, she's with the nanny and I'm freaking out," I laugh. "I'm sure she'll be fine but it's the first time I'm leaving her." I turn into the parking lot of Cole Security Forces and nerves begin to stir.

It's Mark and Jackson, but still. I'm worried that being in there will make his loss even more prominent . . . not that it can be any more apparent. He's dead. I'm alone and a single mother.

"You okay?" Liam asks, and I realize I've been silent.

With my eyes closed, I shake my head. Am I okay? I don't remember the last time I felt okay. "I'm fine."

You can almost feel the disapproval over the phone. He hates that word, but it's my crutch. "I figured. How about I bring a pizza over tonight? We can go over some of the papers for the sale of his car and now the quad."

"Sounds good."

"Good, see you around seven."

"Seven it is." This is awkward. I feel like there's something neither of us is saying but neither of us knows how to proceed. "Okay, I gotta get in to work."

There's some rustling in the background and Liam's hand covers the phone, "I'll see you later. Good luck today."

"Thanks, see you later," I reply and hang up the phone.

I'm going to need a lot of luck.

Exiting the car, my nerves flare again. These men have been a part of my life for years, yet it's as if I'm just meeting them. Things have changed over the course of seven months. Jackson and Mark still call and check on me, but our friendships have changed. Hell, I've changed. Mark came around a lot in the beginning, but as life happens, he's moved on or pulled away. Liam, however, has stayed constant.

Here goes nothing.

"Lee!" Mark exclaims and comes walking over. "I saw you pull in and I was coming out to get you. Thought maybe you didn't know where the door was." He angles in and drops his voice, "It'll be okay."

I nod and press my lips together. "I've missed you guys."

"There are some papers in the conference room we need you to fill out and then I'll show you your office and go over what we need done, sound good?"

I look at my friend, the man who carried my husband for a mile when he was hurt on a mission, the one who is my daughter's godfather and also the man who destroyed my world, and see his hurt. The pain in his eyes is prevalent because it mirrors mine. As hard as this is for me, this can't be easy on them either. Mark, Jackson, and the rest of the men here were his friends. Seeing me is probably difficult for them as well.

My hand grips his arm. "I'm happy to see you."

Mark in his true fashion smirks, "I'm not a bad view, eh, Lee?"

These guys are all the same. Morons. "Sure, you're the most handsome man I've seen in weeks . . . well, besides my mailman. He's pretty dreamy."

"I think I could take him."

"Pretty sure that's a federal offense."

"He can't touch these guns," he retorts and flexes.

I roll my eyes and snort, "Oh, dear God."

I laugh as we walk to the conference room and I notice the stares, but I pretend not to.

Mark notices my unease, "I know this is going to be awkward, but give it a few days and you'll be one of the guys."

"Do I really want that?"

"I can make up a cute name for you . . . let's see," he sits in the chair and looks deep in thought.

"I'm worried you'll burn what little brain cells you have left if you keep thinking that hard," I taunt him. Being around Mark is like being around a puppy. He naturally brings out the fun and playful side. And he's caring yet strong and has this undeniable pull that makes you want to be near him.

"Keep it up and your name will be something you don't like," his brow raises and his lip curls. "You know you don't get to pick. Call signs are given. They're a rite of passage and you get no say. I mean, you think I wanted to be called Twilight?"

Leaning in my chair, I tap the pen. "I don't know, I mean, you look like you could have a thing for vampires."

He laughs and I follow. "Fill out the paperwork and then I'll be back." He walks over and places his hand on my shoulder. "I'm glad you're here. We need the help with Muffin gone."

My hand rests on his. "I know it's hard having them both gone." In a matter of a few months, Mark lost his two best friends in a manner of speaking. Aaron and he were extremely close. They spent weekends rebuilding Aaron's car, barbeques on the beach, and then Jackson moved to California. I can't imagine it's been easy for him either.

"You know me," he replies and removes his hand. I look at the paper and I hear the door click closed. Aaron's death has rocked our worlds and none of us are acknowledging it.

Once I finish filling out what feels like three hundred forms, I head out to find Mark.

Not paying any attention, I open the door and hear a deep voice, "Hey."

I drop the papers and look up to see Jackson. My hand clutches my chest, "Hey, you scared the shit out of me." I give a nervous laugh.

Well, this is unexpected. Jackson called the other day to see how we were doing and make sure I was still planning to come to work for him. He towers over me with his six-foot-three frame. I'm not short by any means, but he makes me feel tiny. He crouches and picks up the papers.

"Sorry about that. Catherine says I do the same thing," he laughs and his eyes light up when he says her name.

"How's she doing?" I ask. I've spoken to her a few times since her move to California, but with the time difference, we seem to miss each other.

Jackson's joy is prevalent in his features. His eyes brighten, his lips lift, and my heart cracks. I remember being that in love. "Great, we're great."

I laugh to cover the pain that's building. "I didn't ask about you," nudging him, I say playfully.

"Yeah, yeah. Everyone cares about her and couldn't care less about me," he winks. "How are you doing?" he asks, wrapping his arm around my shoulder and pulling me in. He's carried immense guilt for all that's happened and offered me a job any time I wanted to work. The flexibility and ability to make my own hours was more than appealing. As a journalist, I had to go when the story came. There would've been way too many nights I wouldn't be able to put Aarabelle to sleep.

I let out a slow breath as he releases me. "I'm living. Liam's been around taking care of things around the house. He's helped a lot with the stupid, mundane stuff."

"Dempsey's a good guy. I spoke with him last week."

"Oh," I reply, a little surprised. I didn't know they were friends like that.

Jackson chuckles at my response. "I have to check on you somehow since you won't answer my calls."

"I answer!" I exclaim defensively. "Well, sometimes . . ." I trail off.

"It's okay. I know you're busy and Demps says you lie anyway," he gives me a knowing look. Jackson is good at reading people. They all are. Sometimes being friends with all SEALs isn't all that great. Sure, I'm always safe and protected, but it's impossible to hide anything. Aaron being gone for a while has made me a little lost as to how to act. I drew my strength from him, now I have to rely on my own. Which I think I've done a pretty good job at.

"I don't lie . . . I'm just tired of saying the same thing over and over."

"Yeah, I remember that feeling," Jackson replies.

Oh, how could I forget? Jackson knows better than anyone else. He's been exactly where I am when his wife died. I'm an idiot and insensitive. "Jackson," I place my hand on his arm, "I can't believe I've been so stupid."

He gives a short laugh and guides me into his office. "Sit," he says with authority, but still gentle.

It always amazes me how Jackson can be so hard because he has the biggest heart of anyone I know. He'd literally cut off his arm so someone else didn't have to be in pain. Aaron always admired him and said it was an honor to serve with him. I think he'd be proud that I've come to work for Jackson, even if he died because of the job he was doing for him.

Jackson sits across from me, "I'm not one to talk about Maddie and all that happened. I've been better since Catherine, but it's still something I work through.

I know you say you're fine, and that's okay, but you don't have to be fine with me. Or Liam," he gives me a pointed look.

"I don't know what everyone expects, you know?" I ask. "I mean, do people expect me to be doing cartwheels down the halls? In love already? Married? Or would they prefer me drunk so I don't have to feel?"

He huffs, "No, they don't expect that. They don't know what to expect either. I refused to date after her death. I never wanted to have a fucking woman near me."

I smile, because I know where he's going.

"Yeah, yeah. Don't even say it." Jackson's grin grows again.

"You're cute in love," I lean back and smirk.

He crosses his arms and mimics my stance, "I'm always cute, but that's not the point."

I roll my eyes at his arrogance. They all need therapy. "Between you and Mark, I don't know how anyone can get any work done."

"Why?" he asks, confused where I'm going.

"Well, I mean you're both *sooo* good-looking. I'm sure everyone just stares all day," I reply sarcastically.

Jackson's laugh echoes in the room. "You'll get used to it," he winks.

"Cat deserves a medal for putting up with you. One day she'll see the truth."

"I'll marry her before that happens. I just need to convince her that I'm worth being around forever." Jackson is always honest. It's the one thing we can count on.

"How are you guys doing?" I think Catherine is good for him. She keeps him on his toes and he complements her.

"Good, she's doing her thing and I'm happy to be

back in California. I'm close enough to San Diego, which worked out well. Anyway, enough about me . . . we were talking about you."

"Let's not."

Jackson puts his hands up in surrender. "I'm just saying you have to do whatever you need to in order to survive, but after a while, surviving isn't enough. Catherine showed me that. I could've been in a much better place if I hadn't lived in limbo for two years."

There's not much I can say. I know he means well, and I know he genuinely understands how I'm feeling. Even I don't understand what the hell I'm feeling or why, but still. "Thanks, Jackson."

"Enough heavy shit. How's my beautiful goddaughter?"

The smile at the thought of Aarabelle is automatic. I love that little girl more than my own life. "Thankfully, after the medicine knocked out the infection, she's been good. You should come see her."

He laughs, "I was coming whether you offered or not. I had Mark get your office put together last week. I meant what I said about being flexible . . . if you need to work from home because she's sick or whatever the case, you can do that. We want you to be happy here and if you need something, feel free to drive Mark absolutely insane until you get it."

"I'll be sure to do that just for fun."

Jackson stands and extends his arm forward. He escorts me to my office.

We enter and I stop short. It's bigger than his office. I would think this is a conference room. "Wow, Jackson, what the hell?" I question him. "This office is huge. Mark, who's basically running things from here, is in a cubicle.

This is nuts." I'm blown away and it's completely unexpected. I'm a receptionist. I won't go on missions or do anything but file some paperwork and get their ridiculous filing system in order. Honestly, it's highway robbery for what he's offered as a salary.

"You may have to bring her here once in a while. We all agreed you'd need something bigger," Jackson states without batting an eye. "I left some things on your desk if you want to get started. Shoot me an email when you're ready to leave."

"Ummm, sure." I stand gaping at this room. It's crazy and completely overboard. I should've expected it though since Jackson Cole does nothing half-assed.

Time to get to work.

chapter

thirteen

"HELLO?" I HEAR Liam's raspy voice call out.
"In the kitchen!"

Aarabelle sits in her highchair as I feed her dinner. She's growing so fast. Already she's eating cereal and a little baby food. Soon she'll be crawling and I have no one to celebrate with. Her father will never see these milestones and it breaks me apart.

"You should really lock the door," Liam huffs as he throws his coat over the chair.

"But then I'd have to get up to let you in," I state matter-of-factly and go back to feeding the baby, trying to put aside my worries. The fact is . . . this is reality. I have to deal with it.

"Uh huh. Hey, Pumpkin," his eyes alight as he crouches down by Aara. It's adorable hearing grown men use a baby voice. It gets a little softer and higher pitched.

The corners of her mouth lift and she throws her arms in the air when he gets close. My heart sputters seeing how happy she gets seeing him. Liam kisses her head and she giggles.

"At least someone is happy to see me," he says playfully.

"I'd be happy if you brought me a present," I joke.

He laughs and goes into the pocket of his coat. "Just so happens I did, but since that's the only way you'll be nice, I'll hold on to this until you've earned it."

Practically leaping out of my chair, I rush over. "What is it?" I try to peer around his back as he holds the mystery item.

Liam's lips curl as he sees how much I want this. I don't even know what it is. Jeez, I'm an idiot. "Nope. We eat first, then maybe you'll get it."

"Watch, it's a freaking Pez dispenser or something stupid."

"Guess you'll have to be nice to find out." He shoves the item into his back pocket and I fight the urge to reach and get it. "How was work?"

We spend the next thirty minutes going over my day and Jackson's return. Liam never mentioned that they spoke, but he's surprised to hear he's in Virginia. After we finish the pizza, Liam somehow convinces me we should watch a movie. I get Aarabelle to bed and come down to find him sprawled out on the couch.

"By all means, make yourself comfortable."

Liam pulls his beanie higher on his forehead and his eyes glimmer with amusement. He sits up and puts the TV on. "I picked the movie."

"What?" I ask with mock incredulity. "It's my house. Why do you get to pick the movie?"

"Ummm, I'm the guest." He shrugs as if this should be an obvious answer.

I groan and lean back. "What crappy, shoot-'em-up movie do I have to endure?"

"You'll see. It's a classic." Liam wraps his arm around me and pulls me to his side.

I cuddle into his chest without thinking. After

practically sleeping on top of him in the hospital, I have no qualms about cuddling. I miss cuddling and if he's one of the rare men who enjoy it, I'm good with that. The selfish part of me likes him touching me. Yet I don't want to like it. It's wrong to enjoy another man's arms around me so soon.

The movie begins and I want to tear my eyes out. "No!" I yell and sit up. "No. No, no, no. I'm not watching this horrible crap," shaking my head vehemently, reaching for the remote.

"'Friday After Next' is Oscar-worthy." Liam snatches the remote and tucks it in his pants.

"Are you serious? Did you just shove my remote in your pants?"

Liam sits there daring me to go get it. Infuriating man.

"Now, are you ready to watch the best movie ever?"

"I hate you."

"I can live with that." He pulls me back down and I seriously contemplate getting the remote. "One day you'll realize how much you love me."

"Doubtful."

Maybe he'll enjoy when he has to watch 'Pitch Perfect' on our next date. Date? Wait. I called this a date. This is just two friends snuggling and watching movies after dinner. Oh my God. Between the hospital, him calling, taking care of me, and all of the other things, it starts to click. No. He's my friend and he doesn't feel that way.

I don't feel that way.

I mean, sure he's good-looking, but he's off limits. He's Liam. The best man in our wedding. The man who helped move Aaron and I into our first home. Lines can't be blurred. My body tenses and Liam notices.

"If you really hate this, we don't have to watch," he

offers.

I look into his blue eyes and fear flutters in my stomach.

"No, I'm fine. Let's watch."

"Now, come get comfortable so I can school you on the top flight security of the world," he says in his best movie imitation.

"Can I have my present?" I ask.

Liam reaches in his back pocket and pulls out a pack of gum. I give him my best resting bitch face and he laughs. "I never said what it was."

"You really know how to woo a girl."

"You'll know when I'm actually trying, babe."

He pulls me against his side and starts the movie. I pray he doesn't sense the change in me. The tension rolls off me, but I try to relax and enjoy tonight.

CHAPTER FOURTEEN

LIAM

SHE FITS INTO my side like she was meant to be here. I should've left. Hell, I never should've come over, but I wanted to see Aarabelle. Well, that's the bullshit I keep telling myself. The truth is I missed Natalie.

And that makes me a douchebag.

"This movie is so dumb," she mutters next to me.

Some women should get a handbook on movies men will never hate. This would be one. "Top Gun" would be another. That movie has hot chicks and bad ass Navy shit. "It would be a lot better if you weren't complaining," I reply, thankful for the distraction.

"Asshole," she mumbles under her breath, but then wraps her arm around my stomach.

I want to give a smartass comeback, but I don't want her to move. The feel of her body against mine makes me want more. It's wrong on so many levels. I'm breaking the ultimate man-code, but I can't stop myself. I can only hope that Aaron would want her to be with someone like me. The fuck if I know why I'm even thinking about any of this . . . she doesn't want me. She wants her husband, and I'm just her asshole friend who won't go away.

Natalie's arm rubs against my stomach and I try to stop the hard-on forming.

Nuns.

Spiders.

Justin Bieber.

Grandma.

I shudder from that last one, but thankfully that did it.

I would never be able to explain my dick getting hard from this freaking movie. She'd know for sure what's up. Her fucking hand being that close to my junk causes me to have to breathe through the list again. I need to focus and stop thinking.

The movie plays on and she begins laughing at it instead of letting me know how stupid everything is.

"See, I told you. Comedic gold." I lean back a little more and smirk at her.

She looks at me and then looks away quickly. I saw it though, the way she stared at my lips a little longer than a beat.

Natalie shakes her head and when she looks back at me, she has her mask firmly in place. "When I force you to watch 'Pitch Perfect' or 'The Notebook,' we'll see how you feel about cinematic gold."

"You'll have to tie me down and gag me to make that shit happen, sweetheart. The only chick movie I'll ever watch is 'Lethal Weapon,'" I reply smugly.

"First of all, 'Lethal Weapon' is not a chick flick." She stays put, but I feel her stir. Natalie is easy to wind up. When she gets heated, I see a piece of her old self coming back. Not this fake happy bullshit.

"I have to disagree." My hand falls and rests on her back.

"You would."

"You just fail to see the epic romance."

Natalie scoffs, "You're an idiot. There's no romance at all! It's two cops trying to not get fired."

I laugh and pull her close, "Mel Gibson is trying to get what's-her-face to be with him."

"That's a subplot. It's not even the basis of the movie."

"Total chick flick. I win." I grin knowing that I have absolutely no argument. It was just the first movie I thought of and I'm totally grasping at straws.

She lets out a deep sigh. "I give up. You can't fix stupid."

I'll let her slide on that one—this time.

My fingers start to rub her back as we both quiet down and return to watching the movie. I don't even notice I'm doing it until I feel her tense. Her breathing stops and she sits up. Which further proves my point about her not wanting me.

"Want something to drink or maybe popcorn?" she asks.

The way she tucks her hair behind her ear, her eyes looking at the floor, and her perfect lip in her teeth shows me everything. She needs to get away and gain some distance.

"Popcorn would be great."

I need some distance myself.

chapter

fifteen

natalie

"WHAT THE HELL is wrong with me?" I say out loud while grabbing the popcorn in the kitchen. I just got all stupid over nothing. There's this *thing* happening to me. I don't understand it. The pull between us grows stronger and as much as I want to fight it, I feel helpless. I want to be around him. I want him to come over and be here, but then I don't, and honestly the only reason is that I'm scared.

Scared of having feelings for another man, and a man exactly like my husband. One who will lay down his life for another. It's the same fate I'm living now, and I don't know that I could endure this again. I definitely don't want my daughter to ever know the hurt of losing yet another man in her life. Only this time, it would be so much worse. She would actually *know* Liam. So I have to stop this—whatever it is.

I head back out into the living room with the bowl and sit next to Liam. His stance is ridiculously rigid as my obvious diversion must not have gone unnoticed. "Want some?" I ask, handing him the bowl.

He laughs and digs his hand in, tossing a few kernels at me. "Smooth, Lee." Liam chuckles and I laugh despite my embarrassment. "Come here, let's finish our movie."

Taking a grounding breath, I lean back into him.

The movie drags on forever. I will never understand how I got stuck watching this. This was one of Aaron's favorite movies too. He and Mark would recite lines to each other any time they could. I miss the little things. A tear pricks and confliction overtakes me once again.

I settle in and try to let my mind stop turning. It's crazy how easy and domestic this moment is. Lying in Liam's arms, watching television after working all day. How we had dinner, put Aarabelle to bed, and now we're just spending time together. It's only felt weird because I've made it weird. It's felt . . . right. I could do this every day and be content.

I shouldn't want this.

But I do.

I shouldn't be comfortable in his arms.

But I am.

I should make him leave and put some distance between us.

But I can't.

I hear the line Aaron used to recite from the movie, *"Hold up, wait a minute, let me put some pimpin' in it."*

I burst out laughing and so does Liam. I look at him as I remember. I remember how he used to sound, how his face was after he'd say it. The way his eyes crinkled and he'd smile when I'd roll my eyes. I remember it all and I start crying. Not tears from laughing, but full out tears. It hurts to remember. The pain crashes over me like waves on the shore. They roll in one after the other and each one breaks my heart a little more. I want the pain to stop.

Liam's eyes go wide when he realizes I'm not laughing. He immediately takes me into his arms and holds me close. "Lee? What's wrong?" The panic is clear in his voice.

"Oh my God!" I cry louder and it doesn't stop. "I can't," I say in between breaths. Holy shit, I'm falling apart. "I can't breathe."

Guilt assaults me for thinking of a life with Liam while I'm still so fresh to this new life, making it hard to breathe.

Liam holds my face in his hands and wipes my tears with his thumbs. "Why are you crying? What happened?" he asks confused.

I keep crying as he stares at me like I'm a wounded animal. Which is exactly what I must look like.

He shuts the movie off and the tears continue to fall. "I can't," I say and he grips my face again.

"Tell me what to do. I don't know why you're crying," Liam's voice trembles and he's looking around frantically for . . . *something,* anything that would help. "Natalie, calm down."

"I don't know. I just . . . it hurts. I don't want to hurt anymore!" I exclaim as my breathing becomes more labored. I'm having a fucking panic attack. "Make it stop hurting," I beg.

Liam's eyes drop and he pulls my face to his slowly. He looks at me as his mouth gets closer and I snap out of whatever the hell that was. "Liam!" I say and pull back. "What are you doing?"

He leans back and grips his neck. "You were crying and I just . . ." he says quickly. "I don't know. I mean, tears and girls . . ." Liam rambles and gets up. He stands there and wipes his hand down his face. "Guys don't know what to do with tears!" he says, frustrated.

I smother my enjoyment at the situation. I really do, but he looks ridiculous and endearing.

"Lee, I'm sorry. You were begging me to make it stop." He starts to pace and speaks fast. "I mean, Jesus."

"Yeah, but why did you think you should kiss me?" I ask, trying to not smile again. But right now, he's adorable. He's flustered and out of his element. I stand and put my hand on his arm to stop him from pacing.

"I don't know. I mean, what the hell? You were crying. Like full blown tears! I'm a guy. We don't do tears." He throws his hands up and starts to mumble to himself about women. "Fucking tears. I mean, I just thought . . . if I kissed you then you'd stop fucking crying."

I burst out laughing again and grip his face. "You're so dumb," I laugh and he relaxes. "Next time a girl is crying, just hold her."

"Don't cry anymore. Ever. I'm not equipped to deal with that shit."

"I can't promise that," I look into his eyes.

Liam's arms wrap around my back and the urge to kiss him rises. "I hated seeing it," he murmurs.

"What?"

"Watching you cry. I've never felt so helpless." Liam shakes his head and then looks down. "I'm sorry I tried to kiss you."

I pull his face back to me.

"Liam, I . . . it . . ." I want to see. I want to kiss him and ease his embarrassment, but more than that I want to kiss *him*. I may hate myself later, but I'm not sure about anything right now. Liam makes me feel safe. Aaron is gone. I look into his eyes, and battling the need to feel this man, to feel desired, to be kissed by him becomes insurmountable.

Slowly, I lean in. His eyes watch mine as I pull his head closer and he lets me. He allows me to lead this and I see the desire build behind his eyes. I watch the storm pass across his face as he processes, and I measure what I'm doing.

"Natalie . . ." he says low and reverent.

The way my name rolls from his lips makes me want him more. We breathe in each other's breaths. Taking and giving this moment, my stomach tightens as I press my lips to his. I don't think. I try not to focus on the differences. The way his lips are firm but yielding. The way he doesn't move and every part of him is stiff. I don't allow myself to compare the differences in height. How I have to lift up on my toes to reach him. My fingers glide to the back of his head and thread in his hair. I want him to kiss me, but right now he stands like a statue. Tilting my head, I try to get him to respond, but the only thing I feel are his hands tightening against my back as he grips my shirt. I break away and we both open our eyes.

Whatever he's looking for in my eyes, he finds, and Liam's resolve cracks. His hand moves to my upper back as his mouth is on mine. This kiss is his. This kiss isn't asking—it's taking. His lips press against mine, firm and strong. I sigh unconsciously and he takes that as permission. I feel his tongue brush against mine and the muscles in my stomach clench. Liam holds me against him and holds me together. I lose myself in his touch. Even in this moment, he gives to me. He pulls me closer and my fingers tangle in his hair and grip. I don't want to stop.

I want him.

I want this.

I need this.

I hate this.

Conflict stirs suddenly as realization dawns on me.

I'm kissing Liam Dempsey and I like it.

chapter

sixteen

MY FINGERS LOOSEN and then his grip does. Liam releases me and we both try to catch our breath. I look at him and his eyes drift to the mantel. He stares at the flag and my insides hurt.

"Natalie," he grumbles in a low tone. He's upset. "I . . . fuck . . . I just . . ."

"Please, don't," I request hoping he won't say this was a mistake or that he's sorry. I hate the word "sorry" and I sure as hell don't want to hear it from his mouth. I'm tired of people apologizing. You're not sorry. You don't know what to say and I'm over hearing it.

"No, listen," his hand grips my arm as I try to turn. "Fucking listen. I don't know what this is. I mean, you're . . . well . . . you!" he exclaims and drops his hand. "We've been friends for a long time and you've always been his wife. I don't know if I'm making any sense."

This whole situation is confusing. There's a part of me—a big part—that's weighted and suffocating in guilt. I feel in some small way as if I cheated on my husband. I know I didn't. I know that he's gone, and hell, he wanted me to move on, but it's there. Deep in my gut, I'm tormented that this was wrong. Then there's the other side of me—the woman side—that wanted and needed to be touched. I enjoyed the way his lips felt against mine. The way Liam took me in his arms and the way my body molded to his. It was everything I needed and nothing I wanted to need. But I initiated it. I went to him and I would do it again.

"I'm not sure what to say," I reply honestly. "I wanted to kiss you. I wanted to not want to kiss you," I give a half laugh.

Liam steps forward and pulls me against him. "I wanted to not want to want you, but I do. I don't know how or when, but I have these feelings for you. I don't know if we should do this. I don't know that either of us is ready for this," Liam says quietly as we hold each other.

"I don't either. Maybe we should take all of this one day at a time. I don't know that I'm ready." I look at him as he gazes into my eyes. "I know I don't want you to stop coming around, but I don't know what I'm capable of. I mean, it's not even been a year and I just . . ." Tears pool in my eyes as I try to process what happened. I kissed my friend. I kissed Aaron's friend, and I'm not sure if it's wrong.

"You're not getting rid of me. And I don't want to push you. But I want to kiss you again. Unless you want me to stop?" He waits and my breathing increases.

The anticipation builds inside. It roils and grows, taking up every inch of my soul. I want this. I measure the parts of myself, trying to see whether it's guilt scraping its way through me or whether it's desire. The desire pools and smothers any guilt. My heart wants this and so does my body. I inhale and close my eyes, taking in each note of spice and sandalwood. The feel of strong arms wrapped around me. I shiver even though there's not one part of me that's cold.

"Do you want me to stop, Lee?" Liam's voice is husky and laced with want.

Liam's hands make their way up my spine and then back down around my hips. He lifts me off the ground and his breath warms my face. I can feel him grow closer and closer. "Now's the time, sweetheart," he says, practically touching my lips.

"No," I breathe the word.

"No, you don't want me to stop, or no, you do?" he asks, his nose brushing against mine. His lips are a millimeter from mine and one nudge and we'd be touching.

"No, I just . . ."

He pulls back the slightest bit. "Just what? What do you want?"

What do I want? I want it all. I want to not hurt anymore, and when I'm around Liam, it's not so hard. He makes me smile and laugh when I feel like I'm drowning in sorrow. But the best part of him is that he doesn't even realize he's doing it. It just happens when he's around.

"Kiss me."

He presses his lips to mine softly. There's no rush, no urgency, he kisses me like I'm delicate and breakable. Liam cherishes me as he holds me in his arms and gives a piece of himself to me. I'm open and vulnerable and this kiss shows me he knows that. He's not pushing me. He's giving me strength and understanding.

All too soon he pulls back and presses his forehead against mine. We stand embraced and his hand rubs my back. "I'm going to get going. You have to work tomorrow."

"Okay," I say and keep my eyes closed while he holds me. "Maybe you can come over again this week?" I ask awkwardly. I mean, I don't know how all this works. Do I invite him over or does he keep showing up like he has the last month and a half?

He pulls me close again and chuckles. "How about we go out on Friday night?"

I look at him and my heart rate picks up. I'm not sure I'm ready to go out.

"Lee, we don't have to go on a date. I just meant maybe we can go out with friends as friends."

Liam's hands drop and I let out a deep breath. "I don't know if I can leave Aarabelle."

"Think about it. We can all go and celebrate you going back to work. Mark and Jackson are here, you said. I'm sure everyone would love to go out."

I nod and wring my hands. "I'll think about it."

"Okay, I'll call you soon," Liam says as he grabs his stuff.

"Okay," I mutter. This all of a sudden has become weird.

He walks to the door and pauses with his hand on the door. Slowly, Liam turns and his eyes glimmer with sincerity. "No matter what, I want you to know that your friendship means everything. I'll always be here for you and we never have to mention tonight again if you don't want to. We can pretend nothing ever happened. I want you to be happy, and if you needed to kiss me because you needed something, I won't be upset."

"Liam, I . . ."

His hand lifts to stop me and he gives a reassuring smile, "I'll let you use me if you need that. I don't know when things changed for either of us, but whatever you need—tell me. If you want to forget tonight, if you want to be friends, or if you want to see whatever this is—I'm here. I'll let you lead for now."

Before I can respond, Liam turns the doorknob and walks out. I walk to the door and place my hand on it and close my eyes.

Now I need to figure out how to lead a dance I don't know the steps to.

I head up the stairs and look at the pictures that line the walls. My wedding photo, our first date, and my maternity shoot all stare at me as I take each step. My lips tingle from our kiss and my mind reels. I kissed another man, and not just any man, but someone who was there for most of these memories.

How could I do this? Can I do this? I pause at the top of the step where Aaron's photo hangs in a dark frame. It has his shadow box with all his medals and ribbons under it. My hand touches the cool glass and a tear falls. Here I stand staring at the man I loved while my mouth still tastes of Liam.

I grab the photo of Aaron off the wall and lie in my bed with my husband in my arms and fall asleep wishing this guilt would stop.

"SPARKLES, CAN YOU bring in the new contract that was faxed over a few minutes ago and head into Jackson's office?" Mark pauses at my office door and then rushes away.

I grab the papers and head over to his office. It's been two weeks since I've been working here and so far it's been great. They realized quickly I was definitely overqualified and I'm now handling all the scheduling and mission preparation.

"Hey," I say as I walk in. Jackson and Mark are

laughing at God knows what.

"Hey, come in," Jackson instructs and he slaps Mark. "I need to see how many guys we have open to send if we get the Africa mission."

I nod and hand over the papers I brought with me. The way Jackson was able to start this company and handle complex missions is seriously impressive. They've been getting more requests and aren't able to fulfill them all due to staffing. Apparently Aaron handled recruiting and they've not filled his position.

"I think you guys need to do a recruiting session or something. There have been a lot of inquiries and you're turning clients away," I suggest and they both glance at me with a pensive look.

"Lee," Jackson says with caution. "I know you just started, and let's face it, you're doing way more than what we hired you for. I need someone who's smart, who can read these guys, and get some new blood in here. I'll turn away business before I'll send anyone unprepared or understaffed."

"Are you offering me another promotion?" This is by far the fastest anyone has ever moved up in a company.

Jackson nods and Mark laughs. "I'm sure you're bored out of your fucking mind answering a phone that rings once every hour. Besides, dickface leaves in a few days and I need someone with a brain."

I look out into the office where there are others who've been here for a long time. They bust their asses and have been dedicated to the company far longer than me. "What about the others?"

Mark glances over, and for the first time, looks serious. "There's a lot you don't know regarding what they do. They aren't administrative."

"Okay," I say confused, but I let it drop. "What all does this entail? I mean, I have Aarabelle and I didn't even want to come back to work."

Jackson stands and heads over to the wall of pictures. "I would never let this take away from Aara. Mark and I will make sure of that. You just have to be honest with us and let us know." He rubs his hand down his face. "If you take it, there are going to be some background and clearance things I'll need you to do."

Mark kicks his feet up on Jackson's desk and gives a taunting look. "Don't make Muffin suffer too long. He's already starting to go grey."

"Fuck off."

"Do I get to referee you two?" I ask and slap Mark's leg.

Mark laughs and drops his legs. "I always win."

Jackson scoffs and walks behind us, slapping Mark in the back of the head. I swear these two are like children. It's some kind of genetic tic they all have.

"Okay, if you think I'm the right person, Jackson, I'll do whatever you need."

Both of their demeanors shift slightly. I can feel the tension from both of them. "Lee," Jackson says drawing my attention to him, "You'll have access to a lot of information and files. Things that are locked on your computer now because of your clearance. When we do this, you'll no longer be locked out."

"Ummm, okay?"

"I don't have any doubts you'll get the clearance, so I want to tell you about one."

Mark puts his hand on my shoulder, "It's about Aaron."

chapter

seventeen

"WHAT ABOUT AARON?" I ask hesitantly. What could they possibly have in a file that I don't know about? It was an IED . . . there's not much else to have in a secret file.

Jackson sits on the edge of his desk and the serious look in his eyes scares me. "We've been investigating the attack on his vehicle. I think it was targeted."

"Targeted how? I mean, who would target him?"

He grips the bridge of his nose and exhales. "Not him. I think they wanted to attack me. I don't know. At this point, we don't have much info, but there's a file and I didn't want you to find out about it from someone or some other way."

"I don't understand," I say conflicted. I was told his death was just that—a death. It doesn't make any sense as to why they'd be looking into it.

"Natalie," Mark calls my attention to him. "No one kills a member of this team without us following up. There were issues with our supply drop. Aaron went out there to investigate and then he died. Then, we go out and Muff gets himself shot. It doesn't add up." The tone of his voice is commanding and yet still the Mark I know.

I should've known they weren't going to let this go,

and honestly, I'm glad. These are good men, honorable men who won't let someone's life go without having answers. However, this isn't going to be easy for me. I've started to feel again, to live, and then this thing with Liam. Hell, I don't even know if it is a thing.

"I'm not sure what to say."

Jackson tilts forward, "I'm telling you that no member of this team gets killed and we just let it go lightly. Someone will pay for his death. Someone will pay for almost killing me. I didn't want you to be blindsided."

Every part of me wants to tell them to stop. To let it go because no matter what, it won't change a thing. The cruel hands of fate have already slapped me once. I really don't know if I can survive another round.

"Okay, I guess thanks for the heads up." I battle with myself if I should ask for more information. If there is a file, then there is something inside of it. I'm not sure I have the restraint not to look. "Jackson?" I ask hesitantly.

"You want to know?"

"Yes and no. I just need to know if there's anything in there I should know because I don't know how much I can handle," I respond honestly. My heart is pounding and my mouth goes dry as I wait.

Jackson and Mark look at each other and they both shift uncomfortably. Mark clears his throat, "All we know at this point is we think our company is being targeted. Also, we think they believed Jackson would be in that car."

My hand flies to my chest and I gasp. "Why?" I stutter. "Why would anyone want to target you?" The words fly out of my mouth and I stand. These are my friends. This was my husband and my family that were caught in the crossfire.

"We don't know, but we'll find out. This isn't

something we're going to drop." Mark stands and pulls me into his arms. "He was one of us."

I nod and step back. This is a lot to process and I'm not sure there is anything that will make this okay. Regardless, my husband was murdered, so finding out why, for me, is irrelevant. It won't bring him back.

"Okay, let's get to the meeting. I have a lot to think about and I want to be able to focus on work. I have to take tomorrow off to bring Aarabelle to the doctor for a follow-up." Her appointment is later in the day tomorrow, but I want to spend some time with her since I feel like I'm missing out being back at work. Plus, I don't want to talk about Aaron . . . not today.

We wrap up the rest of our meeting and go through some things that need to be done. I flop in my chair and spin so I'm looking out the window. What a clusterfuck this all is. My heart was starting to heal. I was finding a way to put one foot in front of the other without stumbling, but now I'm on shaky ground again.

My office phone rings, halting my inner turmoil.

"Hello, this is Natalie."

"Hello, Natalie," his gruff baritone voice causes my heart to falter.

"Hello, Liam," I say as my lips turn up on their own accord. I sink into my chair and twirl the chord. Jesus, just him saying hello has reduced me to a teenage girl.

"What are you doing?"

"Working," I reply sarcastically.

"Smart ass. I'm calling to ask you on a date."

Liam's been gone the last week. They had a training mission that required them to go to Florida. We haven't spoken much while he was gone other than a few quick text messages, but I feel better about what happened between us. Reanell and I spoke at great length and she helped me see everything clearly.

Liam cares or he wouldn't give me the space I need. He knows me after years of friendship, and also Aaron was his best friend. I don't think he's capable of tarnishing his memory. There's not a part of Liam that wants to take my love that I shared with Aaron away.

"You are? A date?" I grin and bite my lip as I toy with him a little.

He laughs, "I am. Are you available?"

"I don't have a babysitter. I kind of need a little more than a few hours' notice, but maybe tomorrow."

"Check your text messages," Liam instructs.

"Ummm, okay."

I grab my phone to check and sure enough, I have a text from Rea.

Hey, I've got Aarabelle tonight. Have fun. Have sex . . . or don't, but you know, you could.

"Well?" Liam asks already knowing the answer.

"Huh, well, what do you know? A friend is abducting my daughter."

"I'll pick you up at seven." Liam's confidence is thick through his voice. Part of me wants to slap him, the other part wants to plant my lips against his again. "Oh, Natalie?" he asks and his voice is low and gravelly.

"Hmmm?"

"Wear a dress," Liam says and then disconnects the call.

I shoot a quick text to Reanell.

It seems you've made a new friend.

It seems you've got yourself a boyfriend.

What are we, twelve? I don't even know if people call them boyfriends. I mean, we're not exclusive. Or maybe we are and I'm just stupid—which is possible. My palms start to sweat as I think about this. I'm not sure I'm ready to have a boyfriend.

No, we're friends. He's just taking me out.

Okay. Whatever you say. I'll grab Aarabelle from the sitter's on my way home. Have fun. Love you.

I love her so much. She's the closest thing I have to a sister. She was there holding my hand when I delivered Aarabelle, she slept in my bed for three days when I found out Aaron died. I don't know how I'd survive without her.

Love you more! I'll call you tonight.

Or don't. That could get awkward.

She's crazy if she thinks that's happening. Oh my God, what if that's what I'm supposed to do?

I need a drink.

CHAPTER EIGHTEEN

LIAM

"**H**AVE YOU LOST your fucking mind?" Quinn stands at my truck giving me shit about going out with Natalie tonight. "Natalie Gilcher? As in your best friend's *wife?*"

"Fuck off. It's not like you think."

He shakes his head and claps me on the shoulder. "You're going on a date with Aaron's wife. Let me know where I'm missing something. Because it seems crystal clear to me."

I shrug him off. He has no room to talk since he was screwing one of our buddy's wives, but apparently he has short-term memory loss. "Maybe we should talk to Bueno about missing something. You seemed to be awfully confused when you slipped your dick there."

"I was drunk." He steps back and shakes his head.

I'm not going to sit back and let him give me shit. I do that enough myself. I don't want to be that guy. The one who fucks his boy's wife. Shit, up until the last month, I never even looked at Natalie that way. It's not like I was chasing her skirt when he was alive. We're friends and it fucking happened.

"Whatever, man. I'm just saying don't give me shit. I'm not doing anything wrong. We're friends and I'm taking her out so she has a night away for once. It's been nine months since he died."

"Did you fuck her?"

I step forward and ball my fists. "Watch your fucking mouth." First of all, it's none of his damn business. Second of all, if that happens, I don't plan on telling him. "If and when we do . . . it sure as shit won't be fucking."

Some of the team guys are worse than a bunch of women. I'll have to listen to all their opinions and unsolicited advice. I don't want to hear how either they agree or don't. It's not up to them. As far as I know, I'll show up tonight and she'll tell me to fuck off—which is quite possible.

Quinn shakes his head. "Be careful, man. That's all I'm saying."

"I'm always careful."

"Yeah, well, this time you're playing with fire. It's not just some girl. It's *his* girl and *his* kid."

"I'm going to be kinda fucking obvious here, man. He's dead. I'm not doing anything to tarnish his memory or life. He was *my* best friend. I would've gladly been in that Humvee when it was hit. I would've traded places with him in a heartbeat. Natalie and I are friends and there's something there. So I'm not doing anything he would disapprove of," I explain and he nods.

"I know you're not like that, but I wouldn't want my wife to marry another SEAL."

"You'd have to find someone dumb enough to marry you first before you need to worry about that." I try to diffuse the situation. I get that Quinn thinks he's helping, but he doesn't see it. He only sees what he wants right now.

"This would be true. And I'd have to give up one-night stands. I'm good." He shakes my hand and laughs. "I'm going to the gym. I'll talk to you later."

"See you later."

Tonight is going to be the first time I've seen her since we kissed. I tried to give her the lead. Let her text me first. I swear I lost my dick and grew a pussy. I'm doing the damn three-day shit. Ridiculous. I want to slap myself or pull my own man card. But she's Natalie. She's got a kid and she's not some girl. I've known her forever. I was at her wedding for Chrissake. I can't just jump the gun and go all caveman on her. She needs to feel in control.

I get home, shower, and make sure everything is set. When I called Reanell to have her watch Aarabelle, she gave me "advice" on what to do tonight. Not that I had a brilliant plan, but apparently Reanell wasn't impressed at all. So, she provided me with the restaurant and where to take her after dinner.

Sixty seconds seem to take forever. The clock is broken because I swear it's not moving. Fuck it. I'm going over now. I'll annoy her until our reservation.

I grab my coat and head out the door.

The ten-minute drive gives me a chance to talk myself out of embarrassing myself. Even though we've been friends for years, this is definitely something else. I've seen her in dresses. I've seen her in a bikini. But this is different.

I park outside her house and open the glove box to grab the gift I got her and the letter from Aaron falls out. Fuck. I forgot about that.

Here I sit outside his house to pick up his wife for a date and I haven't even read what he wanted me to know.

I'm a fucking douchebag. I stuff the letter in my console. Tonight, I want to be with her. I don't want his ghost haunting me and I already have enough guilt about this date.

I think about what Quinn said and how I'm stupid. Partially, I am. She's a widow, a single mom, and trying to put the pieces of her life back together, but there's something there. She draws me in and I don't even realize it's happening. She makes me want to be a better man.

I went from dreaming about guns to thinking of the way her blonde hair looks when she's tired and it falls in her eyes. The way Aarabelle looks when she's asleep and how much I want to have that at some point. I can't explain it. I don't know if there's even a way to put it into words. But she does something and here I sit trying to talk myself into doing something I'm not sure I should. If she'd never been Aaron's wife, I would've been at her door already. I would've had her in my bed, in my arms, and in my heart, but she comes with a warning sign. One I've chosen to ignore because I can't. I'm weak to her and I don't know why.

But I'm going to find out.

chapter

nineteen

natalie

KNOCK, KNOCK, KNOCK.

The sound of the tap on the door causes the fear to stir like a snowstorm inside of me. The way your face grows cold and it hurts to breathe—which is crazy since it's summertime. I know it's not bad this time, but I'm still terrified.

It's a date.

With Liam.

I glance at my dress and press it down with my hands, smoothing the soft, satin fabric and at the same time trying to calm my nerves. I do a quick mirror check, fluff my hair, and pinch my cheeks. I wore my favorite red dress. I was worried after so long it wouldn't fit, but luckily it fits better than the last time I wore it. My breasts are fuller thanks to Aarabelle, and it clings to my curves perfectly. The soft, flowing curls hang to my mid back and I have my nude heels on. It's the first time in months I've taken any time to really look pretty. Usually I'm in sweats and a ponytail. Not much need for vanity around a baby.

"Here goes nothing," I say to myself before opening the door.

Liam stands there with his hand on the frame and my mouth goes dry. Holy shit. He's dressed in black dress pants and a dark blue shirt. His sleeves are rolled showing his forearms and the fabric clings to his muscles. *What is it about a man's forearms that are so damn sexy?* My eyes travel his body and absorb every part of him. It's not normal how good-looking he is. It's not fair. He makes it impossible for any woman to resist him. I make my way up to his face where the grin is painted. He watches me watch him, clearly enjoying himself.

I haven't really *looked* at a man like Liam. I don't usually pay attention, but with him . . . it's impossible not to. He's tall and steadfast, commanding and alluring. Every part of him screams danger, yet I see inside his heart. I see the man who cares for me and Aarabelle. The one who arranged an entire night out after not being able to see each other for a few weeks. I see the heart he wears on his sleeve with me. I want him to push me, but he knows somehow that I need to go to him.

I stand there admiring the insanely sexy man at my door as he stares at me. "Hi," his rich voice is low and seductive. One word and my heart begins to race.

"Hi," my voice cracks and I look down.

Liam steps forward and grips my chin. He pulls me so we're eye to eye. "You look breathtaking. I missed you."

"You did?" I ask already knowing he did. He sent me texts the entire time he was away letting me know he was thinking of me and Aara. That's the one thing with Liam—I can't help but let him chip at my walls. He cares for Aarabelle and loves her. When she was sick, he came running. Not out of some stupid obligation, but because he was concerned. You could see it in his eyes and it was another crack in my armor.

He laughs and steps closer so we're toe to toe. "I did. Did you miss me?" Liam's finger lightly travels down my arm, leaving goosebumps in its wake.

I shrug and reply playfully, "Eh, you know. I needed someone to hang a couple of new photos, so I guess I did . . ."

Liam's hand flies to his chest in mock horror. "I'm the handyman. I'm crushed."

I take a small step forward and wrap my arms around his torso and hold tight. "I missed you."

His strong, thick arms wrap around me and my body molds to his. "We're going to be late," he says and presses his lips to the top of my head.

I look into his blue eyes that glimmer in the moonlight. "Where are we going?"

"That's a surprise."

"Wow, you're really going for the kill."

"I don't know how many of these I may get, so I'm going to make it count." Liam's lip rises and he wraps his arm around my waist and guides me to the car.

"Keep this up and you may get a few more dates," I joke and nudge him.

"We'll see. I'm not the only one on probation," Liam simpers and I slap him in his chest.

"Yeah, okay. You wish, buddy."

He laughs and I follow as we walk arm in arm down the driveway.

"God, I love your car," I say aloud as I climb in. He has a 1968 Dodge Charger that he restored with his dad. It's candy apple red with tan interior. Every part of this car screams Liam. It's sexy, mysterious, loud, and yet it fits him in some odd way.

"You match," he muses as I settle into the seat. "Robin's been good to me. She never lets me down," he says as he grips the wheel. "We have an understanding."

"You named your car?"

"And this surprises you? She's my baby. You wouldn't not name your child, would you?" Liam asks completely serious.

"That's stupid."

"No, it's not."

I laugh and buckle my seatbelt, "Yeah, it totally is, and why a girl? Why not name the car after a guy?"

Liam smiles and backs out of the driveway. His hand glides over the dashboard as he speaks of his car. "Same reasons ships are named after women. Ships have personality and character. They protect us on the seas and bring us home. They mirror what is beautiful about every woman. Willful, strong, protective, and faithful, and Robin is no different."

"I think I've heard it all."

"Well, I could say it's because it's not the initial expense but the upkeep that will kill you." His mouth curves as I roll my eyes. "But that might be considered sexist."

"Might?" I retort.

I try to fight laughing or smiling. I try but fail.

"See, I can always make you smile."

"And at the same time make me want to punch you."

Liam chuckles and pulls into the parking lot at the Lynnhaven Fish House. Which is one of my absolute favorite restaurants in Virginia Beach. "It's a gift—at least that's what my mother says."

"She's biased."

"Natalie?" Liam asks slightly apprehensively. I look over and he sits with his hand on the door. "I'm glad you agreed to come out tonight."

Not that I had much of a choice, but of course I did. I could've told him no and gone home to Aarabelle. There were a hundred other things I could have chosen, but instead, I put on a dress and went blindly with him. "Me too."

"Stay here," Liam requests and exits the car quickly.

My lips widen in approval as he opens my car door a few seconds later. He extends his hand and I place my palm to his. I don't know that I've ever had a date be so chivalrous. No. I will not compare. I need to be here in the moment.

"Thank you," I say and kiss his cheek. "By the way, how did you know I love the Fish House?"

"Lucky guess," he says but I sense there's something more to that.

We enter the restaurant and are seated at the window overlooking the bay. It doesn't matter that my house backs up to this view, I'll never tire of it. The way each wave brings new water to the sand, washing away the footprints we leave and giving everything a new chance. It's . . . hopeful.

Once we order and get our wine, Liam grabs my hand that's resting on the table. "You okay?"

"I'm great. Why?" I ask, perplexed.

"You've just been quiet." He looks out to the ocean and then back to me.

I smile tentatively and flip my hand over so we're palm to palm. "Is this weird for you? I mean, it's *us*."

Liam sighs and his finger whispers over the skin on my wrist. "Weird? No. Unexpected? Yes."

That's a good word to describe what all of this is. Neither of us thought we'd be sitting here on a date, yet that's exactly what we're doing. "It's a good unexpected though, right?"

"Natalie, I wouldn't want to be sitting here with anyone else," he answers and the truth shines through his eyes.

I want to reply *me either*. I want to say the words, but they die on my tongue. Aaron's face flashes in my mind and my stomach drops. The guilt begins to grow heavy and sits on my chest. It weighs on my heart and begins to crush it. I'm on a date with another man at the restaurant my husband took me to on our anniversary every year.

"Lee?" Liam asks as tears pool in my eyes. "What's wrong?"

"This . . . this place," I say and try to get myself under control.

"Did I fuck up?" he asks and comes around the table, crouching in front of me.

"No," I say and dab my eyes. "It's just . . . Aaron." I look away because I hate even saying this. "He . . ."

"He took you here?" Liam asks, not sounding upset, but concerned.

"Yeah," I look back at him as a tear falls. "I'm so sorry."

"You don't have to apologize. You don't have to pretend with me." Liam grabs my hand and turns my chair so I have to look at him. "Listen to me. He was your husband, the father of your child, and my best friend. You don't have to pretend he isn't here between us. If you think he's not in my mind every time I look at you, you're wrong. I'm struggling with thinking of you the way I do. Imagining doing things with you that he'd beat my fucking ass for."

Again, a part of my heart breaks, but this time for Liam. This thing between us isn't easy for me, but I never thought about how it would be for him. I wonder if we're doomed from the start. I don't know if it's even possible for the two of us to have a chance at this. There aren't simply two scarred hearts trying to find a way. There's also a ghost between us.

"I don't know how to do this," I reply honestly.

"Me either. That's why I said we take this slow. You can talk to me though. If you're missing him or if you want to talk about him. He's not an off-limit topic. You never mention him with me. Why?" Liam grabs my hands as we sit in this beautiful restaurant and people look at us. He doesn't waver from me. Instead, he kneels on the ground, holding my hand, while I have a mini breakdown.

I pull my hands from his and rest them upon his face. The short beard he keeps is trimmed and it tickles my hand. I brush my thumb back and forth and stifle the emotions that were stirring. I lean forward and kiss his lips gently. "Thank you."

His brows set into a straight line and looks away. "I don't know what for. I made you cry again . . . which I begged you never to do again. Although," he stops and gives a quick laugh, "You tend to kiss me when you cry, so maybe I should rethink this. But you didn't answer my question."

"I don't know. I feel like it's wrong to talk about him with you. I loved him so much and now I have these feelings for you and . . ." I trail off unsure of what to say.

Liam's eyes never falter. He stays trained on me, waiting for me to finish. "You need to tell me because I promise I can't read your mind. I can try. I can read your body. I can tell right now you're nervous. Your heart is racing, your eyes are shifting, and the way you're stuttering tells me everything I need to know. But I don't know what is going on in your mind or your heart."

"I just wish he was here, and then when I'm with you, I don't think about him so much. It makes me feel like I'm a horrible wife."

"You're not horrible. I don't think what we're doing is horrible. Neither of us thought we'd be here. I think with my good looks and charm you were doomed." Liam winks and his mood shifts to playful.

I laugh and wipe my face with the napkin. "You're a mess. Now please get off the floor and let's have dinner."

Liam returns to his seat and I place my hand out asking for his in return. He wants me to lead this and right now his touch soothes me. I'm not going to think about why that is, I'm just going to enjoy it. This is our time tonight and I want to be in the moment for the remainder of it.

"Okay, let's just enjoy our date," Liam says as the waitress walks over.

Liam orders practically everything off the menu. I swear he's feeding someone under the table. No human can consume this much food. By the time dinner is served, I'm totally full but he's still going.

I joke with him about his appetite and laugh as he tells me the stories from their training mission. Some of the guys Aaron was close with are still in the teams. I know their wives and families and it takes me back a little. I've missed these stories.

"How's work going?" Liam asks.

"Good. I got promoted again. I swear it's the fastest anyone's ever gone from entry-level to management in history," I say and take a bite of my lobster.

"Muffin's a smart guy. I'm sure you were never hired with the expectation of staying entry-level," Liam says as he sits back. "What do they have you doing now?"

I put my fork down and take a deep breath. I know Liam said Aaron isn't off limits, but I still feel uncomfortable. On the other hand, Liam deserves to know in some way too. "I'm doing all their mission prep. I'll handle all the logistics and make sure everything is properly staffed and they have all their supplies. Which apparently was the issue that sent Aaron to Afghanistan to begin with. But today I learned some other stuff . . ." I trail off.

"Like?" Liam's hand covers mine. It's as if he knows I need the extra support.

"They're investigating Aaron's death. I mean . . . I don't know what they're going to find. It was pretty clear-cut to me. It was an IED . . . what is there to investigate?" I ask and Liam's eyes move a tiny bit to the left. I wouldn't normally care, but I know that's his tell. "Liam?"

"Look, I thought all along something wasn't right. I mean, not the IED . . . that stuff is common, but then when Jackson got shot over there, it was a red flag for me. That region wasn't on our radar, but then two Cole Security guys were injured or killed? I don't know. It's the skeptical part of me that questions it," Liam says and links our fingers.

"Should I be worried?"

Liam squeezes my hand. "I wouldn't be okay with you working there if I didn't think it was safe. I'd make up some bullshit and sabotage it. There's no way I'd let you be in danger, and neither would Jackson or Mark."

I take a deep breath and release it. He's right. No one would ever put me in harm's way, but the questions nag at me.

chapter

twenty

"OKAY, YOU READY?" Liam asks as he has me blindfolded for our next part of the date. I focus on everything around me. I can smell hay or maybe it's just that clean, open air . . . I think. I can't place it, but there's no noise at all. It's completely quiet. I breathe in again, and grass and flowers register.

"Where are we?"

I feel him behind me. He stands there not touching me, but I can feel the heat of his body. It sheaths me and the anticipation builds. I lean back so I feel him and he chuckles.

His hands graze my bare arms as the tips of his fingers glide across my skin. My head falls back on his shoulder and my breathing accelerates. "When I was stationed here the first time, I found this place. It's where I came after we kissed. I come here when I need to remember how small I am in this world." Liam breathes against my neck. "Sometimes our problems feel so big that we forget how to be grounded and humble." His hands move to my shoulders. The touch is tender and sensual.

He unties the blindfold and my eyes adjust. It's pitch black except for the stars and moon above us. It illuminates the beauty that I'm surrounded by. Trees line the field and tall grass encompasses the entire area. It's untouched except for the small circular patch we stand in. Liam's arms wrap around me from behind and I take it in. "Wow," I breathe. "It's so beautiful and yet so desolate."

"You're not alone," he says, and I sag into him. My head rests against his chest as he holds me tight. "No matter what happens, you'll have me. As a friend or whatever this becomes or doesn't."

"It scares me. I feel like it's so soon. I miss him still, Liam." I turn in his arms so I can see his profile. "I loved him my whole life and the idea of moving on terrifies me. I don't know that I won't get gun shy and pull away."

His hands cradle my face. "I'll never push you. I know he was your world. I saw the love you two shared and I would be full of shit if I said it doesn't scare me. You're supposed to be untouchable, and yet here you are in my arms. I don't know if I'm lucky or a fucking idiot. I just know that when we're together, it feels right. It feels like we're supposed to be."

Even in the dark, Liam's eyes shine bright. He won't hurt me. He won't betray me. He'll be patient and kind because that's who he is. My hands tangle in his hair as we stand together. Our foreheads touch and he holds my face as I hold on to this moment. I'm at peace in this very second. No hurt consumes me, no fear, just Liam. I close my eyes and allow myself to feel and pray.

Please, Aaron, be okay with this. Please understand I'll always love you, but Liam makes it a little bit better. He'll be good to me. So please, forgive me.

I lift my head and press my lips against his. His hand cradles my cheek and he holds me as we kiss. I grab his neck and feel the weightlessness from letting a little part of myself go. He kisses me adoringly and cautiously, allowing me to lead but still commanding me. I lose myself a little more as I moan when his hand presses against the small of my back.

"Let go," he says against my mouth. "Let me take it for you."

Before I can say anything, his mouth is on mine again. Our tongues thrash against each other as the kiss becomes hungry. He pulls me close so there's no space between us. The low sound resonates through his chest, sending shivers down my spine. It's sexy, and before I know it, my hands are traveling to his chest. I pull his shirt out and my fingers trail up his chest. I want to feel his skin.

Liam breaks the kiss. "Natalie," my name is both a plea and a request.

"Shhh," I instruct him as I unbutton his shirt. "I want to feel your heart."

My hands glide up and he trembles beneath my touch. We stand here with my fingers resting on his chest, feeling his heart beat beneath me. He's alive and here with me. His hands stay at his sides as he once again lets me decide where I'm going with this.

"I want to touch you so bad," he admits and his hand lifts then drops. "I'm fighting every muscle in my body right now."

"Stop fighting," I say without thinking.

Liam grips my arm and pulls my hand down as his lips find mine again. He kisses me roughly. Taking from me whatever I'm willing to give. I don't know how far I can go, but right now I'm lost to him. I don't see, feel, or want anything but him. My mind shuts off completely and for once I'm living in this moment. In the field with him, I'm not drowning. Liam breathes the air into my lungs for me. The life that left my soul months ago, when it was ripped from me, starts to find its way back. I'm alive in his arms. His touch elicits the part of me I closed off to come back and ignite.

"Liam," I sigh when his lips leave mine and he kisses my neck.

"Tell me to stop."

"Liam," I breathe his name again as I feel his tongue glide against my collarbone.

"Tell me this isn't wrong," he says in between kisses.

I grab his face and force him to look at me. I need him to see it in my eyes. I want him to know I'm here with him and only him. "This isn't wrong."

He closes his eyes and pulls me against his chest. We hold each other as our breathing comes back to normal. It's crazy how much he frees me from myself.

"I could stay here forever," Liam says, breaking the quiet.

"I'd love to see it during the day."

"One day, sweetheart. Let's head back to the car before I do something stupid." Liam releases me and takes my hand and we start to walk back up the path. "I've come once during the day, but at night you feel the peace. You can see the light through the black. The stars and the moon remind me that life is short and I need to live each day. My job demands I respect death."

"Respect death? How can you say that?" I ask with doubt dripping from my voice.

He stops and stands before me. "Without death there is no life." Liam pauses as if weighing his next words. "When one of us dies, it's not in vain. We don't go lightly and if I don't respect the sacrifice someone made in honor, then what?" Liam asks.

"There's no respect in death for me. It takes from you.

It makes things go dark and gray because there is no solace for the remaining. I'm left here, picking up the pieces of my destroyed life because of death." I choke on the words as he shifts uncomfortably.

Liam steps forward and I instantly regret my words. "Your life isn't ruined. It's altered. Things didn't go the way you thought, but you have Aarabelle, you have friends who love you, and hopefully you'll have me. I can never replace him and I never want to. He was my best friend and I'd give anything to have taken his place so you didn't have to hurt."

"Liam," I try to stop him, but he puts his finger to my lips.

"No, I would. I hate seeing you hurt. I hate knowing Aarabelle will grow up not knowing him. I feel guilty getting to touch you, kiss you, and hold you in my arms. But I respect that Aaron saved more lives than we'll ever know. He gave his life because he was going over there to make sure his team had what they needed. He's a hero to the men he helped. A patriot. And for that, I respect death." Liam's hand presses against my shoulder and he opens the car door.

I don't speak because I don't trust myself. I climb in the car and let the weight of his words come down around me.

He was my hero too, and I lost him.

The drive home is quiet as we both feel the emotions settle. There's a lot to be said, but not tonight. Tonight was our first date, and it doesn't slip past me that I spent a good majority in memories or tears. I know that if I were with anyone other than Liam, it would've been the date from hell.

The car stops in my drive and we sit awkwardly.

"Liam? I know it might not seem like it, but tonight was sincerely special to me."

He leans over and grins. "You're special and deserve a night out."

"I just need time to get there. I want us to keep seeing each other. I want to be . . . well, whatever we are." I laugh and wring my hands nervously. This is so uncomfortable it's a little ridiculous.

"We're friends, Lee. Friends who kiss a lot."

I smile and let out a shaky breath. "I like kissing you."

"I'm glad. Now come here and show me just how much." Liam's voice is husky with desire.

I shift slightly and give him exactly what he asks for.

"HEY, BABE!" REANELL screams as she runs over. "You look amazing."

"I look like crap," I reply as I look down at my sweats.

"Yeah, I was being nice. You look like shit."

Leave it to Reanell to be so sweet.

"You ready for the gym?"

Reanell and I decided we needed to get off our butts since it's summer, and if I have to get in a bikini, I'd like to not jiggle so much. Even though there's not an ounce of fat on her five-foot-three frame. She's the kind of woman people hate to be friends with, naturally skinny even though she eats a bag of chips in one sitting. Has long, dark brown hair that always looks as if she spent hours doing it when she just woke up. But her eyes are most coveted—she has hazel eyes framed with the longest black eyelashes. I want to hate her, but then she opens her mouth and is the kindest person I know, so hating her is impossible.

"Can we go out to lunch after?" she asks as she sits on the couch.

I slap her leg and scoff. "Get up or we'll never go, and no, we can't go out to lunch."

"Ugh," she groans. "Such a damn killjoy. Okay, let's go stare at hot men while they work out."

"You're impossible," I laugh and lock the door.

Paige has Aarabelle at the park while I go work out for an hour. I don't know how I ever survived without her. She's sweet, nurturing, and Aarabelle loves her. Plus, she's available every time I call her. I've been working from home a little more frequently since that's a perk Jackson said I have. Being around Aarabelle for the first eight months of her life and then feeling like I never see her anymore has been extremely difficult for me.

"So," Reanell says as we get in the car.

"So?"

"Are you seriously not going to tell me about what's going on with you and Liam?" she asks with raised brows.

I laugh and try to deflect. There's no way to explain because we're not defining anything. Since our date, he's been busy gearing up for another short training mission, so we haven't seen each other. I miss him though, so that's something.

"Not much to say. I mean, we're just taking it one day at time."

She shifts in her seat and faces me. "Is he a good kisser? Did he touch your boobs?"

"I swear." I roll my eyes and focus on the road.

"Oh, give it up," she huffs dramatically.

"Fine," I reluctantly agree. "He took me to dinner and then to this open field. We kissed and then he was a gentleman and took me home."

We kissed a lot, but I'm not about to give her any ammunition. Reanell was half asleep when I went to pick up Aarabelle, so she wasn't pestering me for details. It seems like today is going to be a different story.

"That's it?" she sounds unimpressed. "I mean . . . it sounds adorable and all, but I was hoping for something juicy."

"Sorry to disappoint you." I clench the wheel as we pull in to the gym. When we park, I turn and look at her. I'm tired of how she thinks I should so quickly dismiss my husband and move on. It's not that easy and I'd bet my ass that if it were her, she'd never talk to another man. "I'm pissed at you."

Reanell turns in her seat and her jaw falls slack, "Me? Why?"

"Because you make it seem so fucking easy, Rea. It's not easy."

"I never said it was easy. I just watch you and it's hard. But . . ." She places her hand on my arm and her voice softens. "I hate seeing you like that. You're my best friend and if it were me and Mason died, you'd push too. I think you're so strong. You've handled this all with grace even while you were dead inside."

I look away and she shakes my arm. I wanted to yell at her and now she's making my heart physically ache.

"Look at me," her voice is pleading. "Liam came around and I thought maybe he'd help you take care of things around the house and introduce you to someone. I never thought he'd be the one to open you up. You smile now." Tears pool in her eyes and they mirror mine. "You smile and laugh. I couldn't get you to laugh. I would try and try, but you were just void."

"Rea . . ."

"No, it's just that he did. If Aarabelle had gotten sick before, you would've called me right away and begged me to come running. But you didn't, because Liam was there. Don't you see? It's happening and you're not even trying. I don't want to see you push him away."

"I'm scared," I admit quietly. That's the bottom line. I'm absolutely terrified. He's everything that I shouldn't want. He's a replica of my husband. Honorable, courageous, and willing to die for the greater good. If I let him in my heart, there's no way I can handle losing another man. If I let him into my daughter's world and he leaves too soon, I'll never forgive myself.

Reanell pulls me into her arms and rubs my back. "I know you are. You can't keep this all in, Lee. Talk to me."

Everyone wants me to talk, but when I let even a tiny bit out, I feel like the flood is going to overtake me. I'll wash up on the shore alone and unable to breathe. There are times it feels like the tide is going to wash me away. So much hurt. So much pain. But then Liam comes around and it's a little bit easier.

"When I found out Aaron died, the idea of touching anyone else was beyond my thought process. I'd forgotten how to laugh because it was easier to stay behind the wall." I look at her and the empathy swims in her hazel eyes. "I don't want to hurt anymore."

Her lips turn as a sad smile forms. "I know you don't, but life is having it all. You can't know real love unless you've had true pain. You're life isn't going to fit in some box. We're all bigger than that box. You, me, Aaron, Mason, and even Liam . . . we don't get to define the box. But you," she clenches my arm, "You're loving even through your pain. You're beautiful even when you tried not to be.

When Aaron died and you had Aarabelle, you lived because you're better than the box you've put yourself in."

I listen and let her words comfort me. I take each syllable and savor it, really take it in, because she's right. I know this, but sometimes I forget. The pain and sorrow are easy to get lost in. For some reason, it's almost easier to be unhappy, but I don't want to live a life full of misery. I have a beautiful daughter, a fantastic support group, and I have Liam.

"I don't want to live in a box," I admit with tears streaming.

"I won't let you, but it's not me who opened the lid and for that reason I think he's good for you." Reanell pulls me into a hug then pushes back. "Now, do you still want to go in there or should we go get ice cream?"

I laugh despite the tears and hug her again. "Let's go get our gym on."

She groans and her head falls back against the seat. "You're so damn evil."

"No, I'm just stepping out of the box."

"Fucking box."

"Yup, fucking box."

chapter

twenty-one

I'M DYING. THERE'S no other way to describe the immense pain and discomfort I'm in. I blame the gym. Plus, Aarabelle was sick the last few days and, of course, now I have it. Aches and shivers plague my body and I want to crawl in a hole.

"Aara, please stay in one place," I plead as she starts to head toward the other end of the room. She's crawling, which makes this illness a hundred times worse. And she doesn't nap as often, so I get no time to rest.

Three days of her awake all night was bad enough. Now that I'm thoroughly run down, I get whatever bug she had . . . awesome. Liam is due home today from another work up. I forgot how much I hated the stupid training missions. Gone all the time and then they leave for the deployment. I used to beg Aaron just to go for an extra month so it wasn't one week here and one week gone. Maddening is how I'd describe it.

When they're gone, you have your routine. You know what your day will entail. These small training missions screw up your rhythm. Even though Liam and I don't actually have a rhythm—yet. We speak every night on the phone. He's trying to let me decide the pace, but for right now, I'm happy with how things are. There's no real definition. We enjoy each other's company, he makes me laugh, he's attentive, and caring. Most of all, he's good to Aarabelle, which matters more than anything to me.

"Lee? You in there?" I hear a knock on the door, but I must be hallucinating now. Fantastic, the fever has gotten so bad I now hear voices.

I hear the banging again and Aarabelle squeals. "Okay, okay. Shhh," I beg the door and Aara, since my headache is now full out throbbing.

"Natalie . . . I'm going to use the spare key if you don't open," Liam's voice is warning as I drag my body to the door.

I open it and lean against it. My eyes squint from the bright sun and I moan.

"What the . . . ?" he trails off as he looks at me.

Glancing down at myself I realize what has him mystified. I'm in my grey Navy Wife sweatshirt and orange sweatpants. I lift my hands up to smooth my hair, only to feel that it's half in a ponytail and half out. Well, no going back now.

"If you're going to judge, you can leave." I cough at the end and he steps in the house. "Enter at your own risk. I'm dying."

Liam chuckles and shuts the door. "You're not dying." He steps in and kisses my forehead. "I think you need to take more medicine and go lie down. You're burning up."

Sleep.

Sleep sounds good.

Sleep and drugs.

"Okay . . ." I trail off as I drag my feet. "Wait!" I exclaim and then cough.

"What?" he asks, picking up one of the burp clothes with a pencil.

"Aarabelle. I have to watch Aarabelle," I remind him and start to shuffle back toward the couch.

Liam grabs my shoulders, laughing. "I've got her."

Well, that wakes me up. "Huh?" My eyes are wide as I look at him.

He shrugs and smiles. "I've got Aarabelle, you go to bed. Maybe a shower too," he nags while laughing. *Dick.*

"Bed. Okay. Are you sure?" I question him one more time. This is his last out. Otherwise, I'm going to bed and taking some heavy medication. I need to kick this virus and fast.

"I've fought in wars, survived BUDs, dragged bloody bodies out of firefights, and much worse than a few hours with a kid." Liam cocks his head and the confidence he has rolls off him in waves.

I half laugh and half cough again at his self-assuredness. He has no idea what watching a mobile child is like. But okay, I'm sick as a dog, and honestly, I'm afraid I'll fall asleep with her awake, so at this point he's better than I am. "She just ate, she'll probably be hungry around five. She woke up from her nap a little while ago, so you'll have to entertain her," I say as he scoops her into his arms and she giggles. They grin at each other and Aarabelle slaps her wet hand she had in her mouth on his face.

"Baby slobber," he says and wipes his cheek. "We'll be fine. Go." Liam juts his chin out instructing me to head to bed. "We've got this, right, Aarabelle? Uncle Liam and you are going to watch football while Mommy sleeps." I stand there for a moment and watch the scene before me. The man who I've known for years, the one I never could've imagined feeling anything for in a romantic sense . . . standing here as my heart swells. Each time I wonder if this is right, he does something that smothers my doubt.

Liam owes me nothing. He's here, again, because he cares about us. Last we spoke, he wasn't due home until tomorrow, but he got back and came right here. I lean against the wall as he talks to her and I could cry. Only this time, they're tears of joy and love.

"Okay, the Packers are on and we want them to annihilate the Bears. Say 'Go, Pack, Go!'" Liam plays with Aarabelle and lifts her arm toward the sky.

I tiptoe to my room, take the strongest flu medication I have, and pass out in my bed.

Hours pass and I wake feeling rested and slightly disoriented. It's dark, which means I've slept way past the two-hour nap I'd planned. I climb out of bed and clean up, brush my teeth, and try to fix my face. My hair is unsalvageable, so I do the best I can. I look a little better, but the bags under my eyes are not normal.

I check Aarabelle's room to see if she's in there, but it's empty. Afraid of what I might find, I head to the living room where nothing could've prepared me for what I see.

Lying on the couch is Liam with Aarabelle fast asleep on his chest. Her tiny hand is wrapped around his and they're both holding on to each other. His huge body shields her as his arm holds her tight. It breaks my heart and mends it at the same time. Two parts of me are pulled apart. The one side that's sad it's not her father. The other part which is grateful it's Liam. Aarabelle shifts a little, and even in his sleep, he moves to accommodate and protect her.

"Feeling better?" Liam's rich voice cuts through the silence and I jump.

"Hi," I whisper and kneel so we're face to face. "I didn't mean to wake you."

His eyes crinkle and he nods. "I don't think I ever sleep fully. I could feel you watching me. Plus," he yawns and shifts Aara, "She moves every five seconds."

"I can take her."

"No, she's fine."

The television is muted but it illuminates the room. Liam's eyes are tired and yet he still won't let me take her. He lies here and lets my daughter listen to his heart. I place my hand on her back and Liam places his over it.

"Thank you," I smile softly.

"I wouldn't thank me yet . . . I made a mess."

I grin and look around the room. He's not kidding. There are bottles, food jars, and about ten diapers strewn around the room. For the first time, I really notice that Aarabelle doesn't have clothes on and I burst out laughing.

"Oh my God," I whisper and try to calm my laughing. "Why does she have two diapers on? And is that rope?"

Liam shifts and cradles Aara into his arms so he holds her like a football. "Who made these stupid things? Those tabs rip off for no reason, then who the hell can figure out which way the thing goes? So I tied it on."

"With rope?"

"I had some in my bag," he whispers and kisses the top of her head. "It works."

"I don't even know what to say to you," I giggle and cough a little.

"How about . . . 'Oh, Liam, you're so amazing, sexy, funny, and I owe you a lifetime of favors which you can collect at any time,'" he quirks his brow.

"Not likely, dumbass." I stifle my laugh and kiss his cheek. "Give her to me, I'll put her to bed."

He hands Aarabelle over and I grab a diaper as he

stands there with his arms crossed.

"You know how long it took me to put that on?"

I look down and there are at least three knots and the rope is looped around her waist and under her legs. I can't believe she even fell asleep with this thing on.

"Watch how long it takes me to put it on the right way," I laugh and look at the knots. "What the hell kind of knots are these anyway?" I ask while he stands there looking proud of his work.

"Need help?"

"I need a knife to get her out of this!" I whisper-yell. He's insane. I start at the one knot and it lets out. I glare at Liam in mock anger. "I swear if she wakes up, I'm going to tie you up."

He huffs, "I might like that."

"You wish." I sneeze and cough wishing I were back in bed. Liam crouches down and unties the other two knots on the makeshift diaper. I look over at him, "I'm surprised you didn't use duct tape."

"I would've if I knew where it was," Liam scoffs jokingly.

The emotions swirl through me. He could've woken me but he handled it. Yes, he tied a diaper on her, but it's sweet and shows, once again, how lucky I am. We both have fears about going into this, but right now, I don't want to fight it anymore. There are things we have to figure out, but Liam has given me a part of myself I'd forgotten about. He sees me as a woman, not a widow.

"Look," I say as he sits beside me. "It's easy." It takes me literally ten seconds to have the diaper on her.

"I swear I had defective ones."

"Sure you did," I say as I pick up Aarabelle. Liam follows behind me to her room. He kisses her head and says goodnight then I place her in her crib. Every night when I put her to bed, I say a prayer for her and ask her daddy to watch over her. Then we thank him for allowing Liam in our lives and ask for him to help us heal.

When I turn, Liam is standing at her door, leaning against it. I stand across from him and we gaze at each other. Both of us are saying so much right now even though nothing is being spoken. My heart and my eyes tell him everything.

Liam leans forward and brushes the hair from my eyes and lingers a little longer. His thumb brushes across my lip and I sigh.

"Liam," my voice is a breathy whisper.

"I should probably leave," he says as his finger rubs back and forth.

My eyes close and I breathe him in. "You probably should."

I want him to stay, but I need him to go. My defenses are down and I'm not ready.

"Okay," his voice is low and rough. "I should. Plus, you're sick and need to rest."

"Yeah, probably . . ." I grip his shirt and hold on. "Or . . . we could snuggle on the couch?" I say, reluctant to let him go. I want him to stay and this is my safe way of having him close. I know men don't want to freaking snuggle, but I just want to lay with him, and there's no way I'm ready to have him in my bed.

Liam laughs quietly and pulls me in his arms. "Yeah, I could go for that."

chapter

twenty-two

"OKAY, SPARKLES, DO you have the applications for the new team?" Mark requests, walking in my office.

We've taken over for a company that failed at two contracts for support in Africa, and now that Cole Security Forces won them, we need to staff them. I've become extremely passionate about my new role. I feel like I'm ensuring everyone comes home safe. The issues the company had previously were due to poor planning. I now make sure the teams we send over there have all the equipment they need. It's also given me a chance to see that Jackson spares no cost for it. Any time I've asked for more funding for supplies, he grants it with no questions. He'd rather cut funding on our end than on the front lines.

"Yeah, they're right here." I lift a stack of papers and keep writing. "I hate that you somehow have given me the call sign I could kill you for." My middle name is Star thanks to my father's hippie days. Mark found out on my application and said I sparkled like a star.

"It's a gift. You should've seen Catherine the first time I called her 'Kitty.'" He stands there and laughs.

"I hope she punched you."

"Nah, she loves me."

"How is it you manage to drive people insane but they still keep you around?" I ask, still keeping my eyes on the paper I'm trying to fix. The wording is wrong and I want to get it right.

"You know you can take a break *and* we have killer coffee," Mark's New York accent is thick and I can't help but want to mock him. It was the one thing they've always made fun of him for.

"Cawfee?" I smile and mimic him, putting the pen on the desk.

"I see we got jokes."

"Only with you, Twilight."

"See?" Mark says as he sprawls out on the loveseat I have in my office. "We make a good team. You're Sparkles and I'm Twilight. It's like a match made in heaven."

I laugh, "I think you're hitting on me, Mr. Dixon." I know he's not, but it's fun to rile him up.

"No, I'm just kidding." He lifts his hands in mock defense. "I wouldn't disrespect you, Natalie."

"Calm down," I shake my head. "I know you're not. Aaron would kick your ass," I reply jokingly and my hand flies to my mouth. "I meant . . . I . . ."

Mark stands and heads over toward my desk. "He would, and so would Liam. It's okay."

"Did someone say my name?" I hear Liam's voice and my eyes snap up. Oh, great.

"Hey," I greet him and walk over.

"Hey, Dreamboat!" Mark smiles and they shake hands and hug.

"What's up, man? Long time no see."

Liam and Mark finish saying hello and catching up briefly before Mark heads out. I don't know if Liam heard, and if he did, whether it would bother him. Regardless,

I'm surprised to see him here.

"I wasn't expecting you." My voice is wary.

He enters and closes my door. "I know. I sent you a text but you didn't answer. I figured I'd just stop by."

"Well, I'm happy to see you." He steps closer and I take a step back. Why am I retreating from this man?

"You look beautiful."

"You look incredibly sexy in uniform." I appraise him as he approaches. He's wearing his woodland camo. His sleeves rolled up make his already large biceps look huge. The way the top clings to his chest is hot, and I can only image how amazing his ass looks. Something about the uniforms always makes their asses look fantastic. *Maybe I'll have him spin so I can see.*

Liam's lip slowly rises as if he's reading my mind. "What are you thinking about?" he asks as he approaches.

I trail his body with my eyes and then back to his face with a grin. "Your ass."

He laughs and then his eyes darken.

I love the game we play. Playful but seductive. I keep pushing him and soon enough he's not going to be so patient.

"I'd be happy to let you see my ass . . ."

"I bet you would, but I'm at work and that would be all sorts of inappropriate." I giggle and put my hand on his chest to stop his approach. Liam pushes me back slowly as if I'm not even there. "What can I do for you, sailor?"

"The guys are going to a bar tonight," he pauses and I nod. "I haven't gone out with them in a long time."

Another step he pushes me back.

"Okay?" I respond slightly confused where he's going with this.

Liam's eyes lock with mine. The way he's looking at

me leaves me breathless. I take a deep breath but it does nothing to help, all I smell is him. His cologne mixed with a hard day's work filters through my body and makes my head spin. "I want you to come with us. With me."

"I-I . . . but . . ." I trail off and look away. "I don't know if that's a good idea." I keep my eyes down but, of course, Liam isn't having it.

His arms cage me in as he presses me against my desk. "I don't want to go and have to push away random skanks all night. I want you by my side. I want to spend the night with you, Natalie." Liam's lips press against my neck and I shiver. He slowly trails feather-light kisses down my collar, then to my shoulder, and I groan. "I want to walk in and have every motherfucker look at me and think 'damn, how'd he get so lucky?' Then I'll take you in my arms . . ." Another kiss and he moves his way up my neck to my ear. "And I'll . . ."

"You'll . . . ?" I whimper when he bends back.

"You have to tell me if you're going to go first."

It's impossible to say no to him. His blue eyes glimmer with hope and he has me practically trapped between his arms. This date will be different. It's us going out as a couple with mutual friends. People who knew Aaron and then will see me with Liam. I have to choose whether I will let my past define my future.

"Who's going?"

"Does it matter?" he counters.

"Yes," I say looking at him. "Of course it matters. I mean, what do we say?"

Liam's eyes don't waver. "Don't go inside your head. It's just friends, going out for a beer."

"No, it's you and I going out with our friends. Friends that don't know us as us. Plus, you've already told me what you plan to do," I reply with a taunting look.

"Lee," he says cautiously, "This doesn't have to be strange. I'll keep my hands to myself the whole night."

I look at him with raised brows. "Right. After you assaulted me in my office with all your promises."

"Hey, I can keep myself in control. It's you I worry about. I'm prime meat and you may want to mark your territory. And my assault was working?"

The laugh that escapes me is loud and effortless. My head falls back and his lips find my neck again. I sigh and wrap my arms around his shoulders. "You use your sexiness against me."

"All part of the plan, sweetheart."

I squeal and smile, "Okay, you win. I need to see if Paige can watch Aarabelle tonight."

"Mmmm," he groans against my collarbone before looking at me. "Hands to myself, right?"

I lean up and kiss him chastely. "It's not tonight yet."

"No, no, it's not," Liam says before he presses his lips against mine. He reclines me against the cold desk but I only feel heat. His heat. He holds me close and cradles my head in his hands, winding my hair around his fingers. My heart thumps erratically in my chest as he kisses me relentlessly. I claw at his back and pull him closer.

I open my mouth to him and his tongue brushes against mine. And it's like a switch is turned off. He devours me and takes away all the fear I was holding on to. I'm floating from my body as his weight is on top of me. He won't let me hurt. He'll protect me even if it's from my own guilt.

I feel his joy radiate from him. Both of us have found happiness through each other. It's scary but also beautiful. I want to give him more. I want to give him what I know he wants. I'm just not sure I'm ready.

AARABELLE IS ASLEEP when Paige arrives. This girl saves my life being available on zero notice. I'm not sure what to wear since this is the first time I'm hanging out with everyone. I change over ten times, but finally settle on my favorite jeans and an off-the-shoulder purple top. Cute and comfy is my goal for tonight.

I hear Liam's car pull in the drive and I give myself a mental pep talk.

I can do this. It's just friends, and Liam and I aren't doing anything wrong. Hell, we're not even sleeping together. Just a lot of kissing. Really, really good kissing. Amazing kissing.

Before he knocks, I open the door. Once again, this man is too good-looking for his own good. How did I never notice this before?

"Hi, sweetheart." His deep voice is velvety seduction. I melt at the way he draws out the "heart" in "sweetheart" as he appraises me.

"Hi, yourself." I smile and grab my clutch.

"You ready?"

"As I'll ever be." I close the door and reach up to kiss him but he moves away. What the? "Ummm?" I question with my eyes wide.

Liam puts his arm out in a gesture for me to loop mine through, but I stand there waiting for an answer.

"What the hell was that?" My voice is filled with indignation.

"That," he says, tapping my nose, "Was me keeping my promise. You want me to behave, so you can't go starting off the night using me for your pleasure," he informs me, putting his arm back out.

"You're joking."

Liam leans down and his lips barely touch my ear as his voice drops lower, "If I touch you now, the rules are off. I want to be able to have my hands on you tonight, but if I start I won't stop. So you choose. I want you . . . don't doubt that." He pulls away and I know this has to be my choice.

Talk about a decision.

I want him and he makes me happy. "And if I want you to kiss me now?"

"Then I get to kiss you later, when I want."

"What if I don't want you to kiss me later?"

He laughs and moves his lips so they align with mine, "I think you'll like me kissing you now, and I know you'll like me kissing you later."

"Well, since you put it that way," I grip his shirt and pull him flush against me. His lips meet mine and I lose myself in his arms. Liam's hands slide down my body and he cups my ass, lifting me off the ground. Pressed between him and the door, my hands grip his neck and I give him what he wants.

Kissing Liam is unlike anything I've felt before. He's rough, but at the same time tender. His tongue dances with mine as if we've been doing this our whole lives. There's no awkwardness. When he gives, I take, and vice versa. I could spend my entire day kissing him and be completely content.

I moan in his mouth and he grinds his hips against mine. *Oh. My. God.* My body starts to shake and he does it again. My lips break from his and I'm freaking panting.

"We should go," he grumbles against my neck.

"I'm going to need a few beers after this." I shake my head and slide down Liam's body.

"I need a cold shower." Liam grabs my hand and we walk to the car. He opens the car door for me. "Seriously, though," he pauses and waits until our eyes meet, "You're beautiful."

My arms wrap around his neck and our lips press together. "Thank you."

He kisses the top of my head and I climb into his car.

I pray I can make it through tonight without anything exploding.

CHAPTER TWENTY-THREE

LIAM

MY GOD, THIS woman is killing me. She's got me wrapped around her finger, but she doesn't see it. I can't stay away from her no matter what I do. Running is useless anymore. I wind up thinking about her during any song that comes on. The gym is a joke, every blonde that walks past me I compare to how Natalie's body is better. I'm growing a fucking vagina.

She looks at me like I'm saving her. I wish she knew how much she is saving me. I've always been reckless on missions. There hasn't been anyone waiting for me at home, so I'd take a bullet for anyone. Now, during our training, I think about how she'd feel. How it would be for her if something happened to me. Not that she loves me . . . yet. But I know she cares. She sure as hell wouldn't kiss me like that if she didn't.

"So, what fine establishment are you guys meeting at?" Lee asks as she shifts in her seat. Two of my favorite women are with me right now. Robin and Natalie.

"The Banque," I reply and wait for her reaction. The Banque is a country line-dancing bar. It's a little run down, but we get in free thanks to the owner, and there's never a shortage of women willing to give it up.

Natalie tilts back with a groan.

"What's the matter, sweetheart?" I ask a little condescendingly. I know she hates that place. All the wives do.

"It's almost as bad as Hot Tuna. I mean, do you guys even want to try to have some game? Or pick up women who aren't laying it all out there for you?"

She's so adorable when she's like this.

"I'll let that slide."

"Let what slide?"

"I have plenty of game," I let her know. "I've never had to work hard."

She snorts and shakes her head. "Arrogant ass."

"Don't worry, only you get to see my game," I gleam and put my arm behind her seat.

Natalie slaps my chest and smiles. "Well, maybe you should try a new playbook because you're not getting much here, sweetheart."

"That hurt."

"You'll live."

"You'll pay for it."

Natalie laughs, "I'm *sooo* sure. You don't scare me, Liam Dempsey. You're scared of me though."

"Damn fucking right I am," I say under my breath but I'm pretty sure she hears me. I'm terrified of her. She's everything I want and I have no business wanting her. She's got a kid and has already lost a husband. I live a dangerous life. I love my life and won't give it up. There's so much more to fear in this entire thing than just the fact that she's my best friend's wife. Natalie has walls and fears that are valid and I know this. And I'm a selfish prick because I really don't care. If she doesn't want me, then she can say so, but until then . . . I want it all with her.

We drive the next few minutes and she stares out the window. I don't know how to handle her sometimes. Like with the tears. Tears I don't do. When we pull up to the bar, Natalie sighs. She gets so deep in her own worries, it's hard to pull her out. I know this isn't easy and I hate it. I don't have the baggage of worrying what everyone thinks the way she seems to. Quite frankly, I don't give a shit. People will judge no matter what, and Natalie and I are grown adults.

"Lee?" I ask her and her head falls to the side as she looks at me.

"You ready to stake your claim, Dreamboat?" she smiles and my worry fades away.

"Stake my claim?"

"You know . . . let everyone know we're together."

I lean forward and she turns to look at me. "Is this what you want?"

"Liam, of course."

"No, I'm serious." I pause because I want her to actually hear me. "If you need time, if you don't want to keep going, we can just go back to friends. I'm only saying this before I get any closer to you. I've known you a long time and it feels like once we flipped the switch from friends to more, I don't want to slow down." I admit this because I know she needs to hear it. She's had a shit year and I can respect that, but my feelings for her grow each day.

"That's what scares me. I think about you all the time. I worry this isn't normal because it feels so easy." She looks out the front window and then back to me. "I care about you so much. You make me happy and . . . I just . . ."

"Just?"

"I don't want to go too fast and then screw it up. I don't want to lose you either. I have to think about

Aarabelle, and I worry about when we take the next steps, how I know I won't be able to guard my heart from you." Natalie's eyes are open and she's vulnerable. I know how she struggles with letting go and it'll be next to impossible to ignore the feeling that a ghost is watching.

When we're in her house, it's strong. I see Aaron around every corner and it freaks me the fuck out. I can't imagine what it's like for her.

"I'll never hurt you intentionally. You don't have to guard your heart."

Natalie's eyes fill with tears and I feel my body start to go into panic mode. She swipes at her eyes. "You're going to make me fall in love with you, aren't you?"

"I'm pretty sure that's a done deal."

She laughs and opens the car door, breaking the moment. "We'll have to see about that."

When she reaches me on the other side of the car, I pull her against me. "Yeah, we will."

I haven't been to this bar in years, but the place hasn't changed too much. There's a dance floor in the middle and it's surrounded by tables. There are two bars on either side and there's a huge bar in the back of the room. The pool tables are always occupied, but maybe I can convince Natalie to play a game or two. Maybe she'll need me to teach her.

I start to imagine what she'll look like with the stick, bent over the pool table. The way her hair will fall and her eyes will find mine. I'll walk behind her and feel her ass press against my dick. The way she'll wiggle . . .

Nuns.

Puppies.

AK-47s.

Diapers.

Glad I got that back under control. We find the table where a few of the guys are already sitting.

"Hey, fucker!" Quinn stands and claps me on the shoulder, already giving me his bullshit-disapproving stare.

"Hey, where's what's-her-name?" I ask knowing he cycles through women like it's nothing. I don't think he's ever fucked the same girl twice.

"I'm looking for fresh meat today." He gives me a look and turns to Natalie. "Hey, beautiful!" Quinn walks over and gives her a hug. I swear if he upsets her, he's going home to ice his balls.

"Hi, Quinn. I haven't seen you in a long time." Natalie's voice shakes a little. She's nervous, which I try real hard to not let bother me. I'm ready to show everyone where we stand and I wish she was too. I know it's been less than a year and I know it shouldn't bug me. But the problem with knowing and letting are two different things.

We're good together. I've known her for almost nine years and never did I imagine I'd be with her like this. She brings something alive inside of me.

I say hello to the rest of the guys from the team, and when we get to the end, Natalie shrieks.

"Rea!" she runs over and hugs her best friend. "I didn't know you'd be here."

The infamous Reanell Hansen. The two of them giggle and I see Commander Hansen tip his beer to me. Fuck. How the hell did this happen?

"Commander," I say and shake his hand. It's one thing when we're all deployed, but to be drinking with your boss when you're home is another thing.

"Dempsey, today it's just 'Mason,'" he says and

grumbles under his breath.

"Oh, Mason, stop being a dick," Reanell says, and she stands, walking over to me.

"I'm Reanell. It's nice to finally meet you for more than two seconds in passing."

"Nice to meet you, ma'am."

"You did not just 'ma'am' me."

I laugh and immediately like her. "No. Never."

"That's what I thought. Now, sit and let's get some alcohol going so Natalie looks like she can breathe." She smiles and makes us sit.

"Sounds like a plan."

"So, tell me, how much can you bench press?" Reanell tilts her head as she looks me up and down before shifting forward with her chin on her fist.

Natalie slaps her arm so her chin falls off. She and Mason laugh as Reanell gives her the death stare. "Stop being stupid and drink your beer."

"It was a valid question," she says and orders a round for all of us.

Natalie relaxes a bit and begins to talk about her job and Aarabelle. We laugh and enjoy small touches. She places her hand on my leg and looks at me under her long lashes with a shy smile. My hand covers hers and squeezes. The little things like this are hard for her, but I appreciate them. I lean back and put my arm around her and she sinks into my side.

The lights dim, indicating it's a slow song. "Wanna dance?" I ask her quietly for two reasons. One, if she says no, I'll never live it down with these assholes. Two, I don't want her to feel like she has to say yes.

Before she can answer me, a short blonde comes up behind me and places her hand on my shoulder. It takes a second to register.

"Hi, Liam. Would you like to dance?"

Fuck. Brittany.

The girl I almost used to fuck Natalie out of my mind.

chapter

twenty-four

natalie

LIAM SHIFTS AS a really pretty woman stands behind him. They obviously know each other and I swear she looks familiar. I can't place her though.

"No, thanks though," Liam replies.

"I haven't seen you since that night," she says and looks over at me. Well, isn't this nice.

Liam stands and extends his hand to me, making his intentions clear. My palm touches his and he squeezes my hand pulling me up. "Yeah," he tries to brush her off.

"I figured you'd call."

"Listen, Brittany, I'm here with my girl and I appreciate you coming over, but I'm not interested."

Brittany turns to me and extends her hand. "Hi, I'm Brittany Monaco."

I stand and look at her hand. It's bothering me, because I know I've seen her around. "Natalie Gilcher," I reply and her eyes widen quickly but then she looks away and recovers.

Odd.

"I'm—" she begins to speak, but Liam clears his throat dragging my attention to him.

"Come on, sweetheart. We have a dance floor waiting." Liam's eyes never leave mine as he speaks, focusing all his attention on me.

"Okay." My voice wavers a tiny bit. He seems anxious to get me away from her and I wonder. My stomach flutters as we walk toward the wooden square. I want to ask him about her, but I'm not sure I have that right. We're not exclusive—well, I am—but I've never given him that definition.

The wheels spin in my mind, each spoke that passes bringing a new worry. If he did sleep with her . . . does it change anything? He's with me all the time, so I don't even know when he would've had the chance.

"Ask me, Natalie," Liam says as his hand wraps around my back and he pulls me against him. "Just ask me."

I pull back slightly and our eyes lock. I hesitate and look away.

"Ask me, because I know it's killing you."

"Why won't you just tell me?" I ask, still not able to force the words out.

"If you want to know, you're going to have to ask," Liam says, looking deep into my eyes.

Drawing on all the strength I have left, I release a deep sigh and ask, "Did you sleep with her?"

"No." The honesty is clear in his eyes and his voice. He didn't blink or pause. "I wanted to. I won't lie to you, but I never got close."

"When?"

"Before I ever touched you." He pauses and presses

his forehead to mine. The music plays and he holds me close to him. We sway to the music and my heart thumps erratically in my chest. Liam sighs and rubs his nose against mine. "I was thinking about you all the time and I wanted it to stop. I wanted to get you out of my fucking mind." Liam's voice is low and sounds almost angry.

"Why didn't you?" I ask apprehensively.

There's no reason for me to feel threatened, but I do. He's single, incredibly sexy, and has no reason to stay. I have a past, a child, and fears that gnaw at me about getting close to him. He has every excuse at his disposal, nonetheless he keeps coming back.

"Because she wasn't you." I look at him, and his eyes stay closed. He looks pained and I want to ease it. I lift my chin slightly and gently touch my lips to his. Here in the middle of the bar surrounded by our friends, I kiss him. I don't care that I'm sure people are looking. I want him to know how much his words mean. How even though we weren't together, he chose me in some strange way.

He pulls back and rests his head against mine again as we slowly sway to the music. His arms encase me and he guides me through the dance. I can feel the eyes burning holes in my back. The stares of friends who now know where I stand. Where we stand.

"It was the night Aarabelle got sick. I had her in my car," Liam begins to tell me quietly. "The whole time she was sitting in the front seat, I kept thinking how all I wanted was to drop her off and go to you. Tell you how I was starting to feel. And then you called."

"Liam, you don't have to tell me," I murmur.

"I know I don't, sweetheart. But I want you to know everything. I won't keep shit from you." He kisses the tip of my nose and I melt into his embrace. "When I saw your name on my screen, I knew there was no way I wanted to touch her. I turned around before I even answered and then when I heard what was going on . . ." he trails off and I look over at Brittany. She shifts and stares at me, biting her nail. "There was no fucking way I wasn't going to be with you, and if I had touched her," he pulls my chin back toward him, "I would've been wishing it was you."

His words soothe my heart and I smile tenderly. "You make this easy for me. You make it hard to fight because you make sense to me. How can you know exactly what I need all the time?" I ask.

"Because I know you. And this is easy for both of us because it's right. I know your heart, and I won't take that for granted."

"I know you won't," I reply as the song ends. This time it's Liam who kisses me.

We walk hand and hand off the dance floor as Reanell's eyes light up. I'm going to need more beer.

We sit and enjoy a few beers and I even get Liam to dance with me during a couple's dance. I'm not the best dancer by any means, but I do love it. I used to come here with my friends a lot when Aaron was deployed. Liam dances with me even though he has no idea of the steps. I give him an "A" for effort—he really is something special.

Throughout the night we all talk and laugh, and I can't help but look over at Brittany. There's something festering inside of me about her. She looks over a couple of times, but looks away quickly. Maybe it's nothing, but then I don't know. Maybe she did sleep with Liam and he's lying. Which doesn't make sense because he seemed so genuinely honest. Plus, he has no reason to lie to me.

I head off to the bathroom to check my face, and when I get back, Liam and Reanell are dancing. I nearly fall over laughing because while the man can do just about anything—except diapers—he has awful rhythm. Well, there's a flaw I found.

"Having fun?" Quinn plops in the chair next to me. Quinn and Aaron were close when he was active duty. They were in the same section and worked together a lot. He was the one person I was worried about disapproving of this whole situation.

"Yeah, how about you?"

"Where there's beer and boobs, I'm a happy guy."

"You haven't changed a bit." I chuckle and take a drink. Quinn has always been this laidback country boy. He drinks a lot, sleeps around, and has more guns than any human should ever need. His dark hair is buzz cut and you can see the scar behind his ear from when he was injured in Iraq.

"Life's too short to change. I live like I want and if you don't like me, oh fucking well."

"Such a charmer," I playfully respond.

"Listen, I know it's not my place and all, but . . ." Quinn runs his hand down his face. "I'm happy for you. I wasn't at first. I mean, we have a code about wives. But, I think Aaron would be glad you found someone like him. If it helps you at all."

I place my hand on Quinn's. He doesn't know that what he said matters. Or that maybe in some small place in my mind I needed to hear that. I do believe Aaron would be okay with it, it's a matter of whether I'm ready to move forward. If I can live the life of dating a SEAL. Knowing what could happen because I've already had my worst nightmare take place.

"Thanks, Quinn."

"Enough of this . . . you need another beer!" he

exclaims and motions for the waitress.

"Natalie?" I hear my name and Brittany is standing behind me.

Okay, maybe I need shots.

"Yes?"

"I just wanted to say I'm sorry about Aaron," she looks away and my stomach drops. Liam's eyes cut to me and he stops dancing. I'm confused because I thought she knew Liam. Why the hell is she talking about Aaron?

"You knew Aaron?"

I've seen this girl. I know her face and it's driving me insane. The way she looks at me as if she knows me too. Her eyes fill with tears and dread spreads through my veins.

Why would she be crying?

"Yes. I mean, I did. I-I met him and . . ." She stops talking and looks at the ground as a tear falls.

"Okay . . . I don't understand why you're so upset if you only met him." I try to figure this out.

Suddenly, Liam's hand is on my shoulder. "Brittany, you should go." Liam steps forward and pulls me to the side. "I don't know what shit you're trying to pull."

"How did you know Aaron?" I ask and push past him.

"Aaron?" Liam asks, sounding as confused as I am.

She sways slightly and I see Quinn stand and move behind me. "I didn't really. I mean . . . I did . . . but it was . . ."

"Either you did or you didn't," I snap.

"I wanted to say I'm sorry. We were friends."

"You said before you just met him."

"You have a daughter, right?"

She's lying. Woman's intuition rings loud in my head. Something isn't right. Something deep inside my soul is telling me not to trust her. Her face though—I've seen it.

"I've seen you before." And then it hits me. "At his memorial." My eyes flash and I remember the blonde that stood off to the side at his memorial. She rushed out before anyone could talk to her. I saw her crying in Pennsylvania. Why would anyone from Virginia drive up there if they'd only met. "You were there."

"I don't know what you mean." Her voice is shaky and she starts to back away. "I shouldn't have come over here."

"Lee, let's go." Liam is trying to command the situation. I feel dizzy and anger starts to take over.

Reanell's at my side, pulling me back, and my hands start to tremble. "You were at his funeral. I saw you! Why?" I yell. "I-I remember there was a woman crying off to the side. I thought it was strange, but I was so distraught I didn't care. It was *you*."

Liam pulls me against his side and Reanell starts to push past everyone with Mason behind her. "Natalie, there were a lot of people there," she soothes as she turns to Brittany.

"I'm not stupid, Rea. She was there. Why were you there?"

"It wasn't me."

"Why don't you leave now?" Reanell suggests to her.

Brittany turns to leave but I need to know. "How did you know him?" I ask once more and her eyes are filled with hurt.

"It wasn't what you think."

"Is this what you do? You come to a widow and talk about her husband? I mean, it wasn't quiet that my husband was killed overseas. So when you were snubbed by Liam you felt as though you needed to do this?"

Brittany looks away and then back at me, "I knew Aaron very well . . . this isn't a game. I've wanted to meet you for some time."

"Why? Why would you want to meet me?"

"I wanted to apologize to you and meet his wife."

Ice shoots through my body, freezing me in place. "Were you involved with Aaron?" I blurt the question out, unsure if I want the answer, but I need to know. Every muscle in my body clenches in anticipation of her answer.

"We were in love," she says slowly and a tear falls as does my heart.

chapter

twenty-five

"OH MY GOD!" I cry and Liam's arms are around me in a heartbeat. "Let me go!" I push him away.

"Lee, stop." Liam grabs my face and forces me to look at him. "Stop. You don't know anything. She could be full of shit."

"You're a liar! My husband would never cheat on me. We were having a baby! We were happy and in love."

Brittany steps forward, but Reanell pushes her back slightly, keeping herself between us. "I'm sorry. We were together for a few months before he found out you were pregnant."

"You couldn't get to my boyfriend, so now you make up some crazy shit about my husband?!"

"I wish I were making it up. But I loved him."

"Stop saying that!" I bellow. "You're lying. You don't know him." I say to myself, "He wouldn't do that." Liam holds me against his chest as I fight against him. "You have the wrong guy," I say defiantly.

"He had a tattoo on his ribs and he ground his teeth when he slept. I wish it was a lie. He lied to me."

My body shakes, and as much as I want to believe it's a lie, there's a part of me that knows it's not.

"This is low and fucking ridiculous," Liam says and he

wraps his arms around me.

"I wanted to tell you so many times. And when I saw you today . . ."

My eyes close and I want to wake up from this nightmare. It hurts to breathe.

"Natalie," Liam's voice is calm and measured, "All you know is what she's telling you."

I look at him in disbelief. "She was there, Liam! She was at his fucking funeral. Who comes to a funeral for someone they just met? Five fucking states away?" I turn and Reanell has Brittany backed against the wall. I head over needing answers. I want every fucking detail. The man who I've been grieving was a cheater.

"I knew that man and he wouldn't have touched you," Reanell says and points her finger in Brittany's face. The tears forming in Brittany's brown eyes, she looks at me with pity.

"How long?" I ask with rage and disgust piercing their way through me. "How long and how many times?"

Brittany steps out of Reanell's grasp and her face falls. "It wasn't like that. I swear."

"What was it like?" I demand an answer.

"I met him and it just happened. I'm so sorry. I-I just wanted to see you. I wanted you to know I'm not . . ."

"Not what?" I ask with tears falling down my cheeks. They burn and fuel my anger.

This night was supposed to be a step forward. A chance to feel alive a little and be a woman. It was my night with Liam and somehow this has turned into the night from hell. Each word shreds my world into pieces and burns them to ash.

"I loved him. We were together for months before I found out. I didn't want you to find out like this."

"You wanted me to know. You stupid bitch! You wanted me to know!" Liam's arms are vices around me as I flail toward her. "If you cared, you could've not come to talk to me!"

"When I found out he was married, I ended it. But that didn't mean I stopped loving him."

I scoff, "I loved him. You're selfish, do you know that? Months you were together! We have a child."

"I saw her." She looks away ashamed. "I wish things were different."

"Don't look away! You need to see my face when I say this to you," I practically growl the words. I'm so angry! "You could've kept your mouth shut and let me be, but no, you had to come make sure I knew. You stupid, selfish whore!" I scream and I'm ready to punch her in the face.

"Natalie, enough," Liam says as he pulls me away. I'm quaking in anger and disgust. I hate her. I hate everyone.

This can't be real. I tell myself over and over again. I was starting to be me again, and now I find this out. It's not real. Still it is. The cruel joke is on me. The echoes of despair scream loudly through my heart. Hollowness overcomes any emotion and I try to shut down. My mind goes back to when I first found out Aaron was dead and how I trained myself to become numb. I search for that power again, but I come up empty.

"Let me go!" I cry out in Liam's arms.

"Come on, sweetheart." Liam's voice is calm and it enrages me.

"Let go of me!" He practically carries me out of the bar, sets me on the ground, and takes my hand. I look up and pull my hand back. "Did you know?"

"Are you fucking kidding me? No, I didn't know."

Liam extends his hand and I tremble. He looks at me

waiting and I just stand there. I don't want to touch anyone. My mind starts to run crazy circles and the questions assault me. My heart is shattered and my life feels like a lie.

A man I would've lived the rest of my life loving is a lying piece of shit. He slept with another woman when I was pregnant with his child. I cried for months over losing him. I clutched his pillow and sobbed wishing he was home, only to find out he was doing this.

Reanell rushes toward us and places her hand on my shoulder. I look at her and tears continue to fall like rain. "Rea," my voice is barely a whisper.

The torrent of emotions flow from one to another and I can't seem to hold on to the anger. I could handle the anger.

"Let Liam take you home." She nods to Liam who grabs my shoulder and pulls me toward him. "I'll come by later."

"Rea," I say again, begging her to make this a lie. Make this all go away.

"I'll find out the truth. Just go home. Liam has you."

The entire walk to the car is a blur. I keep seeing Brittany's face and imagining my husband kissing her, touching her, and I feel sick. When we reach the car, I lean over and the nausea is too much. My stomach heaves, whether from the news of my husband's infidelity or the alcohol I've drunk, I couldn't say. I cry and let it out.

Liam holds my hair and my shoulders. I want to die. I feel like each bone in my body is shattering. The splinters of my wounds are open and I'm bared for the world to see.

"I hate him!" I cry out as I stand and Liam puts me in the car without saying a word. I hate myself for coming here. I hate Liam for touching her even if it was only her hand. I hate Aaron for his indiscretion and the fact that I'm left with my imagination.

Aaron, the man who wrote me letters. The one who made love to me so sweetly when it was my first time—was a fucking cheater. I made him promises of love and fidelity, to end with him dead and now a liar. I cried for him, wanted to put myself in the ground next to him so I could be close to him.

Did he love her? Was she better than me? When he held me at night and talked to my stomach, was he wishing it was her carrying his child? I can't stop thinking it. It flows through my thoughts over and over. Each memory feels tainted.

Next thing I know, I'm in front of my house and Liam is helping me out of the car. I close my eyes and sit on the deck. The warm air that used to give me solace makes me ill. Liam stands before me, and when I look up, he looks as lost as I am.

"I'm going to let Paige go home," Liam says and walks into the house.

I barely nod.

This day I want to forget.

Paige walks by and waves. I lift my hand and then I feel Liam beside me.

"I'm at a loss here, Lee. I'm not sure what to say or do."

"You think I know?" I say harshly. I'm sitting here crying about my dead husband's newly discovered year-old affair to my current boyfriend. There's no way to make this shit up.

"No, I don't, but do I hold you? Do I tell you that he's a fucking fool?"

I look at him ready to spew my anger, but he looks as

enraged as I am. "I don't know. I can't get answers for any of this. Do you know how this makes me feel?"

"I swear to God, Lee. If he was alive, I'd fucking kill him right now."

"How could he do this to me?" If Liam can give me some answers, I'd really appreciate it.

Hesitantly, Liam moves closer. "I don't know, but I would never be able to touch another woman after you. I'd cut my fucking arm off before it would happen. So I can't answer you because I don't get it. I hate that you're hurting."

I look at him and I feel worse than before. Here's Liam, my boyfriend, consoling me over another man. The word "man" is being used loosely because right now, I don't consider him one.

"I don't know if I can do this with you."

Liam laces his hands behind his head and looks at the sky. "This is going to sound fucked up, but don't let what he did to you define what happens with us. I'm not Aaron. I'm here. I'm standing right here. I didn't touch her and I wasn't married to you. Fuck, we're not even sleeping together and I couldn't do it. So I'm not that guy."

I step toward the door and want to erase this entire evening. Before I open it, I turn to him, "I know you're not Aaron. I know you're here, but right now my heart is broken. It's like I'm back grieving all over again."

He steps forward and grips my face, and I beg him with my eyes not to do it. "You're not grieving. You're hurt and I get that. But if you didn't find any of this out, where would we be tonight? I'd be in your bed with you. I'd be holding you, touching you, showing you how much you mean to me."

"Make me forget him," I say desperately.

"Lee . . ." The apprehension in his voice tells me to stop, but I can't.

"Please, show me how you want me," my voice is dripping with need.

"Don't do this," he begs, staring into my eyes.

I want him to make this all go away. "Make love to me tonight. Please, I need you to show me I'm yours. Make all I can think about be you. Give me this." I try to lean up to kiss him but he backs away. The way he looks at me says it all. I cover my face with my hands. This night just keeps getting better and better.

Liam pulls my hands down. "When we make love for the first time, when I claim you, it's not going to be because you want to forget. It's going to be because you want me. You're mine now." He pulls me close and kisses me. Every emotion Liam's feeling is passed through us. My stomach tightens as I experience them all—anger, hurt, fear, love, and desire. He pours himself into me.

Liam pulls back and looks at me.

My eyes fill with unshed tears. He kisses me gently and walks away, leaving me feeling worse than I did before.

I enter the house and I want to feel nothing. I deserve a break from every emotion that's haunting me. The bottle of Jack Daniels sits mocking me. I grab it and don't bother with a cup.

"Fuck you and your cheating self, Aaron," I say out loud as I take a drink. The burning down my throat ignites my anger. "I hope she was good, fucking bastard," I say at his photo and the flag on the mantel.

I drink another gulp and the alcohol flows through me. After getting sick at the bar and the amount I drank before, my body welcomes the numbness. "I guess I'm a real naïve idiot."

Reanell opens the door and stands there. "Oh, Lee . . . you and Jack don't need to have a date tonight."

"Jack, Johnny, hell, any man will do. Except for Liam, nope . . . he doesn't want me like this." I grab the bottle and pour more down my throat. Might as well, my life went to shit again anyway.

She walks toward me and takes the bottle. Before I can protest, she takes a long drink. "I figure we can both hate life tomorrow."

I snatch the bottle back from her and she glowers. "Mine. I need it more than you."

"Before you grab a straw, I think you should talk to me. Where's Liam?" Reanell looks around and I scoff.

"He left too. I threw myself at him and he left." I see the disapproval through her eyes. Good. She can be pissed at him too. "Maybe he went back to the bar to find Brittany. She seems like she gets around."

"Now you're just being an idiot. Keep talking like that, I'll take your liquor away," she chastises me and I begin to cry. "Oh, Natalie . . ."

The tears stream and the numbness I was hoping for morphs into pain. "How could he do this to me?" I sob and she opens her arms. "I thought he loved me. I was pregnant!"

"I know, I know. Let it out." She doesn't try to console me more than hugging me and letting me drench her shirt.

"I gave him everything. I-I don't get it-t."

"You're hurting and drunk, so go ahead and cry," Rea says as she brushes my hair off my face.

I lie in her lap as she plays with my hair. I mumble incoherently about hating him to wishing I could kill him myself. All this time I thought I was married to a different man.

Once I've gotten to a point where I'm no longer hic-cup-crying, Reanell helps me upstairs. She climbs into bed with me as I lie here wishing I could sleep so I could get a break from my mind. This is what she did after he died. Mason was away and she'd come sleep here so nei-ther of us were alone.

"I wish I could go back in time," I whisper, holding back the sadness that creeps up.

Rea shifts onto her side, "Yeah? To when?"

"I wouldn't have tried to make him sleep with me . . ." My eyes close and I fight the sleepiness. "He didn't even want me."

Reanell shakes my shoulder, waking me. "Liam wants you. Liam cares for you and that's why he didn't sleep with you. You both deserve better than a drunken night of sex because you found out Aaron cheated. Now, shut up and go to sleep. I'm going to owe Mason a blowjob for sleeping here tonight."

My lips attempt to smile but I fail. I close my eyes, drifting to sleep where the hurt can't touch me. I welcome the reprieve and pray Brittany and Aaron don't haunt me in my sleep.

CHAPTER TWENTY-SIX

LIAM

MY HOUSE IS eerily quiet and I fight the urge to go back to her. I sat in my car for an hour after Reanell showed up. Fought with myself to knock on the door but instead I went home. Sitting there wishing I hadn't pushed her to come tonight. Selfishly, I'd wanted to force her to be with me outside of the walls of her home, to go public.

After two hours of staring at the walls, I need to see her and make sure she's okay. The way I left wasn't exactly how I'd planned for the night to end. I wanted to fuck every memory out of her mind. Show her that he's a prick for ever making her feel like this, but I don't want it to be because of him. When I take her for the first time, it'll be because she's ready, but I had to use every ounce of restraint I had to walk away.

What a mess this whole damn situation is . . . I can't really bash Aaron because he was my best friend. But I want to bash him because he's a fool. I can't push Natalie to be with me because the guilt of falling in love with my best friend's wife overwhelms me, but I want her so bad I can barely breathe.

I open the door with the key under the plant. I make

a mental note to have her change that. She's asking for something bad to happen.

First, I see the half-empty bottle of Jack on the living room table. I shouldn't have fucking left her. There was no way in hell I was going to sleep with her tonight. Not that I don't fall asleep thinking about it every damn night, because she's the real deal. The girl you bring home to your mother because you want to spend every day with her. She's not the girl you fuck the night she finds out her husband slept around.

Anger boils inside because he's a prick. The Aaron I thought I knew wasn't so selfish. I can't understand how he could cheat on Lee. She's beautiful, smart, funny, and loving. He was so willing to throw it all away for someone like her? Thank God I never touched that slut.

I check on Aarabelle and see her sound asleep in her crib. I love this little girl. I mean, she's freaking adorable, other than the diaper thing. If she could use the toilet, we'd be golden.

Slowly, I creep open Natalie's door, unsure of what I'm going to find, but I need to see her. She's asleep on her side facing me, but doesn't stir. Her hair falls in her face and she looks perfect. I want to wake her and pull her into my arms. Hold her close. But I refuse to do anything tonight. I look over and see another person on the other side of the bed.

Immediately I want to punch something.

How the fuck can she have someone else in her bed?

Then I see the dark brown hair pulled up and realize it's Reanell. She must've stayed.

I head downstairs and look over at the mantel where the flag sits. I'm conflicted and angry. "Why, man? Why would you do it? After everything that you said about

the guys who fuck around on their wives." I speak quietly but I'm pissed off. "And fucking Brittany?" I only met
her once, but she was more than willing to do whatever I
wanted after one night. Hell, she would've blown me in
the bar if I asked her to. It makes no sense. You trade up,
not slum it.

I sit on the couch and lean my head back. I'm drained,
pissed, and a slew of other feelings I'd rather not think
about.

The bottle of Jack sits there and I grab it, pulling a
long gulp down. I close my eyes and wait for some brilliant idea to strike me on how to handle all this shit. She's
going to pull back. I can feel it. I pushed her away when
she threw herself at me, but I want her to be ready when
we take the next step, because after that . . . there's no
going back.

I relax and my mind goes blank.

Suddenly, I hear footsteps. I jump up disoriented and
realize I fell asleep on her couch.

Shit.

I look over and see Reanell coming down the steps.
She stops and her hand grips her throat until she registers
who I am.

"You're here?" she asks with a knowing look.

"I came by late to check on her, but . . ." I feel stupid.
I should've left after I saw they were okay.

Reanell steps forward and puts her hand on my arm.
"You really do care about her, don't you?"

I let out a deep sigh. "I think that's pretty obvious."

"Do you love her?" She pulls no punches.

"I cared for her all those years we were friends. But
I'm falling in love with her," I admit for the first time to
anyone including myself.

She nods and looks at the bottle of Jack. "She's going to be hurting for a while, but don't give up on her. I see things in her that you've brought out. Her heart will heal, but you'll have to decide how much shit you're willing to put up with in the meantime."

We both sit on the couch and I look at the clock. It's six A.M. and it's way too early to be thinking about this. "I should get going."

"For what it's worth," she puts her hand on my forearm, "I don't think Natalie's willing to see the issues she and Aaron were having. In her mind their life was wonderful, but getting ready to have a baby had her rose-colored glasses firmly in place. When you're a military wife you choose to see things in a certain way. It's easier than dealing with your brooding asses when you go through another shift in attitude." Her face falls and she looks away.

"I can't compete with him."

She looks back and her eyes soften, "I don't think you have to. That's what I'm saying. Give her a few days and let her grieve the loss of the *real* husband she had. She's been mourning an idea . . . which I understand."

"I can't feel like I'm second best to him."

"I understand that. I think in a day or two she'll come to terms with it all. If you love her, you're going to have to realize this is like losing him all over again. The past slapped her pretty hard. And then kicked her a few times." She sighs and looks away. "I also don't think you were ever number two. Once she allowed her heart to let you in, you've been number one, even when you weren't."

"That makes no sense, but I'm exhausted and need some fucking sleep. Plus, I don't want her to see me here."

"You're a good guy. I like you," Reanell says and we

both stand.

"Thanks. I think." I grab my keys and head out the door, careful not to make any noise.

I look at her window and decide I need to let her come to me. I can't keep pushing her and I fear I'll push her away. I love her and that scares the ever-living shit out of me. She needs to decide if it's me she wants. I sure as hell won't be the consolation prize.

chapter

twenty-seven

natalie

MY HEAD IS throbbing. Between the crying and the copious amounts of Jack Daniels I drank on top of the beer, I'm lucky I'm not puking. I roll over and Reanell looks at me with a sad smile.

"Morning, sunshine," she says in a low tone. "Water and aspirin are over there. You should take them."

I groan and press my palm against my skull. "Aarabelle?"

"I already fed her and she's down for her morning nap."

I shoot up and immediately regret doing that. The clock reads eleven and I feel like the world's worst mother. "I didn't even hear her."

"That's because I woke up early and took the monitor out. I think you needed the sleep more than being super mom." Reanell sits up and puts the water bottle in my hand.

Memories from last night flood back and I immediately

wish I was still asleep. I look around the bedroom and anger boils past what's reasonable. "I need to get out of this room," I mutter and take the pills.

"Do you want to talk?" she asks, knowing what I'm feeling. In the beginning of her marriage to Mason, he cheated. They're one of the stories in the teams that gave others hope that they could come out on the other side. Reanell and Mason worked hard to get through it and come out stronger. He paid heavily, but love was never their issue.

"About what? How stupid I am?"

"How the hell are you stupid?" her voice is full of reproach.

I stand and look at the dresser where Aaron's watches sit. I look at his side of the bed that still has his clothes folded neatly. Opening a drawer, I start looking for something. Anything that tells me this happened. The headache throbs on, but I don't care. There are answers here and I'm going to find them.

"Natalie, what are you doing?" she asks me as I start to throw his clothes out.

"I have to know. There has to be something here. Something that tells me my husband was fucking another woman," I explain as I pull a shirt out of the drawer. "I never bought him this . . . maybe she did."

Rea comes up behind me and her hand grips my shoulder, but I shrug it off.

"He wasn't that smart. There's something here," I insist. I grab the picture of us with him behind me holding my shoulders and kissing my cheek. I throw it against the wall with all my might and the glass shatters. "I hate him!" Everything comes flooding back.

Reanell sits back on the bed and crosses her legs.

The next drawer contains his pants. I pull each pair out and rifle through the pockets. Looking for God knows what, but I need something . . . anything. "Stupid bastard." Each time I come up empty, I grow more and more angry.

I rip open his closet door and start pulling more things out. I find a pocketknife in his pants and rage consumes me. I want to tear every emotion out of me. Purge the hurt he's managed to cause from the grave. "I hope she was worth it!" I cry as I cut his favorite suit with his knife. The fabric rips apart and so does a part of my soul.

"You about done?" Reanell asks, while sitting on the bed.

"No!" I rear back and stab his uniform and tear it apart. "How? My entire life I was devoted to you!" The knife rips another shred. I drop it and the clattering against the wood floor is the only sound that penetrates the air.

I stand in his closet and inhale. It hits me like a brick to the chest, I smell him. It's as if he's standing behind me. The clove and musk scent is strong, and instead of sadness . . . I want to see it turned to ash.

"Okay, I'll just go make some popcorn," she leans back against the headboard.

"I hate this house! I want to set it on fucking fire," I cry out and Reanell sits quiet. "Say something!"

"What do you want me to say? Tear it up, burn it down . . . do what you have to so you can start to heal."

I look back in the closet where his shirts are shredded as if an animal tore through them. "Are you happy now?" I grab the shirt and grasp the hole, yanking it further. The pocket tears and I keep ripping apart anything in my sight. I taste the salt from my tears as I continue to assault his belongings. "Do you see me?" I cry out to the ceiling. "Do you see what you've done to me? I hate you! You've ruined me!"

Reanell touches my shoulder and I fall into her arms. "He didn't ruin you. I think he just freed you."

I wipe my eyes and let out a deep breath. "I need a shower."

"Yeah, you do. Go get cleaned up and we'll go get some fresh air and talk."

"GRANDE, NON-FAT, WHITE chocolate mocha please." I order my drink of choice and sit in the chair across from Reanell.

"She could be completely full of shit," she tries to convince me for the third time today.

I look out the window and try to find an answer that doesn't end in "fuck you." "You and I both know she's not. She was at his funeral."

"That day was a blur for you. Are you sure it was really her?"

Aarabelle plays with a smile on her face, throwing the toys out of her stroller as we sit on the deck. "I know it was, but I know it in my heart."

Reanell sits back and shakes her head. "Maybe. I don't know. I knew you and Aaron weren't perfect. I feel like you need to remember that. But I'm going to say this and you can punch me: he's not here anymore, Lee," she lets out a shaky breath. "You have Liam now. Are you willing to let him go?"

"Do you realize how fucked up this is? Legitimately, this is so insane I can't even fully comprehend it." I begin to ramble as it all comes out. "I married Aaron out of high school, followed him all over the place. Made it through how many deployments, work-ups, and all that other crap to have him get out of the Navy. Then, he goes to work for Jackson and somewhere in there he screwed someone else while I was pregnant. Oh, but wait!" I keep going with my hands moving as I speak. "He goes and gets himself blown the fuck up! Yup! That's my life. But no, it gets better, because it wouldn't be fun if I didn't keep going . . . I fall in love with his best friend," I say and then sit back.

Oh my God.

"Love, huh?"

"I said love."

"Yeah, you sure did." Reanell studies me over the rim of her cup and then takes a slow sip of her drink.

"I didn't—" I start to say "I didn't mean it," but the words get stuck in my throat.

"Dadadada!" Aarabelle screams as she throws her pacifier.

"Mamamama," I say as I try to get her to say my name. She laughs and raises her arms. I lift her and hold her close.

"You're going to try to deflect, but you and I both know you and Liam work. You make sense."

I hold my daughter close and kiss her. "How so? We've kissed a few times, so how are we working?" I ask while bouncing Aara up and down. She giggles and my heart that felt broken mends with the love of my child.

"Maybe I'm talking out of my ass. I like him. He's different than Aaron was. I know you think you guys had a good marriage, but do you remember all the bad? What about the nights he was being an asshole and angry at nothing? What about the way he'd go out with Quinn and the other guys and not come home? How easily you forget all of that."

"Aaron and I never had it perfect, but what was wrong is what made us right." I defend my life and feel foolish. He wasn't always great. In fact, if I'm honest, there were many times where I wasn't sure we would make it.

War changes a man. It causes what was once a light heart to become black and cynical. He'd been slightly injured in the firefight in Iraq that took out his team, and that loss affected him greatly. After that mission, he was never the same. I gave him time and space, but when he chose to get out of the Navy, things were bad for quite a while. He was angry, and when I got pregnant, there was a part of him that pulled away from me completely. He wasn't happy, but he pretended. I guess I did a lot of pretending as well. If I avoided the issues I thought they would just go away.

"I know it's not easy, but give yourself some time."

"And you still like him after he left last night? I threw myself at him, begged him to sleep with me, and he said no and then left."

She huffs and looks away, frustrated with me. "Did you actually want to screw him on the night you found out about your husband's affair? Is that what you want to remember? I think he's a fucking hero for telling you no!" Reanell doesn't typically get loud with me, but here she is cursing at me.

"Don't judge me, Rea."

Her eyes narrow and her jaw falls. "Are you high? Because there's no way you would ever say that shit to me. I've never judged you, Natalie. Ever. You have no idea, and for that, you're an asshole."

"Gee, thanks."

My phone rings and I look at the screen and see Liam's name.

"Hello," I answer the call.

"Hey, I wanted to check on you."

Always concerned about me.

"I'm . . . I don't even know. Reanell and I are getting coffee."

"I think we should talk. Do you want to meet up?"

I draw in a breath and let it go. "I don't know. I'm not sure I can handle much today."

No response.

"Liam?"

"I'm here. Let me know when you decide."

"I will," I reply and hang up.

Reanell gives me the knowing eyes and keeps her mouth shut.

"Don't look at me like that. There's only so much one person can take in a day."

Aarabelle demands my attention and I choose her. I'm a mother first and foremost. I need to decide if I'm ready to love again and if that person is Liam. It's not fair to either of us to go forward only to find out later.

"You know, he was there this morning," Reanell blurts out and then folds her arms across her chest.

My face is blank as I try to understand. "At the house?"

"Yup, sleeping on your couch while you were passed out. He came back. He stayed even though you pushed him away."

"I don't . . . I mean . . . why?"

"Why?" She throws her arms up and Aarabelle giggles. "Because maybe he loves you. He was worried about you, so he came to your house in the middle of the night and checked on you. Then fell asleep on your couch. But here's the thing and why you're an asshole . . ." she pauses and stares at me, "He left before you'd see. He could've stayed and made you face him, but instead he did the noble thing and left. He didn't want me to tell you. So yeah, you're an asshole."

He came back even after I made a fool of myself.

"Why does this have to be so friggin' complicated?" I ask the beautiful sky, waiting for some divine intervention.

She huffs, "I think you need to think about what I said and tell me: are you going to screw this up?"

I look back at her and I realize it's my choice. It's up to me. And if Liam and I can't make it work because of my truckload of issues, then so be it. But he's been here, day in and day out. He cared for me when I was sick, was there when Aara was in the hospital, and put me back together when I wouldn't acknowledge I was broken. It was Liam who mended my cracks.

"Can you watch Aarabelle? I need to take care of something."

Reanell just sits back as if she knew this was coming and extends her hands. "I think you should go now." She grabs Aara from me and shoos me. "Go. Run. Now."

I grab my keys and get in the car.

Time to see if we really have a chance.

chapter

twenty-eight

*H*E CAME BACK.
I keep saying it over and over again because it doesn't seem possible. Every time I think I've figured him out, he does something else to throw me off. I battle with what exactly I'm going to say when I do get to his house. There are a lot of things I'm dealing with, and it needs to be him who leads this relationship now. He's what I want, but I need Liam to take the reins. My heart is mangled and it's going to be his decision whether he wants to be the one to mend it.

His apartment is only a few miles away from mine and I wish it was further. I have no idea what to say. The words float through my mind: *sorry, I wish it was different, I want you, I'm a mess.* I don't know which is true, or maybe all of them are. I am a mess. I do want him—so much. I wish that this entire situation wasn't happening and I'm sorry this is where we are.

I park in the drive and try to collect myself. I know two things. One, I care about Liam deeply. Two, I'm going to have to process everything.

The walk to his apartment seems to take forever. It could be that I'm walking at a snail's pace. I go to knock and he opens the door.

Liam stands there in his tight, navy blue t-shirt and dark blue jeans. His light brown beanie is on his head and he leans against the door. "Hi," he says and looks past me.

"Hi, can I come in?" I ask hesitantly.

He opens the door and turns so I can pass him. Well, shit . . . now I have to talk.

Liam follows behind me and I look around. His apartment is modern and practically empty. The typical bachelor pad, complete with the biggest television I've ever seen. I stand in the middle of the room and he waves toward the couch.

"I'm surprised you're here," Liam says as he sits in the seat next to me.

"If I'm keeping you from something . . ."

"It's not important."

I tuck my hair behind my ear and try to decide where to start. "I'm going to talk and I'll probably ramble, but I need to say it." I look up and he nods. "I'm sorry about throwing myself at you like that. It wasn't fair to you or to whatever we've been doing. I care too much about you to do that . . . but I knew you could make it go away. It makes me selfish, and I'm so embarrassed that I did that. When you left, I drank so much and all I could do was replay how you looked at me when I begged you. I understand if you don't want to be with me or don't want m—"

"Don't even say it. Don't say I don't want you. That's not the case. I want you. Every day I want you," Liam cuts me off with his voice razor sharp.

My cheeks flush and my heart begins to race. "Okay, I just meant that I shouldn't have tried to get you to sleep with me last night."

"Look, if all that shit hadn't gone down and you wanted to take that step, I would've been all for it. Trust me,

I want nothing more than to touch you, but not because you want to fuck Aaron out of your mind. I want it to be because you can't stand the idea of me *not* touching you."

He's right but so wrong. "I want to be with you. There's something between us that is beautiful and I don't want to lose that. Even if you had said yes last night—it wouldn't have been that."

"That's exactly what it would've been. Let's be honest, because if we start with lies, this will fail before it even has a chance."

Fear of losing him begins to bubble up. "I don't know how to go from here because I feel like I've taken two steps back. I want to trust you, and I do, but I feel like this affair just destroyed whatever we were building. How could you want me knowing this?"

"Natalie," Liam says and his hand gently cups my face. He pushes me to look at him and I get lost in his eyes. "I've fallen for you and for Aarabelle. I'm not going anywhere until you tell me you're done. I'm done fighting with myself over having any kind of feelings for you. I want you, Lee. And his fuck ups have nothing to do with us."

"But they affect us."

"Only if you want them to. Look, every part of me battles with touching you. It's like I'm the fucking dirtbag here. You were his fucking wife." His hand drops.

"He obviously didn't hold that title very high," I say and grab his hand wrapping my fingers around his. "I'm angry, though, and hurt. He and I weren't perfect, but I didn't think he was capable of infidelity."

"Did you have any idea?"

"No, I mean, we were fighting, but I was pregnant. We had been trying for almost a year to get pregnant with Aarabelle. I could only sleep with him during certain times, and sex was tedious, but I thought we were making the best of it."

Infertility was a huge burden between us. Aaron felt his manhood was being challenged and I thought I was maybe not meant to be a mother. Even through it all, Aaron and I tried to stay close. He wasn't any more distant than normal, and I definitely didn't suspect anything.

"I wish I could take this away from you. I can't though. He was your husband."

I nod in understanding. Liam only knew the side of our marriage everyone saw. The happy, smiling couple that loved each other since they were sixteen. In many ways, it wasn't an act. I did love him, and if he were alive, we'd be together, or at least figuring out where to go from here. But he's gone, and I have Liam.

"In a way, it's also opened my eyes to how my life wasn't exactly what I thought."

"How so?"

"Do we seriously talk about this? Do I really tell you about good and bad in my marriage to your best friend?" I question because it feels almost unnatural. This is the guy who I'm sure listened to Aaron talk about me and now I'm sitting here about to make him listen to me.

"I can't say I'm going to enjoy it, but if we keep avoiding this shit, we're never going to get past it. Look, this is hard as hell for me. Aaron was my best friend. I would've taken a bullet for him, no questions asked. When things started happening with you and I, I felt like a dick." Liam plays with my fingers as we sit and talk. "You're off limits. No one fucks another team guy's wife. It's code. But he's gone and I don't know how we found our way here."

"I battle with the same thing. You were . . . well . . . *you.*

I saw you as a friend. As Aaron's friend. I can remember sewing your patches on and painting your helmet when you were in BUDs. When my feelings started to shift, I tried to stop it." I twist my fingers in his as we both open ourselves up. "Do you know what I'm most upset about?" I muse out loud, but I need to say it.

"What?"

"This whole time . . ." I look away, but Liam's hand pulls my chin toward him.

Liam's eyes are tender but his jaw is tight. "Don't hide from me. Let me in."

My eyes blur with unshed tears as the words begin to form like acid on my tongue. "I've been so blind. In my mind, I blocked out everything bad and I've put him on this pedestal. When I told him I was pregnant, he shrugged and walked away. I forgot about that until last night. I wanted him to be so perfect. I didn't want to remember how we weren't always happy, but we were comfortable. I'm such an idiot."

He's rubs his thumb gently against my skin. I close my eyes to his touch and my hand touches his chest. I lean into his body and he holds me close. "You're not an idiot."

I let out a short, sarcastic laugh. "The hell I'm not. My husband was cheating on me when I was pregnant. I laid in bed crying for days over someone who could've been planning to leave me. My entire life was a lie."

"I don't know what to say. A part of me—the selfish part—wants to tell you he was a fucking moron and you're better off with me. I wouldn't cheat and would tell you how you shouldn't spend another minute thinking of him." I lean up and Liam lets out a deep breath. "The other part of me is fighting against defending the motherfucker. But I won't defend what he did . . . it's so fucked up."

This is what I worry about with us. "Will Aaron always be between us?" I ask and hold my breath.

"I don't know. Tell me . . ." Liam pauses and bends forward. His lips touch mine and he kisses me. His tongue glides across my lips and he pulls back. He waits for me to open my eyes, and the fierceness stops my breath. The tension in his muscles is clear as he gives me what I need. "Do you wish he was here instead of me? Right now, do you wish it were his arms around you? His mouth on yours?"

I hear him speaking, but I can't focus. When his lips touch mine, all that exists is Liam and me. He stops and waits . . . I bring myself back to his question and shake my head no.

"That's not good enough," his low gruff voice is demanding.

"Right now, I'm not thinking of anyone else." My lips ghost against his.

He just barely touches his lips to mine. Liam's head moves side to side as he brushes against my mouth. It's a game of who's stronger at this point. "I didn't ask that."

"I'm not sure how to answer that, Liam. I'm here with you right now. I'm in your arms. I want to be here—with you."

The air is thick between us and he doesn't relax. "He doesn't have to be here. This is you and me."

"I don't want to lose you." The honesty seeps through each syllable. "I'm scared."

Liam lies back on the couch and pulls me against his chest. I lie in his arms pressed against him with our fingers intertwined. "I'm falling in love with you, Natalie." His chest rumbles and I look up. "If I'm not already there. You're not the only one who's got something to lose. I don't want you to say anything back to me. I just want you to know." Liam's fingers roll mine as he waits for me to react.

As afraid as I am about being hurt again, I know I'm not alone. "I'm falling for you too. I just don't know if I can."

His eyes tell me he understands. He pulls me back down and rubs his hand against my back. There's a lot the two of us need to overcome. But right here and now, I'm safe. Liam's strong arms hold me together and I try to think of the last time I felt this way.

Aaron and I were married so young, but we'd had a good marriage. He was gone a lot, and that part sucked, but it made our reunions that much sweeter. Aaron had a temper, but he was never abusive or mean. Hell, half the time I was the one throwing things across the room. He provided for me and I became content. But there were times I could see him distancing himself from me. When he would become belligerent when I would try to talk about what happened overseas. The infertility, PTSD, and his disdain of no longer being a SEAL ate at us. He would spend hours in the garage working on his car and then go to sleep or go out. I put blinders on and thought when I was pregnant with Aarabelle it would fix everything. But the only time Aaron was happy was when other people were around.

Then I wonder about Liam. The fact that I'd be entering a relationship knowing the life I'd live with him and the possible outcome. But I was built for this. I'm a SEAL wife. I know the life, the struggles, and the joys that it can bring. I know I'm able to handle deployments and all that goes with it. I just don't know if I could withstand losing him. Loving Liam comes with a cost.

"What's going through your mind? I can feel you tensing up." Liam breaks the silence.

I lean on my hand that rests upon his chest. His blue eyes sparkle and I give a sad smile. "I'm thinking about all of it. The love, the loss, the affair. I think the fact that I don't have answers is the hardest part."

"Do you want to talk to her? Will that help?" Liam's hand continues to run up and down my back.

"I don't know. A part of me wants to forget it all and call her a liar. What does it even matter?"

Liam kisses the top of my head and lets out a deep sigh.

"Where do we go from here?" I ask.

Liam's hands grip my shoulders and he pulls me on top of him. I'm lying on his chest and we're face to face. "We decide. You decide because I'm here with you, but I need to know you're not there with him."

Pushing my hands up his chest, I rest against his shoulders. "I'm with you right now."

He sits up so quickly I'm not sure how he manages it. He flips me so I'm on my back and he's on top of me. My body warms from his touch and he glides his calloused fingers down my bare arm. "Liam . . ." I sigh his name.

"Tell me when you need me to stop," his voice is low and smooth.

I don't know that I'll ever be able to tell him to stop. I hope he has more control than I do.

chapter

twenty-nine

HIS FINGERS GRAZE my pants where my shirt meets. I squirm in anticipation. Liam pauses and my eyes lock on his. I don't speak or move, but I grant him the permission he seeks. He knows how to read me, my body, my tiny movements that not many would be able to pick up on. It's a blessing and a curse.

The pads of his fingers float across my stomach and my breath stops. Lust flurries and builds as his fingertip moves higher. It skims my ribs and he traces the underside of my breast.

"Tell me if it's too much," his husky voice gravels in my ear.

"It's not enough," the words fall from my lips.

Liam groans and his tongue traces the shell of my ear. My eyes roll back in my head in pure pleasure as he pushes underneath my bra. When his finger grazes my nipple, I nearly buck off the couch.

"You're so perfect," he reassures me and rubs back and forth, my nipple pebbling beneath his adept touch.

Needing to touch him, I run my hands under his shirt, pushing it up. Liam uses one hand and rips it off. My fingers delicately press against his skin. I trace the tattoo on his ribs: *Dulce bellum inexpertis*. I outline the letters and he tenses. "What does that mean?" I ask as he kisses my neck.

He looks up and his blue eyes darken. "It means war is sweet for those who haven't experienced it."

My voice is barely audible, "I'm sorry. I know you've lost a lot."

"I've gained too. War takes from us. It robs us of so much, but if we let it . . . it can save us. You being here in my arms right now is reminding me that sometimes the victory is worth the battle."

Liam bows down as each breath passes between us. As much as he's breathing life into me, I'm doing the same for him. We've both lost because of war. Liam's lost countless friends as well as handling his own demons. "I shouldn't be feeling this way," I say as he brushes the hair out of my eyes.

"What do you feel?" his voice is rich and warm. It heats parts of my body that have been forgotten. "Describe it," he demands.

I close my eyes as his hand floats down my body and back under my shirt. I allow the sensations to overtake my mind and Liam's touch is what I give myself over to. "Your hands are strong, but when you touch me, it's tender." His thumb brushes my nipple and I sigh. "The scraping of your thumb against my skin." He does it again.

"Does it feel good?" he asks gruffly.

"Yes," I moan, as his hand cups my breast and he squeezes.

"Do you want me to keep touching you?" he asks.

Keeping my eyes closed, I stay in the moment. "Please," my voice is low and dripping with need.

His weight shifts and he pulls my shirt over my head. I look at him and his eyes turn to liquid as he appraises me, setting my nerves at ease. Liam groans in approval. "Perfect. Every inch of you is perfection." He pulls my straps down and waits. I tilt and unhook my bra, but leave it in place.

No other man has seen me like this besides Aaron. Aaron was my first and only. Liam seems to understand my hesitation and then he's on top of me again. His mouth fuses to mine and he kisses me eagerly. My fingers pull his beanie off and tangle into his hair. I want him so much right now. Every cell feels like it's on fire and I'll soon become cinders. Burning with need, I get lost again. No thoughts of anything but him exist.

My hands grip his ass as he grinds down on me. I feel his hardness against my core and I begin to throb. His hands start to drift down my side as he pulls the bra from between us, but keeps me covered with his body.

"I'm going to suck on your breasts, Natalie. Do you want that?" he asks and I practically melt into the couch.

I whimper as he reaches behind my back and pulls me with him. He keeps me shielded with his chest. I'm straddling his legs, feeling the exceedingly large bulge between my legs.

He holds me against him and stares into my eyes, "Do you want my mouth on you, or do you want me to stop?" There's no anger or hesitation. He wants me, it's clear, but he's not wanting to push me too far.

"Don't stop," I plead and his hands drift down my back ever so slowly. There's no hurt in my heart right now. I feel alive and adored. My heart races and my core clenches.

Liam carefully extends me onto my back, keeping his eyes on me. His head drops and his tongue circles my nipple. He lavishes it and caresses me. "Oh, oh God." My voice is husky and my breath comes in short bursts.

His mouth moves to the other breast and my hips move against him, creating the friction I'm desperate for. "Your skin tastes like heaven." He sits back and looks at me.

I fight the urge to cover up, and the way his eyes appraise me keeps me still. The tip of my finger slides to the front of him and his head falls back. I rock against him again. It feels too good to stop. "Liam," I sigh his name.

"Tell me to stop or I'm going to flip you over and not be able to control myself."

"Kiss me," I request and he acquiesces. Our mouths come together and my hand rests on his heart. I feel his life beneath my palm. He's alive, real, and he's good to me. Liam was there when Aara was sick, when I was sick, and any other time I've needed him. Liam's mouth never touched Brittany. His hands press against my back and he holds me tightly against him. There's nowhere else I'd rather be than right here in his arms.

We break apart and we stay chest to chest. "I'll never take you for granted. I'll never give another woman a piece of me once you're mine. I'll only be yours."

I look up with tears in my eyes. "I'm not ready, but I'm yours now. I want to give myself to you completely when it can be only about us."

"What makes you think I was offering myself to you?" Liam smirks and the mood shifts from raging desire to playfulness.

"Oh?" I raise my brows in question. "I think if I wanted you, I could have you."

Liam pulls me closer and I nuzzle into his neck. "Are you calling me an easy lay?"

I laugh and he kisses the side of my face. "Never.

There's nothing easy about you."

"Well, except my banging hot body . . . I mean, that's just easy on the eyes."

"Arrogance is not sexy, darling," I tease as his finger makes designs on my back.

"I think you're very sexy," Liam says as his hands make their way to the sides of my breasts.

"Oh?" I reply as my lips press against his neck.

"Should I show you with my mouth?" he inquires while his scruff grates across my shoulder. It prickles my skin and ignites the lust that had dropped to a low simmer.

My phone chimes, interrupting where we were going. I groan and reach over toward my purse. Liam adjusts himself and sits back, looking at my half naked body with a smug smile.

"Shit," I say when I read the text. "I gotta go. Aarabelle is being super fussy and Rea has to run out." I grab my bra and Liam snatches it from my hand. "I need that."

"I'm thinking you wouldn't want to leave the house like that."

I don't want to leave. God knows I want to stay here with him. It's the only time I'm whole. There's no pity in Liam's eyes. When I see myself in him, I'm desired and beautiful. I lean down and kiss him and grab his t-shirt. I throw it over my head and smile.

"Keep the bra. I can wear your clothes."

Liam stands before he takes a measured step, slowly drawing me in. "I'm going to take the coldest shower I can manage. I'll somehow find a way to not think about you in my clothes. Walking around with my shirt clinging to your body and you smelling like my cologne."

I step back and grab my purse. "You may need to take

two showers." I wink and open the front door. I turn back and glance at him over my shoulder. "You know, I might even sleep in it." I turn back and hear him groan as I close the door behind me.

Funny, I didn't think of the pain Aaron caused even once while I was in Liam's arms.

CHAPTER THIRTY

LIAM

"**D**EMPSEY, MY OFFICE now," Commander Hansen orders and I pop tall. What the hell did I do now? "Sir," I say and stand at his desk.

"Take a seat," he instructs me and points to the chair. Commander is the kind of officer we all want to serve under. He's fair and doesn't think he's above everyone. He's a leader you want to follow and it makes taking orders from him pretty easy. "My wife is a pain in my ass. She meddles, and most of the time I'm able to handle her shit, but Natalie is a different story. Gilcher served under me for six years. I knew him and he was like family. So, me calling you in here isn't Commander to Chief. It's man to man."

I nod out of respect and bite back my response. It's no one's business what the hell happens between Natalie and I. The other night was a shit show. What was supposed to be a turning point ended up in complete disaster thanks to a stupid bitch.

"I'm sure you don't give a shit, and honestly, I don't care if you do. I care about Lee and Aarabelle. More than that, my wife makes my life miserable when she gets like this. Rea is worried, so if you need to take a few days and be there, go."

That wasn't what I thought he was going to say. I thought I was going to get the stay-away-from-her speech. To which I would've found a way to tell him to suck my dick . . . respectfully. "How long?"

"If you need to drop leave, I'll approve it. We have the next two weeks where there's nothing going on. Hell, most of you guys will leave before lunch anyway."

"I'll do that, sir. I appreciate it."

Commander looks away and huffs. "Natalie didn't smile, cry, or laugh. For weeks she just sat with no emotions. Reanell was in the delivery room with her and it wasn't until Aarabelle was born that she finally cried. She went back to that way a few weeks after Aaron's memorial." He scratches his face. "Then she started to open up when she thought no one was looking. I attribute that to your arrival."

"I don't know that I had anything to do with it."

"I don't either, but it's a hunch."

This is the most bizarre conversation I've ever had.

Commander stands and walks to the wall. "I suspected something was going on before he left for Afghanistan," he admits. "I think Natalie remembers a different life than what she was living."

Aaron was my best friend. I knew he was struggling with a baby coming and what it meant, but I never thought he was fucking around on her. He and I were living on opposite coasts, so we didn't talk as often, but he sure as fuck never mentioned another woman.

I think about Natalie and how she is already reconstructing her walls. I remember what she felt like, tasted like, and how long it took my dick to go down. Yesterday was another day I didn't expect to happen the way it went, but she opened up to me. The need to claim a part of her was so strong, I wasn't sure I would stop. I had to constantly remind myself that she was in control of how far we went.

She's worth the blue balls.

"I understand, Sir. I'm going to need those few days."

"I was hoping you were the man I thought you were." Commander stands and extends his hand.

"Commander."

"Chief, I'll see you in a few days."

I turn and start to form a plan. One that includes no way out and maybe rope.

"SO, YOU GUYS still together?" Quinn asks as we load the weights on the bar.

"Yeah," I reply and get aligned to lift. I'm going for a personal record and all this dick wants to do is talk about Natalie.

I line up my hands and Quinn pushes down so I can't move. "She's okay with this? The fact that her husband— your best friend—was fucking around on her and she wants to be with you?"

"I'm not sure where you got confused when I said 'yeah.' She and I are together. Aaron fucked up, but he and I are separate."

"If you say so," he scoffs and moves his hand.

He's always got something smart to say. It's irritating and I'm tired of his bullshit. "You know, you're not a part of my fucking life choices. If I want to be with her, I will. If she's okay with it and I'm okay with it, then what the hell do you care?"

Quinn steps back with his hands raised, "I'm just

asking, dude."

I sit up, pissed off. "When you've fucked anything that walks, I never said shit. You've fucked up more than all of us combined." My hands tremble as I clench them into a ball. "Lay off about me and Lee."

He moves toward me. "I won't say another word after I say this. You hurt her and I'll beat the ever-living shit out of you. She's not just some girl. She's his fucking wife and that's his daughter. I know the cost that comes with a single mother."

"I'm not stupid."

"The jury's still out on that one." Quinn slaps me on the shoulder. "I may not have been as close as you and Aaron were, but he was my friend too. I know you're not a piece of shit. I'm saying to make sure you're all in before you go any further." He gives me a pointed look and then morphs back into his normal, jackass self. "Now, let's see if your weak ass can lift this."

We've been friends for a long time. It's probably the longest speech I've ever heard. "You don't have to worry about me hurting her."

"All I wanted to hear. Are we going to work out or do you want to hug it out?" he jokes while waiting.

"Dickhead. Let's go." I get back on the bench and try to focus on getting through the rest of the workout.

Quinn and I finish and decide to go grab lunch. He's smart enough not to bring up my relationship or whatever the fuck this is with Lee. We talk about the upcoming deployment. Having our own squad means we work together but each manage a group of guys. We're hoping our squads aren't split since we understand each other. It's nice to know the guy who's watching your six.

"I heard you're taking a few days off," Quinn mentions

as he grabs his drink.

"Yeah, I'm going to take Natalie and Aarabelle somewhere. I have to figure it out," I laugh. I've racked my brain trying to think of something close that she'd like. Just something for us to get away from all this shit and see if this is something or if it's a matter of circumstance.

"Why don't you take her to my beach house?"

"Where?"

"The one in OBX. I know she lives on the beach and all, but it's a nice house and it's away."

"I gotta admit, man, I'm shocked," I muse and lean back. He's the last person I thought would be helping me out.

"I told you, I wanted to be sure. You care about her and you're taking the kid. I think that says it all. Here," he says and takes the key off his ring. "Take it. Go or don't. I don't care. I'll tell you all the info. It's a few hours, but Corolla is a cool spot. I've seen the wild horses a time or two."

"You're not such a dick after all." I smile as I put the key in my pocket.

"Don't tell anyone."

"Your secret's safe with me," I slap him on the back. "Until you piss me off. Then I'll tell everyone."

"Yeah, I'll tell everyone how you couldn't lift the bar today."

Now, I need to get my bag together and a plan to get Natalie to agree.

This should be fun.

chapter

thirty-one

natalie

"MAMAMAMA," AARABELLE REPEATS over and over, sitting in her highchair. It's music to my ears. She's growing up so fast. I wish I could push pause and freeze frame each tiny moment.

She's truly mobile now, which has been a huge pain in the ass. Plus, everything goes in her mouth, and I swear the child can find the tiniest things.

"Mamamama."

"Hi, beautiful girl." I smile and put another Cheerio on the tray. I've learned one Cheerio gives me time for about one dish to get washed. Timing is everything.

She grins and tries to grab it as I rush back to the sink to keep cleaning before she starts screaming again.

I look out the window and see Liam's car pull up. My happiness is automatic and the butterflies start to flutter in my stomach. It's only been a few days since we've seen each other, but I've missed him.

The time apart gave me a chance to come to terms with my emotions. I'm angry, but I won't allow Aaron's decisions to impact my future. He's gone. He made bad choices and I have to live with that. But he gave me Aarabelle, and in a way, he gave me Liam. The truth is, I have no way of knowing if it even happened. All I have is the word of some woman.

I hear Liam knocking at the door and Aarabelle starts to fuss. Looks like my Cheerio time has expired.

"Come in!" I yell toward the door and hear it open.

"Lock the damn door," Liam grumbles as he enters.

"I live in the safest neighborhood. I also have the nosiest neighbor who camps out on her deck. I think Mrs. DeMatteo would notice and beat you with a bat before you could get in." I smile and Liam squats down and kisses Aarabelle on the cheek.

"Hello, gorgeous," he coos at her and she grins.

"Mamamama," Aara says.

"Give her one Cheerio, please," I instruct Liam and almost get excited that I can do all the dishes while he feeds her.

"Sure thing, but first you better kiss me."

I turn and my arms wrap around his neck. "Hi," I whisper.

"Hi. You look beautiful," Liam says seductively.

"You're all sweaty," I reply as I lift up on my toes. I inch closer to his lips and he leans down slowly.

The tension builds between us and I savor the moment. When a kiss can leave your head spinning and your body tingling . . . I haven't had this in so long.

He stops right before his lips can touch mine. "I like sweaty," he grumbles and then he kisses me.

I hold the back of his neck and he holds me tight as he moves me backwards. My back hits the counter and he pushes against me. The kiss ends as quickly, but leaves me breathless.

"Maaaaaamaaaaa," Aarabelle screams from her chair reminding us of her presence.

I laugh and push against his chest. "No one forgot you, silly girl," I chide playfully and place a Cheerio on Aara's highchair.

She gives me one of her whole-face smiles. Where her eyes glimmer, her nose crinkles a little, and her lips are wide. You can't help but smile back at her.

"So, I have an idea," Liam says as he snakes his arms around my waist.

"Oh?"

Liam releases me and turns me so we're facing each other. "We're on training workups, so you know that the deployment will be coming at some point."

"Yeah, I figured." I know this. I can try to pretend that I'm ignorant, but I'm not. Years of being a SEAL wife has given me the knowledge of how they work. How I'm going to handle him leaving remains to be seen. This is one of my biggest worries. Can I cope with this again?

"Hey," he lifts my chin. "Do you trust me?"

I look into his eyes and my hands rest on his chest. I think it's the one question that I never have to think twice about. Liam has proven time and time again in the last nine months that I can trust him. "Of course I do."

"Okay, then go upstairs and pack a bag for you and Aarabelle."

"What?" I pull back looking at him confused.

"For a few days." Liam kisses the tip of my nose and turns me around.

I turn back but he starts to walk me toward the stairs. "Liam, stop."

"I knew you were going to argue," he mumbles.

Damn right I'm going to argue.

"What the hell am I packing for? Where are you trying to take us? I have to work this week. I have things to do," I start to ramble off without taking a break as my mind reels. "I can't just go away. There's no way I can drop everything. I have meetings and Aarabelle has a play date. I mean, what about . . ."

"Good God, woman. You trust me. So trust me," Liam stands against the wall as I stare at him with pursed lips. "Go! Up the stairs."

"Don't 'woman' me. And don't order me around," I reply defiantly.

He bursts out laughing and I follow. Liam steps forward and grips my hips. My hands wrap around his neck. "Stop being so damn cute. Go pack. I want us to get away from here." He pulls me close and gazes with adoration in his eyes. "Give ourselves a chance to be free of all the shit here and see how we feel. Just us. No ghosts. No memories. Only the three of us."

When he says those last few words, my heart sputters. The three of us. It was never meant to be him in the three of us, but here we are. Liam doesn't just want me. He wants Aarabelle too—even with her diapers and drool. He's not asking to whisk me away on a getaway so he can seduce me. Instead, Liam cares enough to want to build something together and include Aara.

"You really know how to win a girl's heart, Dempsey." I tug on his neck while lifting myself up and press my lips against his.

Liam pulls back but keeps me tight against him. "Only yours. I only care about your heart."

I lean my head against his chest and wish I could stay here. With my eyes closed and holding on to this moment.

In his arms where I'm secure and I know he'll protect me.

"What am I packing for?"

"A few days. Beach gear."

"Beach? Do you see what is off my back deck?" I ask confused.

"Zip it. Go pack." Liam breaks from my hold and slaps my ass. "I've got Aarabelle."

"Oh, that's comforting," I retort and climb the stairs quickly, hoping he won't chase me. Or maybe I do hope that.

I enter my room a little giddy. A vacation—with Liam. It's kind of surreal and completely unexpected. Holy shit, we're going to have to sleep together. Like sleep—in the same bed. I mean, I wouldn't want him to sleep on the couch and we've been moving so slow with everything sexual, but I don't know that I'll be able to be in the same bed. Then, of course, I don't know that I want to keep going slow. I want him and it's clear he wants me. I know that my feelings for Liam are real, but still. I've only ever been with Aaron and it worries me that I won't be good.

Panic starts to bubble and I decide I need to focus. I'm getting way ahead of myself here. Packing. That's all I need to worry about. I'm going to have to smack him for this. Women need days to pack for a trip, not minutes, and that's when they know where they're going. I try to make a mental list of all the things I'll need for Aara and myself.

Piling different clothes on the bed, I start to feel a little better. I have outfits for whatever may happen, and I at least have the beach necessities. Aaron's closet has all our luggage in it. I haven't come back to this closet since the day I shredded his clothes. There's nothing inside of here that I want to open again, but I have to. My hand rests on the door handle and I draw a steadying breath, then open it. It still smells like Aaron. Spice and musk assail my senses and I fight the tears. He's hurt me so deeply, even from his grave. "Why didn't you tell me?" I ask aloud. "I won't let you destroy me. My heart was yours but you decided it wasn't good enough so I'm taking it back. I'll always love you but I'm not yours anymore." I lean against the door and hope he hears me.

I allow a solitary tear to fall as I grab the suitcase from the top shelf. When I pull it down, I see a torn piece of paper that sits on the floor.

Hesitantly, I squat and grasp the paper. I turn it over afraid of what I might find, but all that's written is "I'm sorry."

More questions begin to take shape. "Sorry for what, Aaron? Or to who?" I yell and kick the door closed. The loud smack of the door echoes through the room. Leaning my back against it, I slink to the ground and hold my knees. My head falls forward and I begin to cry. Dissolution of a marriage is always hard. Becoming a widow and having that marriage taken from you is the most difficult thing anyone can imagine, but finding out that marriage was a lie—inexplicable.

"Natalie?" I hear Liam call out. "Are you okay?" I feel his hands touch my arm and I slowly lift my head.

There he stands with Aarabelle in his arms.

"No. Yes. I don't know," I say in a hushed voice. I'm trying to hold back the tears. I don't want him to see me like this. Liam is who I want, but I'm still breaking from Aaron. It's not fair to either of us.

"Okay, well . . . let's get packed and we'll figure it out together." Liam stands and puts his hand out for me to take.

I place my hand in his and he lifts me up.

Aarabelle begins to clap her hands and I laugh. "You wanna go on vacation, pretty girl?"

She squeals as if she has any clue what I'm saying and I look at Liam.

"Together," he states again and kisses me on the temple. "Now," his voice shifts to be more animated. "Someone needs a diaper change and I call not it."

I shake my head as he holds her out toward me. "No way, you said you've got Aarabelle and if we're in this whole 'together' thing," I say with air quotes, "You're going to be doing diapers too." I cross my arms and give him a shit-eating grin.

"Over my dead body, sweetheart."

I walk over and my tongue glides across my lips. I watch the intake of Liam's breath, the way his eyes follow my tongue and linger on my lips. He shifts Aarabelle to his other arm and grabs my waist when I get close.

I lean close to his ear and whisper, "No diapers, no naked." Liam groans and I laugh. "Now, I need to finish. No rope!" I yell as he walks out the door.

"You can't make the rules," he yells back and I hear him talk to Aarabelle. "Now, where is Mommy's duct tape?"

chapter
thirty-two

"OKAY, NOW WILL you tell me where we're going?" I ask for the thirtieth time. It's so easy to drive him crazy.

"You're trying to make me frustrated, but it's not going to work. I'm highly trained," Liam throws his arm over the back of my seat. "What can I say? I'm just superior like that."

I look at him waiting for the smirk or something to let me know he's kidding. "Superiorly stupid!" I retort.

"Jealous."

"Of what?" I ask with my jaw hanging.

I wait for him to answer.

And wait.

And wait some more. He continues to drive and looks anywhere but at me. Aarabelle giggles and plays with her toy in the backseat.

This man is maddening.

"Liam!" I shriek and he begins to chuckle. Which of course only fuels my irritation. Fine. I can play.

I lean back and put my feet up on the dash. With my eyes closed, I lean back into the seat and I can feel his eyes. *Yeah, this is going to be good.*

"Sweetheart," Liam says through his teeth.

"Hmmm?" I reply keeping my eyes closed and feet in place. My face stays stoic as I fight the urge to smile.

"Would you be so kind as to take your feet off of Robin," Liam's voice is strained but polite.

I open my one eye and look over. "Oh, I'm quite comfortable."

"That's great, but really, you wouldn't want to lose your foot if we crashed. I'm only thinking of you."

My head rolls to the side lazily and I shrug. "You'll carry me around. I'm good. Thanks for caring though." I bite the inside of my cheek to keep from laughing. I can practically feel the steam building in his head.

"Lee."

I look over coyly. "Liam."

"If I tell you where we're going, will you take your feet off my baby?"

Oh, the joy of winning. Some men are hard to figure out what their trigger is, but Liam is simple: his car. Robin, as he calls her, is his version of a child.

"Do you use rope on Robin?"

Liam tries to smother his smile, but I see his eyes crinkle. "Feet, Natalie."

"Where are we going?" I ask as I shift my legs a little.

No way am I conceding. It's too much fun, first of all. But secondly, it keeps my mind off not knowing where we're going, for how long, and whether or not I'm going to sleep with Liam. My type A personality is going a little crazy not knowing. I'm trying to relax and go with the flow, but that's not in my DNA. Everyone knows I'm the take-the-bull-by-the-horns-and-do kinda girl. I've had to be with Aaron always gone.

"Do you really want to know?" Liam takes my hand and laces his fingers with mine.

I look up and boldly meet his eyes, "Not really. I just like annoying you."

"Women."

"Men," I answer back as I take my feet off the dash.

"She's sound asleep," Liam notes while looking in the rearview mirror.

Glancing back, I see how peaceful she is. Not a care in the world. I envy that kind of serenity. I'd be lying if I said that being away from home right now isn't a little bit of a relief. There's something to be said about leaving your worries behind.

"Thank you for this," I squeeze his hand gently.

Liam lifts our intertwined hands and kisses my fingers. "I'm glad I didn't have to tie you up and carry you out. Let's just focus on relaxing and seeing where this goes. No expectations."

"I can do that."

He laughs, "I'll believe it when I see it."

"Whatever. So, how many days do I need to call out of work for?"

"I already talked to Muff and Twilight. You're good."

I look over with wide eyes. "You did what?"

I'm not sure whether I want to slap him or kiss him. On one hand, it shows he cared enough about my job to even think of it. On the other, it's my job and I should be the one to handle things.

I've only been working for Jackson for a few months and I love it there. I don't want to risk losing my position. Although, I highly doubt that Jackson would ever fire me. I've increased their manpower and reduced costs in some areas. I've also been able to utilize my contacts through my time as a journalist. I did a lot of military reporting and knew a few people who worked in similar companies.

They were all too happy to give me some new people looking to create some areas of opportunity for growth.

"I called Muff and told him my plan. He said—and I quote—take her for as long as you want." Liam pauses and let's that sink in. "So I'm taking you."

I let out a deep breath. Relax and enjoy. Relax and enjoy. I tell myself repeatedly so I don't go postal.

"I'm going to just say thank you."

"There's a first," he grumbles.

"Why does this feel so easy with us?" I ask out of nowhere. I don't know why it came out of my mouth, but I wonder it often. Our relationship feels like it went into hyperdrive. It's not instant because I fought him for months, but when I gave in . . . it just felt natural.

Liam looks over with his brow furrowed. "Easy? I don't know I'd call this easy."

"No, I mean being with you. It's easy and effortless. As if we've been doing it forever," I muse.

"I think it's because it's right. I don't know. Why? Are you wanting me to be difficult? Because I can."

I laugh and shake my head. "I'm sure you can. You already are difficult, but I mean us as a couple. I wonder if this is normal."

Liam's hand grips the inside of my leg. "I've never felt like this with anyone. I think it's because we've been friends for a long time. I know you and you know me. There's no getting-to-know-you phase. I loved you before we were ever more—just not like I feel now. You were one of my close friends, but you were off limits. Doesn't mean I wouldn't have done anything for you, though. Now, it's just different." Liam looks out the window as he tries to figure it out too.

"I loved you, too. That being said, I never thought

about making out with you all the time. This is new to me so I wasn't sure if this is how it happens. To go from friends to lovers and feel as if it's the right choice." I grab his hand and lace our fingers together.

"I stopped fighting feeling wrong about us and it happened. Maybe that's why it feels so easy, because it's right. We're not two strangers who met at a bar. I know your family, friends, and I would've kept being a part of your life even if Aaron hadn't died." He pauses and scratches his jaw. "I never looked at you the way I do now and I can't honestly say when it happened for me. I can pinpoint when I decided it was okay though. In the hospital, after we were flirting, I decided I was allowed to feel for you. I think you were meant to be mine."

"Do you now?"

"I do."

"And how exactly do you think that's the case?"

I love this part of our relationship. We can go from serious to playful in a second.

Liam huffs. Maybe he doesn't love this part so much. "I don't fucking know. I think you were in love with me years ago."

"No, I thought you were hot though. Always have."

He smirks and nods his head. "I'm a catch."

"You know you wanted me."

He turns his head slightly to give me his sexy panty-melting smile. "Oh, I did. You've always been beautiful. Only now, you're mine and I will have you."

"Don't count your chickens before they hatch there, pumpkin. Maybe I'm going to meet a handsome stranger on this trip who's going to whisk me away on his yacht. Show me all the things I'm missing out with you," I joke and watch the muscle in his jaw tick.

Oh, alpha men are all the same.

"I'll fucking kill anyone who tries."

"So scary."

"Keep testing me, woman. Watch what happens," Liam warns and I grin.

Liam smiles and pulls off the highway toward the Outer Banks of North Carolina. I didn't even notice where we were going until now. I knew we were going south, but it didn't dawn on me that we would be going to one of my favorite beaches.

"Why are you smiling?" Liam asks.

I didn't realize I was. "I'm just happy. I love OBX."

"See? Superior."

"Oh, shut up," I laugh and smack his chest.

We drive north a ways and through all the quaint little towns that make up the Outer Banks. There are tons of little shops and restaurants. I love where I live now, it's the old feel of Virginia Beach, but these towns are homey. They have charm and scream beach living. Where my house is still has a lot of tourism. All of these towns thrive on the summer tourists, but they still keep their roots.

Liam enters the town limits of Corolla and I close my eyes and breathe in the salt air. The smell of sun and sand mixed with the sea. It's home to me. We pull into the drive of one of the most breathtaking houses I've ever seen.

"Wow," I say, looking up.

"It's Quinn's family's house."

I look over and Liam looks as surprised as I am. "Who knew?"

"No shit. Aara's still sleeping. Do you want to grab her and I'll get the bags?" Liam offers.

"Sure." He goes to exit the car, but I put my hand on his arm stopping him. He looks over with his mouth slightly open.

"What's wrong?"

I lean across the console practically into his lap. "Thank you," I say and press my lips to his.

The second our lips connect, something shifts. Liam's hands thread into my hair and he kisses me roughly. Our tongues move together and my body ignites. I'm euphoric in this moment as I give my appreciation to him. He holds my face to his and I feel his teeth nip at my lip.

There's no way he's sleeping on the couch.

Liam gently pulls my face back and kisses me tenderly. "You can thank me anytime you want."

My laugh is short and my breathing is heavy. "I bet you'd like that."

"Damn right I would."

"Go get the bags. I'll get the baby," I instruct and climb back over to my side.

I get Aarabelle out of the car miraculously without waking her and look closely at the house. It's a beautiful, blue, two-story house with white plantation shutters. The porch wraps around the left side and sits on stilts. Even though it's old, you can tell it's been well cared for. Through whatever storms it's been dealt, it's strong and stands proud. The front door is white and the sand dunes almost cover the wood stilts. I walk up the stairs and Liam's behind me.

He unlocks the door and allows me the time to take it in. "It's magnificent," I say hushed, careful not to wake Aara. She's napped for about an hour, but if she doesn't wake on her own time, she's a beast.

"Look around. I'm going to bring the bags up."

I nod and start to explore. The kitchen has been recently updated and has beautiful black granite countertops with country white cabinets. I walk forward and the windows make me stop short. Beautiful, cream, satin fabric drapes across the glass and pools on the ground making the blue ocean look bluer. I know I have the view of the ocean at home, but it's as if I've never seen *this* ocean before.

I hold Aarabelle who's fast asleep in my arms and look out at the sea before us. I hear Liam come down the stairs and feel him behind me. His arms wrap around my torso and we both stand looking out.

"Beautiful," he whispers.

"Yeah, it is."

"I was talking about you."

My heart is buoyant and his warmth cocoons me. I lean against his chest and cherish this moment. There's so much I want to say, but this is enough right now. Being in his arms, away from all the shit at home, just spending time with Liam and Aarabelle. This is contentment.

"YOU READY?" LIAM yells from downstairs. He's had Aarabelle for the last hour while I've gotten ready for dinner. I assume she hasn't peed or pooped since I haven't heard massive amounts of cursing or Aarabelle screaming.

"Almost!"

I have a white eyelet dress on with my hair in a low twist. I spent extra time shaving every inch of my legs and making sure I didn't miss anything. If we do end up where I hope we do, I want to be as perfect as possible.

Standing before the mirror, I look at myself and smile. This trip was everything I needed. I feel alive and refreshed. After we got settled into the house, we took a walk on the beach. Liam carried Aarabelle while I held on to his arm. Aara was giggly, especially when Liam started to run into the water with her. She would squeal and laugh, then he would run back out.

A part of my heart became his in that moment. I'm hoping tonight another part will be his as well.

"I'm going to eat baby food soon!" Liam's loud voice carries through the halls.

Men.

I grab my bag and head down the stairs.

"I'm ready. Sheesh," I chide as I enter the living room area.

Liam stands there with his khaki pants and navy blue shirt. The muscles in his arms tug at the fabric, stretching it so the shirt looks almost uncomfortable. His blue eyes are deeper than normal, but still mesmerizing. The scruff he usually has is clean-shaven and his beanie that I love so much is missing. He's ridiculously sexy.

"I'm not going to make it through dinner," Liam grumbles.

"What?"

"Can't you wear sweatpants?" he asks, looking at my legs.

I scoff, "I'm not wearing sweatpants to dinner. I got dressed up, you're going to have to learn to control yourself, Mister I'm-so-superior."

Of course there's a part of me that's more than giddy that he seems to be having a hard time with my dress. I didn't wear it to drive him crazy, but it's a perk. I forgot what it was like to have a man's sole attention be you. How it makes you feel when you're desired. Liam awoke that inside me. He brought the woman in me back to life.

When I turn around, his breath hitches. The dress is a halter top, and the back drops to the small of my back.

"Fuck no," Liam says and gently grips my arm. "Please tell me you have a sweater or a poncho for that dress."

I turn slowly with a sly smile. "Nope. It's warm out."

"I'm gonna need a minute." He lets out a deep breath and holds Aarbelle out for me to take.

I grab her and laugh, "Come on, Dreamboat. Let's go eat before you lose your mind."

We head over to a small seafood restaurant, which seems to be one of the only places in town. Liam had to stop for gas and we grabbed a town map. Tomorrow we plan to use the beach cruisers that we found in the house and check out the other local spots.

They seat us at a table by the windows with an ocean view. Aarabelle sits in the highchair between us.

"Mamamamama," she says looking at Liam.

"I'm not your mama. I'm the fun one."

"Fun? You tied her up."

"And she lived and didn't pee all over."

I shake my head, "It's okay, my love. Liam doesn't know how to handle a little diaper," I mock him and Aarabelle is her happy self.

Liam looks off and Aarabelle yells, bringing his attention back to her.

"Someone is just like her mommy," his playful voice is animated. "I see you." Liam gives Aara his hand and she slaps it a few times.

He gives her his attention and I sit in awe. They say the way to a man's heart is his stomach, but mine is Aarabelle. She's my world. There is nothing else that matters other than my daughter. A man can leave, die, cheat, but she'll always be my child. Loving and accepting her is not only important, but without it, no man will ever have me.

Our food arrives and we eat and make small talk. I tell Liam about some of the things I've been handling at work and he tells me about the stupid things the teams have done. I laugh at his new game with Quinn of who's the stronger one. It seems to be helping him with working out on a schedule again.

"Aarabelle's birthday is coming up. Are you going to do a party?" Liam asks once we've finished dinner.

"I want to do something fun. Jackson said he and Catherine would fly in and I know my parents will come too. I should probably start planning."

I have some time, but Liam's known me long enough to know that my parties are Martha Stewart on crack. I go overboard and love to have extravagant events with each minute detail planned. Usually it takes me about a month to hand-make all the decorations. I have issues.

"I would volunteer to help but . . ." he trails off. "I've been to your shindigs . . . and I'll bring the beer."

"I don't think so," I state with a smile. "You're with me, you have to help."

Liam mumbles under his breath as the waitress brings the check.

We decide to take another walk on the beach since it's beautiful out. Liam pays the bill and lifts Aarabelle into his arms.

"Come on, sweetheart." He stands with his hand extended.

I place my hand in his and we exit to the beach. Liam has Aarabelle in his one arm and wraps his other around me. I walk surrounded by him as his body shields me from the wind. This is one of the things I love most. We don't have to talk. Liam is okay with the silence and so am I.

Neither of us has the need to fill the quiet, we can simply find comfort in each other.

As we walk, Aarabelle tucks her head onto his shoulder and he protects her. My heart fills with love watching him care for her. He loves Aara and I love him. I've always cared for him as a friend, but today there's no doubt that my feelings of friendship have formed into something much deeper.

"Liam," I say tenderly.

He stops and we face each other. I want to tell him. I want him to know how much I care.

"What's wrong?"

"Nothing," I say feeling awkward. I look down and move the sand with my toes.

"Hey," he says and pulls my attention back to him.

I take a deep breath. Liam isn't Aaron. There's no guarantee he won't suffer the same fate, but the bottom line is that he's different. Our relationship is much different as well. I was a kid when I met Aaron, we grew up together, and in some ways, we grew apart. The losses in his life caused him to put me in a different place in his heart. Maybe he didn't want to hurt anymore, so he chose to hurt me instead. I'll never know that answer, but I have to move forward.

I never planned to love again. But Liam . . . I can't fight him. I don't want to fight it either.

"I love you." I say the words and I see the joy reflected in his eyes. Tears fill my own eyes as I let the love free in my heart. "I do. I love you. You make me happy and you make me feel safe."

Liam steps closer and cups my cheek, "I love you, Natalie. I'll always keep you safe." My face tilts into his hand and he wipes a tear that descends down my cheek. "Don't cry, sweetheart."

"I'm not sad. I just . . . there are things that scare me with loving you," I admit.

"Like what?" Liam's voice is tender and curious.

He must know the fears that I face. Or maybe he doesn't. They immerse themselves in this world where they think they're untouchable. Even though they live and breathe death.

"You're an active duty Navy SEAL. I'm already a SEAL widow." The words seep out and so does fear.

"I can't make you promises. I'd be a liar and a fool to tell you it can't happen to me. I know you know that. You knew when we started feeling more than friendship what it would mean. Deployments, training, dangerous things I can't tell you about." Liam's words are measured, and his voice is strong and steady. He keeps his hand caressing my face, and my hand rests on his chest. "I can tell you all the bullshit you want to hear, but it'll just be that. I want a life with you, Lee. I want to build something with you and Aarabelle. I want to spend my days thinking about coming home to you. I want to feel your body beneath me when I make love to you."

I look up and my chest tightens.

"I want it all. I love you and Aarabelle, but it comes with a cost. I knew this was going to be something we have to work through. Loving me comes with the risk of knowing I might not come back home."

A tear falls from my eye as the image flashes before me. Another knock on the door telling me he's gone. Another flag on the mantel where I have to look at the only two men I loved taken from me. I can't. I don't think I could do it.

"I can't lose you like that."

"I can't promise you won't, but I can promise I'll fight everything to make sure it doesn't. I'll do anything I can so you never have to feel that way. That's the only promise I can make."

Aarabelle sleeps soundly on Liam's shoulder and I know the choice before me. Either I walk away from Liam now, save whatever is left of the heart I have left. Guard myself and be careful about who I let in, or give everything I have to him. Take the chance to end up with nothing or maybe the greatest love I've ever known. Liam and I have a chance to create a new love that I never had.

Aaron was easy and known. He was comfort and stability. I think even with his affair he wouldn't have left me. We would've maybe found a way to get through it. It wouldn't have been easy, but we have a kid, a life, a marriage together. I'll never know those answers or whether it would've been true, but I loved him. Even now, as hurt as I am, Aaron holds an intangible piece of my heart and soul. It'll always be his.

"If we do this," I hesitate, "You'll be careful?" It's a stupid question, and that word is abhorrent to them. They don't know how to be careful. It's a hero complex, but he needs to know I need that.

"Natalie, I'll do everything I can to come home to you."

"Then let's go back to the house. I'm ready for bed."

I take his hand and we walk back to the car.

chapter

thirty-three

*N*ERVES START TO take hold as we get back to the house. I try to tell myself it's only Liam, but then again—it's Liam.

"I'm going to put her down." My voice trembles. *Smooth, Natalie.*

"I'll come with you," he offers and places his hand on my back.

Great.

We climb the stairs and reach the spare bedroom where I've set up her portacrib. It faces the back of the house so the sun shouldn't wake her first thing in the morning. I hold her a little longer than normal and kiss her forehead. I'm stalling.

Liam kisses her cheek, then kisses mine. He leaves the room and I let out a deep breath.

I need a fucking drink.

"Here goes nothing," I say to myself and place her in her crib. "Sleep all night, my little princess."

Mommy's going to be busy.

Well, now where do I go? The bedroom? The bathroom? Do I have to slip into something? I feel like a dipshit.

I decide I really do need a drink and head to the

kitchen. Liam is standing against the counter sipping a beer.

"Seems I'm not the only one," I say with a laugh and grab the beer from his hand.

He grabs my waist and pulls me against him.

"You don't have to be nervous. We don't have to do anything you don't want," he says against my neck. His nose trails from my neck to my shoulder, and I place the bottle down on the counter behind him. Slowly his fingers dip into the fabric where my back isn't exposed. He lingers there, grazing against my skin, while his tongue traces my neck up to my ear.

I shiver and heat pools in my core.

"I want to go slow. I want to savor every moment with you. I want to touch you, taste you, feel you, and then we'll do it again." His deep voice is rich and full of promise.

I melt in his arms.

"Liam, I've . . ." I stop speaking when his tongue traces the shell of my ear.

"You what, sweetheart?"

"I've . . ." I let out a shaky breath. "I've only ever been with Aaron," I admit and tense. To some this might be a turn off. I don't know. I only know how to do what Aaron liked and maybe I didn't do it well. Maybe that's why he sought another woman. "What if . . ."

Liam's hands drift up my back and grip my shoulders from behind. He pulls me back so we're eye to eye. "What if?"

"What if I suck?"

"I'm going to keep my first thought in check," he replies with a smartass grin.

I stand waiting for him to be serious.

"Natalie, stop it. You're perfect and we'll talk. If you

don't like something, just tell me." Liam's eyes don't waver. He waits until I nod.

Then he scoops me into his arms and pulls me against his chest.

"Put me down."

"Hush."

"I can—" I start to say, but he silences me with his lips.

Liam carries me with almost no effort up the stairs. We enter the bedroom and he carefully kicks it closed with his foot. He holds me and kisses me nonstop as he lays me on the bed.

"I love you," he assures me.

"I love you."

"I'm going to show you how much," Liam's eyes don't leave mine as his hand travels from my face all the way along my body. He leans down allowing me to feel his weight.

I'm warm everywhere. I want him to touch me, kiss me, and I want to feel him inside of me. The want to be claimed by him is so fierce it rocks me to my core. He strokes the skin on my leg with his fingers. Gradually gliding up and down while staring at me. He inches higher and higher until he's at the hem of my dress.

"Kiss me," I request and he does.

Our tongues volley between each other and he pushes me deeper into the bed. His weight covers me and I want more. I hold his face and kiss him with everything I have. My heart thumps in my chest and my pulse races when his fingers skim across my underwear. Liam deepens the kiss and his hands trail higher until he's rubbing the underside of my breast. The fabric is too tight and he retreats.

He sits up and pulls me with him. Deftly he unties the knot behind my neck and the straps fall, leaving my bare chest exposed. Liam looks down before his hands cup my breasts. Leaning in close, his lips are at my ear. "I've waited to do this again. I've dreamt of you lying naked before me. I hope you're ready for a sleepless night, sweetheart." He rolls my nipple between his fingers and I moan.

"Take your shirt off." My voice is desperate. I want to feel his skin against mine again.

I help him by pulling it up and he removes it. The pads of my fingers trace the tattoo again and I remember how much he's been through. Before I can think too much, his lips wrap around my nipple and his tongue circles it. My hands grip his head and hold him there.

"Oh," I sigh as his teeth gently bite down. "Liam."

He stops, "Say it again."

I look into his eyes confused.

"Say my name."

"Liam," I say it again.

He groans and then lavishes the other breast. His hand snakes to my back and pulls my dress off. He throws it on the floor and lies me back down. His mouth returns to my breasts and then he begins to sink lower. I tense as fear begins to take over.

Liam doesn't miss the change in me though. He knows too well how to read people. "Relax, sweetheart. I want to make you feel good."

I let his words wash over me and focus on staying in the moment. His fingers hook in my white simple thong and he leisurely pulls it off. I'm completely bared to him. I'm open and exposed, but all I see is awe in his eyes. He looks at me like I'm a prize, a gift for him.

With his eyes trained on mine, he lowers his head and

kisses my stomach. Then an inch lower he places another kiss. Another inch receives the same attention before he's settling between my legs.

He watches me as I lean up on my elbows.

His head dips and mine falls back. Liam's tongue swirls against my clit and every part of me comes to life. He sucks and then his tongue enters me. I jump up, but he anchors me. My arms give out as I squirm against him, but he doesn't relent. Each swipe of his tongue brings me higher. I build toward my orgasm and he moans against me.

"So close," I start to chant.

It's been so long. I swear I've never come this quickly. I'm right there when he lifts his mouth.

My eyes fly open and my mouth is slack as I look at him in frustration.

"Not yet," is all he says and then he returns. He starts slowly and his tongue is feather light. I fight the urge to push his head where I need it most.

"Liam, please," I beg.

I feel his finger press against my opening and he slowly enters me. I don't know whether to cry or laugh. He starts to move and his tongue is exactly where I need it. I climb, and I swear if he stops, I'm going to bite him. He moves creating the friction I need. Heaven. This is fucking heaven. My nerve endings burn with the need to release. My muscles lock and I let go.

Each part of me tingles and feels heavy. I'm panting and still throbbing as Liam continues to draw out every ounce of pleasure my body can give. He pushes up and stares down at me. "You're even more beautiful when you come."

"Now it's your turn," I say flipping over and climbing

on top of him. My fingers touch his lips and I trace all the way to his sternum. I travel over every ridge and plane of his six-pack. Sliding down his body, I admire the man beneath me. He's strong, sexy, caring, and I'm going to do everything I can to make this night memorable for him.

Touching him feels right.

Being with him feels like it's meant to be.

I loosen his belt and remove his pants. He lies there with a lazy smile as I take my time removing his boxers. I take a moment to admire him. His long, thick cock throbs before me and the need to be filled overwhelms me. I want him to take me. But first, I want to explore him.

"Natalie, if you keep looking at me like that, I'm not going to be able to control myself," Liam warns and I want to defy him.

I love that I can test his limits. It's a sense of power I've never known.

My hand wraps around him and I lean up and nip at his ear. "You're not the only one testing their strength," I say low and seductive. "I want you inside of me so bad I could cry. Make me yours, Liam."

A switch flips inside of him and he turns me onto my back. "You're already mine."

My eyes close and he waits.

"Look at me," he demands.

I open my eyes and see the love shine through him. "Do I need a condom?"

"No." I don't tell him that the chances of me conceiving are slim to none. The only way I can get pregnant is through infertility treatments.

"I want to feel you. Only you. I want you to feel me. Don't close your eyes."

Each breath I take feels like an eternity passes waiting

for him to enter me. He goes slowly and I feel the tip of him. "I love you. I love every part of you. I wanted to fight it, but I can't fight you." He comforts me as he pushes deeper inside. My eyes stay on his and I give over all my heart. "You're supposed to be mine and I won't lose you." Liam's eyes close as he enters me fully.

My breathing is short as I try to adjust. He stays still and then presses his lips to mine. I relax and get lost in the kiss and then we begin to move together. Liam thrusts and I hold on to his back as he slowly rocks inside of me. I push against him and he groans.

I take everything about him in. The way his jaw is tight and his muscles are taut as he moves. His eyes shift from dark blue to light, his eyes open in pleasure. My hands memorize the way his ass fits in my palm as he moves with me. Pushing and pulling me apart. We fit together as if we've been doing this forever.

He flips me over so I'm on top and my hands trail his body. "You feel incredible," I say as I rock back and forth. "I don't want this to stop," breathless as I start to climb again. "It feels so good," I whisper against his mouth and he kisses me again.

His hand dips between us as he finds my clit. The pressure from his finger and the way his dick hits the spot inside of me . . . I'm a goner.

"I'm gonna come, Lee. You feel so fucking good," he warns me.

"Oh my God," I moan as my orgasm is so close. I close my eyes and free my mind. I focus only on the way Liam is touching me.

I shatter apart and I swear my body just exploded.

He flips me back over and pounds relentlessly as he follows my orgasm with his own.

Liam and I made love and I never want it to end.

We lie here trying to catch our breath and I start to come down from my high. I get up and head to the bathroom. I stare at myself in the mirror after cleaning up and try to notice anything different. My hair is a mess and I try to fix it, but I'm still the same. The insides of me are changed though. I'm no longer just Aaron's girl. I've given myself to another man—a good man. A man that I hope will be around for a long time.

I climb back into bed and he wraps the blanket around us. I lie there staring at him with adoration.

His head lolls over and his face lights up. "That was . . ." Liam struggles for words.

"Good?" I ask apprehensively.

He takes my hand. "No, sweetheart. That was better than good."

I beam and close my eyes. My mind drifts without permission to my first time with Aaron. It was nothing like that. We were both inexperienced teenagers who were trying to recreate a movie. I don't want to think of him. Liam deserves to have me here and not in my past right now.

"Liam?" I ask, trying to divert my thoughts.

"Hmmm?" He takes my hand and places it against his chest.

I don't know after this how much we'll see each other. I wonder if he's leaving soon for a deployment or if it's just training. Even before our relationship progressed, I missed him when he was gone. I don't know how I'm going to handle it now. I have to remember he's a SEAL and I'm back to that life. Previously, I wouldn't even notice when Aaron was gone, but Liam and I are so attuned.

"What's your schedule for the next few weeks? I'm

not a needy person, but I want to know how much we'll see each other."

"I have to leave in a few days for about two weeks. Then I'm home for a bit. I'll be here for Aara's birthday and then probably have to leave after that."

"I'll miss you."

Liam shifts, pulling me on top of him. His fingers trace down my nose to the side of my face. My chin quivers a tiny bit thinking of him leaving for six months. We're so new and I don't want him to go. "I'll see you every day. When I close my eyes, I'll see your blue eyes, blonde hair, and your beautiful face. You've done this, you know it's not forever," Liam stops, catching himself on that phrase. "I'm sorry, I didn't mean it like that."

"I know you didn't," I reassure him and roll over. "But it can sometimes be forever."

Liam pulls me to his side and I close my eyes. He holds me close and I dare to hope that this forever won't be the same fate as the last man I loved.

I wake the next morning and my hand reaches for Liam, but all I get are cold sheets. Again.

No.

I sit up and look around. *Please don't let this be a dream.* It's definitely not my bedroom. I'm in North Carolina. "Okay," I tell myself, "Just take deep breaths."

Climbing out of bed, I feel the aches of the muscles I hadn't used in a while. I'm sore but I welcome it. It reminds me of the complete ecstasy I felt in Liam's arms. The sun shines through the window and I go to see where he is.

I walk past Aarabelle's room to check on her, but she's not there. I rush down the stairs and see them on the couch. Liam has Aara tucked into his side and she has food all over her face. She's elated and smiling, watching television with him. Leaning against the wall, I watch them.

She starts to wiggle and he places her on his lap. "Okay, Mommy's still sleeping, and I'm pretty sure you're going to need a new diaper after the amount of food you ate. We're going to keep that between us."

She stands on his legs and bounces.

"So if you could not poop, that would be really great," he tries to convince her. "I mean, I can buy you a doll or whatever it is you kids are into. Want a pony? There are wild ones running around. I'm sure I can snag one if you can keep up your end of the bargain."

"Mamamama," Aarabelle coos and Liam tries to occupy her.

"Your mama is way better looking than me. Can you say Liam?" he asks and she eats her fingers. "Probably not but you could try."

I stifle my laugh as she eats her hand and bounces, oblivious. If he's already bribing her with ponies, we're going to need to nip this in the bud.

"A pony?" I say as I come into view.

"Oh, thank God. I was worried she was going to shit and I don't have rope or tape."

"There's so much wrong with this situation." I smile and walk toward them. If this is a glimpse of my mornings with Liam, I'll be a very happy woman. He sits shirtless and I do my best not to ogle, but his body is hard to tear my eyes away from. His chest is broad and shoulders strong. I know what it feels like to have his strong arms wrapped around me.

In fact, I would like to have that right now. I saunter over, wearing his long t-shirt that I found on the floor.

Remembering how much he liked me leaving in it the first time we fooled around, I figured he wouldn't mind.

"Good morning," he gazes at me as I stand in front of him.

"Morning." I scrunch down and kiss him and then kiss Aara. "Morning, Princess."

I lift her into my arms and make myself comfortable on his lap.

"My two favorite girls." Liam wraps his arms around us and squeezes.

"Thank you for waking up with her."

Aarabelle babbles on as I nestle her into my chest. She looks at Liam and her whole face lights up.

Liam shuts the television off and pushes the hair off my face. "I went for my run and when I got back I heard her talking in her crib. I must've worn you out last night," he says with pride.

Rolling my eyes, I snuggle into his chest. "What time is it?"

"Ten,"

"Ten?" I yell out as I jump up. "You let me sleep till ten? What the hell?" I ask and look at Aara. "Did you feed her?"

"Yes, I fed her," he scoffs. "I'm not a total idiot."

"What the hell is on her face?" I ask, swiping the dark brown smear on her face. "Is this chocolate?"

Liam stands and ignores my question. "I'm gonna hop in the shower."

"Liam! You gave her chocolate for breakfast?"

"Feel free to join me," he says while walking up the stairs.

"You're going to change every shitty diaper she has!"

"Love you!"

"Ugh!" I groan and look at her all happy and clueless. It's hard to be mad at him since he let me sleep in, but still. He has so much to learn and hopefully he'll be around for me to teach him.

chapter

thirty-four

"DON'T LET HER get too close!" I call out from my beach chair. Liam is letting Aarabelle play near the water and I can't help but get a little antsy.

"Calm down. I know how to swim—well!" he lets me know in an annoyed tone.

I've gotten to actually enjoy the beach for the first time since Arabelle's been born. I don't know what to do with myself. Plus, I get to look at Liam shirtless. Really, I'm winning anyway you look at this.

My phone rings and I look at the number. California?

"Hello," I answer.

"Natalie? It's Catherine."

"Cat! Hey!"

I haven't talked to her in so long. Between her working insane hours and the fact that my life is nuts, we just miss each other. I do get to talk to her through Jackson though . . . I guess that's something.

"Hey! I had a few minutes and was thinking of you. I think I'm going to come back east next time Jackson comes to Virginia and I'd love to see you."

I laugh as Aara throws sand at Liam. "Yeah, that would be great."

"You sound happy," she notices.

"I am. I'm actually away until tomorrow. Liam and I came to the Outer Banks."

She goes silent for a second. "Things are good then? With Liam?"

I sigh and the smile that forms is natural. "Yeah, things are really good. I'm content, Cat. He's sweet and he loves Aarabelle and me. It's strange and we're adjusting, but I'm in love with him."

"Oh, that's amazing. Seriously! I'm so happy for you. And after finding everything out?"

Jackson and Mark found out about the affair, I assume through Liam or Quinn. Jackson pulled me aside and assured me they knew nothing. He and Mark were both angry, but they've also seen it so many times. Cheating isn't uncommon in the SEAL community. I was grateful that I wasn't the only person who was blindsided by it.

"It sucked."

"Trust me, I know. I know it's awful, but I promise you, in time, the affair can even become a blessing. When I walked in on my ex cheating on me with his whore, I didn't think I could love again. It was the most horrific thing, but because of that . . . I met Jackson. Maybe Liam is your lobster." We both laugh at the *Friends* reference.

"I think he could be. I'm taking things one day at a time, but you know. Oh," I remember to tell her about Aara's party. "In about a month, I'm going to have Aarabelle's first birthday party. I know it's a little early, but I'd love if you and Jackson could be there."

"Oh, for sure! Jackson wouldn't want to miss it. Okay, babe, I gotta run. I have a meeting in a few, but I'm glad we could catch up a little," Catherine says, sounding rushed.

"Me too! I can't wait to see you."

"I can't wait either. Kiss that precious little girl and

we'll chat again soon."

I disconnect the call and think about what she said. Her ex did a real number on her. At least I never had to walk in on Aaron and Brittany, but at least Catherine wasn't married and having a baby. It sucks no matter which way you slice it. Infidelity takes a part of your heart and tarnishes it forever. I can polish it up, but it'll always have a dull spot.

Liam and Aarabelle head back and I appreciate the way he moves. Even the way he walks is lithe. The muscles in his arms enlarge as he lifts the baby. I stand up and head over to them.

"Dadada," Aarabelle babbles and rubs her eyes.

Liam and I glance at each other and then down to Aara. She gazes at the house and I wonder if she is just making noises or if she seriously called him some form of Daddy. It would make sense. He's the only man in her life. Neither of us speak as I wait to see if she says it again.

"Did she?" I question aloud.

"We probably misunderstood."

I nod and blow it off. She might have said something else and we are being silly. We both stay silent for a few beats and watch her as if she'll say something again. After a few minutes, Liam reaches for my hand and laces his fingers with mine.

The sun warms my face and I close my eyes.

"You should really be wearing something else," Liam chastises, breaking me from my peaceful moment.

"What's wrong with my bathing suit?" I ask looking down.

I know it's not the body I had before kids, but I don't think I'm fat. I have on a deep burgundy strapless bikini. It hugs my new curves but hides the tiny pooch I'll never get rid of.

"Nothing's wrong. I'm just having a hard time not wanting to carry you over my shoulder and bury myself inside of you again," Liam says and I literally shudder.

My stomach tightens and I need a minute to think again. That was definitely not what I was expecting to hear.

"Okay," I manage to say. "What time are we leaving tomorrow?"

"I need to get some stuff ready before I leave, so probably after breakfast. And after morning sex."

"So sure I'm going to give it up, huh?" I play with him a little.

"I think I've proven myself."

"I'm not so sure."

He's more than proven himself, but it's not in my nature to let him gloat.

"I'd be careful. Aarabelle is yawning and I can think of something to do during her nap time."

I look at the baby and wonder if it's too early for her nap.

"I have some other things I really wanted to do, like catch up on my TV shows.

Maybe another time though."

Liam lunges forward and practically knocks me out of my chair. "I'd start stretching, sweetheart." He kisses the side of my neck and his warm breath causes goosebumps to form. "I'm going to make you come many, many times."

I try to manage my breathing and appear in control. "I'm counting on that."

He's going to make me suffer, but in the absolute best way.

An hour later, we pack the few things we brought to

the beach and head back toward the house. I feed Aarabelle and get her ready for her nap. She's exhausted, and after her oh-so-healthy breakfast, getting her to eat lunch was not fun. Once everything's cleaned up and I get her settled, I'm not sure what to do.

Do I go and look for him? I mean, he alluded to what we'd be doing. Then I feel awkward because I'm not sure if this is normal. I feel like a horny teenager worrying about having sex all over again. I've never had an adult relationship where you date.

"Trying to avoid me?" Liam says and I leap out of my skin.

"What is with all of you? Do they train every one of you to scare the shit out of people? Fucking hell." I try to calm my heart, but it's been almost a year since he died . . . it's been a year.

It's a year.

Today.

And I didn't even realize it. It's been one year today since Aaron died.

I look at Liam with tears building. I'm here on vacation with Liam—making love, having fun, and I didn't realize it's the anniversary of my husband's death.

"I didn't mean to scare you. Are you okay?" he asks concerned.

"Liam," I say with my hand on his arm. "I don't know . . . I mean . . . today is a year. Today makes one year since he died." I look up with despair. I'm an awful person. I mean, I didn't even know. I didn't think about it or him. Yes, he hurt me, but still. Shouldn't I be in Pennsylvania? I suddenly want to vomit.

Liam stands there and doesn't say a word. Guilt for two men becomes too much for me. I'm standing here on vacation with my boyfriend crying over my dead husband. The day after we had sex for the first time. Oh my God. I'm going to lose it.

"I need a minute," I say and rush down the stairs.

There are no answers here to ease my mind. Nothing is right and yet nothing is wrong. I made my peace with Aaron. I made my choice with Liam, but at this moment, my two worlds are colliding and nothing fits.

I burst through the door onto the beach and fall to my knees. I'm more upset that I forgot. I don't know what the protocol on mourning is, but shouldn't I have remembered?

I think about the note I found with the apology. Maybe he was sorry about the affair. Maybe he was sorry he married me and was unhappy. Even though I don't think that. Sure, we had hard times—all marriages do—but we had a lot of happy. We had laughs, love, and we had a family. I take this time here on the beach to forgive him and forgive myself. If I go off his letter, he wanted me to be free and to love again. I want that too.

And I have that.

I look toward the ocean and there are three wild horses trotting along the water. I've never seen the horses when I've been on the beach. They're majestic and the three of them move a little slower for a moment.

The dark brown horse seems to be in charge as it leads the pack. There's a light tan horse who's in between the two darker horses. The other horse pushes past and is almost black. It's the tallest of the three. It moves in front and the tan horse perks up.

I sit and watch them and can't help but feel for the tan horse. I decide it's a she. She has two male horses vying to lead her. But she's wild and doesn't want to be led. Again,

I decide all of this. She wants to love, but feels torn between the two horses. When I've written their entire story in my mind, the dark brown horse turns and leaves her.

"I'm sorry too, Aaron. You left me."

The two horses run in the opposite direction and I feel like somehow he just answered me.

Standing, I brush the sand off my legs and decide to find Liam. He deserves an explanation. When I turn, I see him standing a few feet behind me. His arms are at his sides and his eyes are sad.

"Liam," I say as a plea.

He puts his hand up and then pinches the bridge of his nose. "I didn't realize it either. I didn't fucking remember." He steps forward.

"I'm sorry I ran out like that. It's not your fault. I felt like I was an awful person. Here I am," I walk toward him, "Happy and in love. Falling asleep in your arms and wanting to be there again. It's overwhelming all on its own. And then when I realized what today is, I felt this pang of guilt. But I choose you, Liam. I want to be in your arms. I want to be here with you. It's you who has my heart."

His eyes meet mine and he pulls me against him. Neither of us speaks and I wonder if he saw the horses. The symmetry between those three horses and myself spoke volumes to me. One of them would always have to be alone. They had to make choices about who should lead and who she should follow. But I don't have to choose because one left, leaving my path clear.

I vow to myself to enjoy the rest of our trip together. To allow myself the break from the life that awaits me when I'm home. Liam is who I want to spend my time with. He's who I love. I look forward to him calling, coming over, and he gives me everything I need. Liam and I may have been friends but I can't help but wonder if this was how it was always meant to be.

"GOOD MORNING, SLEEPYHEAD." Liam's hot breath is against my ear. I curl into a ball and want desperately to be asleep.

"It's still dark out," I grumble. I open one eye and want to slap him for waking me. Last night we spent our time just the three of us holed up in the living room. We played with Aarabelle and then he held me for hours.

We didn't speak about what the day had held. I think each of us needed to process it on our own. A year changed a lot for me. I learned a lot about life, love, grief, and that there are no real answers for any of it. Love can hurt and heal. Aaron hurt me deeper than I knew was possible, but Liam showed me it's okay to forgive. Grief ate at me, formed pockets of guilt and anger so deep I didn't think I'd find a way out, but I did. There are still times I'm angry, but I won't let it define me. Each day I have to choose the life I want to live.

"I'm going to go for my run, but then I thought maybe we could exercise together," his voice penetrates deep into my core.

God, his voice is sexy.

"What did you have in mind?"

His lips glide over my ear and he pulls my hair back exposing my neck. He gently bites the skin there and I moan. Slowly, his tongue slides across the skin he just nipped. "Maybe some cardio?" he suggests. "Or stretching . . ." he says as he bites another sensitive area.

"I . . ." My voice is breathless when his hand snakes

across my chest. "I . . ." I can't get the words out.

Liam's hand squeezes my breast as his mouth explores my neck and ear. "You what?" he breathes the words into my ear.

His fingers pull at my nipples and my ass rocks against him. I'm already wet. I want him so bad. "I want you," I say in a voice that even I don't recognize. I'm needy and begging for him, though he's barely touched me.

"How bad?"

I moan as his hand finds my other breast. I try to roll over, but his body keeps me where I am. Completely at his mercy.

"How bad do you want me, Natalie?"

"More than my next breath."

His hand dips lower and he pushes my legs apart. When his finger finds my clit, I moan out in ecstasy. He pushes and swirls while I lay panting. My hand reaches back and I push his shorts and underwear off. I want to lead this one.

My hand wraps around his dick and I pump him up and down as he swells beneath my touch.

"I want to do something," I say as he continues to insert a finger inside.

"Do anything you want," he offers.

I sit up and take my top off. Liam's eyes shine in the low light entering from the moon. Morning, my ass.

I pull his pants off and he shifts on the bed. Leaning down, I wrap my lips around his cock. Liam groans and his fingers tangle in my hair.

"Holy fuck," he moans.

My mouth glides up and down his length as I focus on every breath hitch and sound he makes. I focus on taking him deep and know he must enjoy it based on how his hand tightens in my hair. I slide back up and then take him deeper, and Liam moans again.

"Natalie, you need to stop." He pulls me and flips me on my back. "I'm going to fucking drive you insane."

I have no doubt.

He pulls my legs over his shoulders and wastes no time. Liam's mouth is on me in a moment and my head falls back. He licks and devours me. There's no finesse. It's savage and feels incredible. His finger enters me and he pumps inside of me, twisting his hand while his mouth sucks at my clit.

"I'm gonna come," I say as he takes me higher.

He doesn't relent and slips another finger inside that moves at the same pace as his tongue. My breathing is erratic and I'm growing closer to release. I can taste it. I need it. Liam sucks harder and I fall apart. I squirm and pant as he continues to draw everything I have.

"So fucking gorgeous," he says and slowly climbs his way up my body.

My hand grips his neck and I pull his mouth to mine. Our tongues meld together and he slips inside me.

"Oh," I break apart as he pushes deep and waits. "Move. Please, move," I beg as he rests fully seated inside of me.

He waits with eyes closed as if he's memorizing this feeling. I'm full and want him to take me.

"I want to live inside of you," he says and then pulls back. "You're made for me." He continues to talk as he pushes deeper than before. Liam slides back and forth as he fills my heart and my body. "I want to love you all day."

My eyes close as I savor the sensations of him inside of me. When I look up, I rest my hands against his face. "You already do," I say softly. "You love me all day." He slows his pace but continues to move as I tell him how I feel. "You give me so much without even knowing it. You healed me. You gave me the strength to be the woman I once was." Liam's eyes stay locked on mine as he pours himself into me and I pour my heart out to him. "You showed me how to love again. So you do love me all day, and I love you."

We both stare at each other as we make love. A tear falls from my eyes as we both fall over the edge together without saying a word. Liam holds me against him as I cry, overcome with love and happiness. This is a moment I'll never forget. It's the moment I realized just how deeply in love I am with Liam Dempsey.

chapter

thirty-five

"HEY, CAN YOU head into the conference room?" Mark asks. It's my first day back to work after our vacation. There were piles of papers on my desk and I saw on the calendar that Jackson is flying in again.

"Sure."

"Thanks," he replies, already gone.

I'm assuming something is going on because everyone is running around like lunatics. I grab my notebook and try not to notice the weird looks I'm getting. I wonder if I'm getting fired.

"What's going on?" I ask as soon as I enter the door.

"There's an issue with an account. Jackson is on his way here and then we're heading out. It'll be me, Jackson, and three other guys," Mark says, still looking at a paper.

"Where are you guys headed?"

"Overseas," he answers quickly and seems extremely distracted.

"Okay . . ." I trail off feeling a little out of the loop. "Did I screw something up?"

Mark's head snaps up. "No, not at all. This is fairly normal. Our overseas accounts are always a little strange. This account is in Dubai and the Navy wants us to provide asset protection. They want us to come out and see what's going on firsthand and give them an assessment on what we can do to ensure it doesn't get fucked up. Muff wants to make sure you can handle the office while I'm gone."

"I'm sure I can."

"Okay, we'll be out of reach most of the time, so you'll have to be able to figure out anything while we're away. I wanted to give you these files before I leave in a few days. Plus, go over a few of the financial things."

It says a lot to me that they want me to handle the office in their absence. It doesn't make sense why they'll be unreachable, but far be it from me to understand everything that goes on here.

Mike knocks, "Charlie's on the line for you, Twilight."

Mark looks over at me, "I need to take this. We're leaving in a day or two, but I'll shoot you an email with everything in case things are hectic beforehand."

"Okay," I stand awkwardly and head out of the room. Mark is usually a pretty calm guy but he seems keyed up. I hope he's being honest and that I didn't do something wrong. I handled the Dubai account and made sure they had the manpower they requested.

Heading back to my office, I see I have a missed call from Aaron's mom. It's the first time I've heard from her in a year. She cut me and Aarabelle off completely, and no matter how many times I've tried, she never reciprocates.

I sent out Aarabelle's birthday invitations the other day. Maybe she's going to come.

I dial her number and someone picks up.

"Patti?" I ask.

"Lee," she says my name with a sigh. "I'm so sorry. I've been an awful mother-in-law. I should've called. It's just been so hard," Patti starts to ramble and my heart aches for her.

"There are no guidelines on grief. I wish you would've let me grieve with you, but I understand." I want to ease her mind. It's a hard place to be and I can't begrudge how she chose to live with it.

"I got the invitation with her photo. She looks so much like him."

"She does," I agree.

"How are you doing?"

We chat and catch up. She tells me she wants to come out for her birthday party and would love to talk again. I've missed her. She was like a mother to me since I was sixteen.

"Are you happy?" The question stops me short. I want to be honest with her, but I worry she's going to hate me.

"I am. There's a lot that's happened in the past year, but I'm moving on. I don't have any other choice." I choose not to tell her too much. She doesn't need to know about Aaron's affair. I decide to let her memory of her son stay unsullied.

"I'm glad for you. I think he'd be happy too." Patti sniffles but holds it together. "I'll let you get back to work and I'll see you in a few weeks."

We disconnect the call and I sit back in my chair. I've got a lot to be thankful for.

The rest of the day passes without any issues. I go over all the files Mark emails over. Reanell texts me and asks me to meet her for lunch. She's been so busy with the command side of the team that we haven't seen much of each other. I'm excited to get to spend a little girl time with her, and since everyone in the office is nuts, no one will miss me.

I pull up to our favorite restaurant that serves break-fast all day. Citrus always has a wait, but we're good friends with the owner. I called her and let her know we'd be coming, so she saved us a place at the bar.

"Hey, sexy mama," Reanell says as she finds me on my stool.

"I've missed you!" I exclaim and pull her into a hug.

She hugs me tight and we act as if it's been years rather than a week or two. "How's everything? Vacation seems to have agreed with you."

"Yeah, it was great." I smile thinking about the time with Liam. It really was great. I know Reanell well enough to see the wheels turning in her head. I give it five seconds before she goes from chewing on her nail to berating me.

"Seriously? That's all I get?"

Or maybe less.

I laugh and grab my drink, giving me a few extra seconds and also giving her frustration a little nudge. "I'm happy, Rea. He makes me feel like I can do anything."

"I'm happy. How are you with the whole SEAL thing and the thing with Aaron?"

She's the first person to bring it up. She's also the only person who watched me go a little crazy and shred his shit.

The truth is . . . I'm not sure how to handle either issue. Aaron isn't here, so I can't get answers from him. Liam is a SEAL, so I can't do anything about that either. My choices aren't really favorable.

"They are what they are."

"You are a liar." Reanell laughs and puts her head on her hand. "It's me. No need to fool me."

"I can't do anything about either. I'm still upset about the affair. I was pregnant and he slept with someone else. We'd been trying to have Aarabelle for so long and I know it took a toll on us, but still," I pause as it all comes boiling back up. "I can't even pinpoint when things might've happened."

The hair on the back of my neck stands. I can't explain what has my senses heightened, but I look around, trying to see if I'm being watched.

"What is it?" Rea asks and looks around too.

"I don't know, I just got a weird feeling." I look around again but I don't recognize anyone.

We enjoy our lunch and I tell her about Aarabelle's birthday party. She laughs and tells me I'm going overboard, but knows there's no stopping me. I want to celebrate where we've come in a year. Aara may not know the life she's had isn't exactly sunshine and roses, but she's had a life filled with love.

"I gotta get back to work," I say and put a ten-dollar bill down. "The guys are all leaving and I need to make sure everything is in order."

"First, you're going to sit here and tell me about the sex." She crosses her arms and waits expectantly.

I thought I'd gotten away with it, but apparently not.

"I really don't have to tell you anything." My smile fades almost immediately when I look at the end of the bar and Brittany is sitting there. "I'm leaving," I inform her and start to grab my bag.

"Why?" Rea looks and sees her.

Brittany looks over and stands.

Anger flows through my veins. I walk over to her and she averts her eyes. "Don't look away. Are you following me?"

"Following you? No!" she says and goes to gather her things. "I swear, I don't want to cause trouble."

"What do you want?" I ask, because this is the part that still gets me. She wanted me to know about her and

Aaron. She could've let me go on living my ignorant life, but instead, she made me aware. "I'm trying to move on from all of this, but it's obvious we're going to see each other."

Brittany leans against the chair and sighs. "I want to move on with my life, but there's a lot causing me not to."

"I feel the same."

"Look, I didn't want to tell you. I didn't set out for you to find out, but don't you see? I'm the same as you. I'm in pain." She nearly chokes on the last word.

"I wish I could say I care . . . but I don't."

"I know you don't care and I wish I wasn't the other woman. I just don't know how to move on . . ." she admits and her eyes fill with tears.

Reanell stands behind me and places her hand on my shoulder.

"Can you answer some questions for me?" I ask. I can't even believe I'm entertaining the idea of talking to her, but maybe we can both find a way to move past this.

"I can try."

"When did you start seeing him?"

She looks away and then back to me as she tries to collect herself. "We were together about a year before he died. We met at a bar and started talking."

"Wow." It's as if I've been punched in the gut. He was seeing her when we were trying to get pregnant. "When did you find out about me?" I look at her and wait for the answer that has bothered me since I found out.

Brittany pushes her blonde hair behind her shoulder. "A few weeks before he died. When I found out I was pregnant."

My eyes snap up and I fight back the nausea that threatens to escape. "Pregnant?" I ask looking down at her stomach.

"Yes, I was eight weeks pregnant when I lost the baby." She looks at me with sadness in her eyes.

I grasp my throat and try to breathe. "I-I don't . . ." I'm not sure what to say. "When?"

"I lost the baby a week after he died."

And the hits keep coming.

So she would've had a baby with my husband. Awesome. After three failed pregnancies and countless months of infertility, I find this out. Each time I start to think this can't get any worse, it does.

"I think I'm going to be sick." I turn to Reanell and she pulls me into her arms.

"I love him. I wasn't just some girl."

I turn and look at her. "Yes, you were. He didn't tell you he was married. He never told me about you. The man you loved was a lie. I've known him since he was sixteen. I went to his senior prom, was at his boot camp graduation, married him. You weren't his life." I spew the words out.

"You weren't either," Brittany rebuts.

I wish I could argue with her. I wish I could yell and scream, but she's right. I wasn't his life. I was his wife who got pregnant and maybe trapped him.

Brittany wipes her eyes and rights herself. "I'm sorry. I should go."

Reanell steps forward. "I know you're hurting, but this," she points to me, "Isn't the right way."

Brittany starts to walk away and I grab her arm. The words taste like vinegar on my tongue. I fight with myself whether to say them, but I've lost a child. I know the pain and how hard I held on to each loss as my own personal failure. Each baby that didn't make it ate at me. "I'm sorry you lost a child," I say as tears fall.

The tears she had stopped start to flow and slide down her cheek. She doesn't say a word as she gathers her bag and leaves.

"A baby," is all I can say as Reanell pulls me into her arms. "She was going to have his baby."

chapter

thiry-six

TWO WEEKS PASS and I do my best to put Brittany and her bomb to the back of my mind. Liam has been gone, so it's given me time to grieve the news in my own way. I've come to some kind of peace regarding it, although I don't know I'll ever completely be at peace with it. I hate myself for being relieved she lost the baby. It's not something I'm proud of, but Reanell has been great with helping me understand my feelings.

This last training session was supposed to be three days, but they extended it to seven so they could get some shooting qualifications. I don't miss this shit.

He came home late last night and had a lot to finish, so we agreed for a late dinner tonight.

"Hey, sweetheart," Liam says as he comes in the kitchen with a bag of Chinese food. I can smell the yumminess.

"My hero." I give a dramatic sigh and clutch my chest. "Did you get me an eggroll?"

"Do I get a prize if I did?"

"You get a kiss and maybe I'll get naked for you."

"Maybe?" he asks with a raised brow.

"Fine, you'll get nookie if I get an eggroll," I acquiesce.

Liam digs through the bag and his face says it all. They forgot the eggroll. Ha! I'm so going to make him pay for this.

"Eggroll, Dreamboat." I put my hand out waiting. He continues to dig.

"If I don't get laid because there's no fucking eggroll, I'm going to kill someone," he says out loud and I smile.

There's no eggroll and he's going to be upset. Oh, how I enjoy late dinners.

"Is that all I am to you?" I quip. "Sex?"

He looks over and grimaces. Looks like someone isn't happy. "I'm not even going to answer you. I'll be back," he says and starts to walk away.

"Oh, stop!" I say laughing. "Don't be an idiot."

Liam's arms cage me in as he leans down. "I'll make it up to you." His voice is full of promise.

"I'll be sure you do."

"I missed you," he says as his lips barely touch mine.

"I'd miss me too."

"And you say I'm arrogant." He smiles against my mouth.

I smile back and kiss him gently. "I just know how lucky you are."

He kisses me again and laughs.

We eat our dinner and fill each other in on our time away. I miss hearing the field stories. Things that happened and all the dumb things they do. Liam tells me about Quinn and the pranks he pulled on some new guys who checked in this week. I laugh and tell him about work and then I fill him in on my talk with Brittany.

"She was pregnant?" he asks with his jaw hanging open.

"Apparently. I don't know what the hell to believe anymore. It's all ridiculous."

Liam pulls my chair so I'm sitting with my legs

between his. "Are you okay?"

I know it's not easy for him to shift into this conversation. I mean, here we are again, talking about Aaron in
some way. Even I grow annoyed with it. The flip side is
that Aaron wasn't just some ex for me and he wasn't some
guy to him. There's a lot of history for both of us.

"It was a shock. It was a big shock," I say in a hushed
tone.

"I'm sure, but that doesn't answer my question."

"I'm fine."

"Oh, good. You're fine again." Liam throws his hands
up and they come down with a slap.

I look up as I hear the chair grate against the floor.
He moves away from me and starts to eat again. I sit here
stunned.

"Why are you pissed?" I ask, a little pissed myself.

He drops the fork and looks over and huffs. "You're
fine? We're going back to that? You find out your husband
was having a baby with the woman he was fucking behind
your back—and you're fine?"

Fuck him. I can be fine or whatever else I want to be.

"I've had a few days to process it all, Liam. I'm sorry
I don't want to tell you all the shit that went through my
mind. I'm fine with it now—is that better?" I sneer the
words and shake my head.

"I have a lot on my mind."

"That's no excuse to be an ass to me. I didn't have to
tell you about Brittany and their love child. But I'm trying
to be honest with you. You said we should talk about this
crap."

"I know."

"That's your cue to say 'I'm sorry,'" I instruct him.

He looks over and pulls my chair back. His eyes

sparkle in the light and he gives a dramatic sigh. "My darling, Natalie," Liam pauses and then lifts my hands between us, "I'm forever sorry for being an ass. I promise to only fight with you when it's acceptable and you grant me permission. Will you forgive me?"

"I hate you."

"No, you don't."

"I'm pretty sure I do."

"You'll live."

"You might not," I threaten.

Liam's lips rise as he fights his smile. "I'll take my chances."

He could probably kill me in half a second, but he'd have to catch me first. We both sit in silence and I allow myself a few moments to gather myself after our argument. I wonder how long we can seriously go like this.

Liam starts to shift a little and I notice he seems to be somewhere else. Normally I would push him, but it's unlike him to be uncomfortable. Liam exudes confidence. He knows how to handle most situations before they even happen. Maybe I really upset him with our disagreement.

"Are you okay?" I finally ask after a long bout of silence.

"Yeah, I told you I have a lot on my mind," he explains. I sit and wait for him to expand on that. He lifts his head to the sky and lets out a deep breath. "We got our deployment orders today." He looks over at me and waits.

I know what this means and the fact that he's this unhappy tells me all I need to know. It's soon and I'm going to need to start preparing for it. I try to dig deep into my old ways. Think later—smile now. I need to lock down my own concerns and be his support. He can't see my fear, he can't see my sadness. He has to hear the words that will keep him safe. Time to rely on my own training of being the one who gets left behind.

"When do you leave?"

Liam grabs my hand. "Right after Aarabelle's birthday."

"Oh, really soon," I say and try to fortify myself behind the wall of indifference. It's been a long time since I've had to deal with deployments.

"I'm sorry."

"For what?" I ask surprised. He didn't do anything wrong. This is the life. It's time I get used to it again because Liam is in for a long time.

He stands and begins to pace. "I know you're not okay about this. Fuck. I'm not happy either."

"Am I happy? No. But it's your life. I understand."

"I think we should go away for a week before I leave. I have stand-down leave before. We can go back to Corolla and just be us."

The picture he paints is something I can't refuse, but I took off work not too long ago. "I don't know. I mean, I have a lot going on." I chew on my nail and battle my own wants. Another trip would be great to be able to just be us again. But I'm trying to move forward in all parts of my life, including working.

"Lee, I think it's important for us to do this before I go."

"We just got back though."

"I know, but I want to spend a week together. Just the three of us. I want to soak up as much time as I can with you and Aarabelle."

The pleading in his eyes makes it almost impossible to resist him.

I stand and put my arms around his waist. "Liam, I'm

not going anywhere. I don't need some trip to reaffirm how much I love you." I wait for him to look at me. "I don't know that I can get away again."

Liam's hands glide down and he grips my thighs, lifting me. I hang on to him as my legs wrap around him. "I'll just steal you."

"I'm not stealable," I joke and make up the word.

"I've already stolen you." He kisses the tip of my nose.

And he has. He knows it too. I don't want to fight tonight, and I think I can talk him out of the trip later on . . . but tonight, I want to be with only him. I don't want to think about babies or deployments. I want to just be us.

"Where's my eggroll?" I ask and he smirks.

"In my pants."

My eyes widen as I try to keep from laughing. "Is it a big one?"

"I'd say so," he retorts with a smile.

"I may have to see for myself."

"I can arrange that."

I press my lips on his and he carries me out of the kitchen. I keep kissing him as he moves with me in his arms. A tiny pang of stage fright hits me again as I realize this will be the first time Liam has ever been in my bed. The bed I shared with my husband.

He slowly lowers me as we get to my door. "I don't have to stay," he somehow reads my mind.

"Don't be stupid. I want you here." I take his hand and open the door. He holds my hand as we enter my bedroom.

There are a lot of memories in this room, but I want to make new ones. I deserve new ones. Corolla was beautiful, but this is where our life is. We need to be a couple in our real life.

Liam holds my hand as I pull him to the bed. I look around at the room and am grateful for my tirade. It allowed it so there aren't any pictures other than of Aarabelle. I didn't want to look at him after I found out about Brittany. I sure as hell don't want to feel like he's looking at me now.

His hand holds my face as he slowly inches close before he kisses me. I lie back on the bed and pull him on top of me. Pushing the beanie off his head, my fingers slide through his hair. The scruff I love so much is back and it scratches my neck as he begins to move his mouth there. I could fall apart so easily in his arms. He gives me such comfort and security.

"I hate the idea of leaving you," he says against my skin.

I hate it too, but I focus on the words floating around before speaking them. I have to tread carefully before I say things. I'm in the tiptoe stage where I have to guard his heart and my own.

"It'll be okay."

Of course I don't know that. Our lives are constantly hanging on a precipice, ready to tip over the edge and shatter. He could die at any point. I could decide it's too much stress. But if we can love each other enough, we have a chance.

Liam pulls my shirt over my head and holds me close. It's like he's holding on to more than just this moment. Unease begins to build and I start to question what we're doing. If he's dreading it already, do we even have a chance?

His lips trail down my collarbone and I try to alleviate my worries. I want to stay in the moment with him. Give myself over and let him take me from my own mind.

"Stay with me," he orders in his deep, husky voice.

I close my eyes as his mouth wraps around my nipple. He sucks and nips at it as I writhe beneath him. His hand travels down my body beneath my shorts. He moves slowly, and I catalog each movement he makes. The way his finger brushes against my hip. Each swipe across my clit as he toys with me.

Liam strips me of my defenses so I'm open and exposed to him. He can see through my layers of bullshit and straight to my heart. "Liam, kiss me." I want to hide back behind my walls.

"Let me love you. Let me in." His voice leaves no room for question. He knows I'm scared. He knows me. I close my eyes and he pushes his finger inside me. "I've got you. I won't let you fall."

"Feels so good," I moan as he uses his thumb against my clit.

Suddenly his hand retreats and I'm left feeling empty. My eyes fly open and I whimper. He gazes at me as he removes his clothes.

I sit up and push his hands away, "Let me."

My fingers gently pull at his shirt. I go slow, savoring him and knowing what lies beneath his clothing. A man too beautiful for words. I trail down his now bare chest and use my nails to scrape at his skin. He hisses as I run my finger across his stomach.

"No other man has my heart," I murmur. "No other man has my body." My eyes lock on his as I remove his pants. They slide down and he moves me back beneath him.

"And no other man will ever have them again."

His lips crash against mine and his tongue presses into my mouth. I kiss him with everything I am. He commands my body and I allow him. Liam is claiming me and I'm claiming him. We are each other's and no matter what happens, I can't go back.

I don't want to go back.

He pulls my pants off completely and hovers above me.

"I love you." My voice is strong and I need him to know. "I'm yours."

He enters me in one push and I nearly cry out from the feeling. His eyes stay trained on mine and he rears back and slowly pushes forward.

"Liam!" I cry out as emotions and physical sensations become too much.

"No other man will be inside of you," he says aloud but I can't tell if he's trying to convince himself or me.

"No one . . . only you," I say.

"No other woman will have my heart," Liam assures me. "No one else ever had my heart. Only you, Natalie." His eyes close as he slides back and forth.

From the words and the feelings, it's too much. Liam has stolen every resolve I had to keep something for myself. He knows what I need and he gives it to me. With his body and with his words.

I soar high as he flips me onto my stomach. His hand wraps around and he applies pressure on the bundle of nerves. He pounds me from behind as I push back against him. I need him to lose it. I want to drive him so hard that he can't think of anything but how good this feels.

"Fuck me," I cry out as I push myself back to meet his thrusts.

He nearly loses it as he grips the back of my neck and the sound of skin slapping overtakes the room. Heavy breathing, moaning, and our love making echoes. I close my eyes as he grips me tight and fucks me relentlessly. It's heaven and hell. I fight my orgasm off, as I want to go over the edge together.

"Let go, goddamnit," he says angrily. "Let me feel you lose it."

He swirls his hips and circles my clit and I'm gone.

I moan and let myself go. Liam kisses my back and follows me over the edge a minute later. I fall flat on the bed, sated and exhausted.

"You're incredible," Liam says as he rubs my back.

I roll over and smile lazily. "You're pretty incredible yourself. I'll be right back."

I sit up and head into the bathroom. I wrap my robe around me and look at the left side of the sink. Aaron's old razor and toothbrush. They've been a part of the house and I forgot to get rid of them. I pick them up and hold them in my hand. I don't feel anything though. No sadness, no anger just resignation.

Liam opens the door and sees me. He looks at my hand and then closes the door.

"Liam!" I call out and rush toward him.

"I'm going to go."

"No! Please, it's not like that," I try to explain. I wasn't mourning or anything, I saw it and picked it up. "Please, stop. Let me explain."

He's throwing his clothes on and tears start to form in my eyes. "I'm sorry. I need to go."

"Stop!" I cry out and he turns. "I wasn't upset. I wasn't crying over his razor. I just saw it and I don't know . . . I picked it up. It wasn't like that."

"What was it like?" He looks away, but I see the hurt in his eyes.

"I don't know. I can't explain it."

Liam grabs my hand and I look up. "Try."

"I saw it there, but I didn't feel anything. I won't feel bad though. You can't expect me to be so unfeeling. You're the first man to be in my bed other than him. You have to have some sympathy for that." I wait for him to fully register what I've said.

"You think I don't have sympathy for what you feel? You're fucking kidding me. I've never said a word, but I'm fighting a damn ghost." Liam's words are sharp and he's clearly upset.

"You're fighting something on your own. I've never made you feel that way."

His eyes meet mine before he turns away again. "Maybe not, but seeing you with that razor. Clutching it to your chest wasn't my imagination."

"You have two choices," I say determined to end this, because he's making it something it's not. "You can either trust me when I say you have nothing to worry about or you can leave."

"So easy for you?"

"Don't." I say with no room for an argument. "Don't you dare make this my fault. This is all you."

Liam steps toward the door and my heart sinks. His hand rests on the doorknob and he turns to me. "I just need a minute. I'll be right back."

I nod, understanding. "I can handle a minute."

He steps toward me, and in an instant, I'm in his arms. He holds me close and breathes me in. "It'll never be more than that," he vows and then releases me.

I climb into bed and wait for his minute to pass.

chapter

thirty-seven

"NO, MOM, I hear you," I say while trying to put the food we need for Corolla in the bag. I figure if we're going for a week, we should pack what we can.

"Are you going to be back in time for her party?" she asks.

She's flying in three days before Aarabelle's birthday party to help. The flight from Arkansas isn't cheap, and no matter how many times I explain I'll be back a full week beforehand, she isn't grasping it.

"Mom, everything will be fine. It's a two-hour drive and Liam has to be back to work after that anyway."

"I'm ecstatic you guys are going away again," she admits. My mother has been extremely supportive of my relationship with Liam. She's always loved him and knowing how great he is with Aarabelle is enough for her.

"Liam pretty much demanded it. I feel like shit taking off work again, but I'm going to do some stuff from there. I think it's important though."

I'm really looking forward to the trip. After about a week of arguing with him on how I didn't think it was fair to request time off again, Liam made a valid point. I work with a team of former SEALs. All of them have had deployments and work ups, they all know what it's like to be the one leaving and wouldn't begrudge me a chance to spend the time with him.

Of course Mark gave me no argument and said he didn't even need to run it by Jackson. I still felt guilty and almost hoped they would say no.

"Well, I can't wait to see you and that beautiful grand-daughter of mine."

"We can't wait to see you either. I'll call you when I get back from Corolla." I grab some snacks to throw in the bag. We leave in three days and at least this time I've had time to pack.

"Okay, have fun. Love you."

We disconnect and I hear a car pull in the drive. The purr of the loud engine lets me know it's Robin. Great, now he even has me calling the stupid car by its name. I head out toward the deck to see why Liam's here. He told me he was super busy with training before the leave periods start.

"Hey," I say, pulling the blanket I grabbed off the couch around my shoulders.

"Hey, sorry I only had a few minutes and I figured you'd rather hear it from me." Liam looks pissed and de-termined. He pulls the brim of his uniform cover lower, so I can't see his eyes.

"Okay? What's wrong?"

He kicks his foot and I can already tell I'm not going to be happy. "I'm leaving tonight."

"What?" I exclaim.

"I have to head out for a few days. We have a mission and they need us to go."

"But your leave starts tomorrow. We were leaving for Corolla," I say and pull the blanket tighter.

He looks up and I see the resolution. He doesn't have

a choice. "I know. I'll try to be back . . . they said it's a day or two. If we can't leave on Friday, we'll go as soon as I get back."

"I'm not taking off more time. I was having trouble with taking the five days."

Liam steps forward and places his hands on my shoulders. "I know. I'm not happy either, but I have to go. It's a small team of guys."

"And you can't give it to the other chief?" I ask, knowing he couldn't.

Life of a military girlfriend. Job comes first and we come second.

"Natalie," he says my name and he grips tight. "I *have* to be the one to go."

"Okay, I mean, I don't have a choice. I hate this. I'm pissed, but it is what it is."

Liam pulls me close and his lips press against mine. He holds me tight against his body and keeps his mouth fused to mine. This kiss is desperate as if he's memorizing me. His hands hold like vises around my arms. He doesn't let up and I can't help but think how this feels like goodbye. It's like that kiss where you're not sure you'll ever have another one. I fight the urge to cry because I feel it in the tips of my toes. It's hurting and I try to break away, but Liam keeps me against him.

Finally, he pulls back. My breath is coming in short bursts. "What was that?" I ask.

"I'll see you as soon as I can. I'll try to make it back before we were supposed to leave." He brushes his hand across my cheek.

"Liam," I try to stop him but he keeps going. "Liam! Stop!" I start to jog after him and he stops. "You can't kiss me like it was our last and then leave like that." I hold my arms across my chest and he turns and looks at me.

"I've never had to leave someone behind. I don't know how this works," he explains.

I haven't thought about how this would be for him. He's been single.

I step forward and wrap my arms around his stomach. "Well," I say sweetly, "You tell me you love me and that you'll see me soon. You kiss me tenderly and feel free to tell me how every minute you're away from me will suck." I grin and Liam's arms encase me.

"Oh, is that all?" he relaxes a little.

"Well, any compliments will work."

"How about this . . . every second I'm away from you I'll feel like my heart is missing."

"You can do better . . ." I smirk.

He looks behind me and chuckles, "I will think of you every moment of every second."

"Better, but I could use a little swooning."

"Oh, Natalie, love of my life . . . I will hold my breath until I can breathe the same air as you and even then it will not be good enough because my lungs will be dead."

I laugh and pull him close. "Now you're just being silly."

"I love you."

"I love you, more," I say and lift up on my toes and kiss him. "Hurry back."

He doesn't say another word and releases me. I stand here and watch him get in his car. The sound of the engine makes me jump and I fight the tears. I won't let him see me cry. He waves and I wave back as he drives out of sight.

I can do this. He'll be back. I can handle it.

DAYS PASS AND I don't hear from him. I should be in Corolla right now, but instead I'm working from home while Aarabelle is at the sitter. I hate not being able to hear his voice. The training missions were different because he would call.

Instead, now I sit and wonder. I worry that I'm going to turn on the news and see something has happened.

God, I didn't miss this part.

I head out to the deck to get some sun. It's still funny to me how we take this view for granted. I stare out at the horizon and get lost in my thoughts. My life is in a wonderful place. I have a beautiful daughter who makes my life worth living, a man who loves me and who I love, and a great job.

My family will be here soon and then they can all see just how great things are. Faith works in mysterious ways. A year ago, I was unwilling to think I could be here. I thought I was destined to live alone and sad.

I stand here looking out at the ocean, feeling a sense of serenity until I hear the sound of a car pulling into the driveway and I turn. The smile is instantaneous. He's home. I need to lay eyes on him. I want to kiss him and hug him.

I rush down the driveway and see Jackson and Mark walking up first. They look at the ground and walk slowly as if they're about to destroy my world.

No.

No.

Not again.

No.

My heart falters as they approach without looking at

me. "No!" I scream out and begin to step backwards. "I can't." I begin to shake, but Mark moves to the side and I see Liam.

He's okay. "Oh my God, you're okay!" I scream and rush toward him with tears falling. "I was so scared!" I begin to run and then Liam puts his hand up to stop me.

My feet don't move as Liam approaches, but doesn't say a word. He just looks at me with so much pain in his eyes, I'm afraid he's going to break.

Oh, please tell me they didn't lose someone.

"Liam?" I ask hesitantly and take his face in my hands. "What's wrong?" I feel his scruff against my palm and lean in to kiss him, but he jerks back slightly. I stare at him with wide eyes trying to figure out why he's so forlorn. "Hey," I say again. Still, he doesn't speak.

He closes his eyes while pulling my hands from his face. My fingers fall as he steps to the side, and then I see him.

"Aaron?" my voice shakes.

My chest heaves and I stare at his dark brown eyes and long hair. My husband . . . Oh, God.

Aaron steps toward me and my heart stops beating.

"Hi, baby."

TO BE CONTINUED . . .

books by

corinne michaels

the Belonging Duet

Beloved (Book One)
Beholden (Book Two)

the Consolation Duet

Consolation
Conviction ~ Coming May 27th

cknowledgements

OU'D THINK BY the third time I'd have this down pat, however, it still is the hardest part. If I forget you, I'm sure I'll hear about it but know I love you.

My betas: Mandi, Jennifer, Melissa, Holly, Roxana, Megan, & Linda—I love you all and I couldn't do this without you. Each time I send you the mini cliffhangers you come back for more. I love torturing you and making you smile. Thank you for your friendship!

Christy Peckham: I couldn't do this without you. You put up with all my crazy and still stick around. I'm so blessed to have you in my life and I don't take that for granted. You make me smile when I want to cry, laugh when I'm already crying, and if I'm really gone, you get me pissed which helps. I love you!

Melissa & Sharon: Melissa, thank you for not wanting to kill me or at least not actually doing it. I'm blessed to have a publicist like you. Every author should be so lucky as to work with you. Sharon, oh my love! You make me laugh and keep me anchored. Love you both Maleficent & Satan.

Claire Contreras: They say people come into your life for a reason . . . I think it was to teach me the kind of woman I want to be. Your strength is astounding, your friendship never wavers and each day I'm grateful to know you. Love you to the moon!

FYW: You're the first place I go, the last place I go, and my in between. I'm so blessed to know such a fantastic group of women. You're all fun, beautiful and Funk-y and I love you.

Bloggers: Without you, our books would never get seen. Thank you for taking the time to read and review, promote tirelessly, and for all your love and support.

Stabby Birds: You girls are my rocks. I couldn't imagine a place without each of you.

Corinne Michaels Book Group: You guys are so much fun. Thank you for loving me and all my crazy. You truly make me smile each day I come in to check on the group. The words of encouragement and friendship overwhelm me each day.

My test readers: Thank you for dropping whatever you are reading to let me know how you feel. You can't imagine how much I appreciate you.

A huge thank you to my editor, formatter, proofreader, and cover designer for making this book all that it is.

Thank you, The Rockstars of Romance, for hosting everything for Consolation. I love you girl so much!

Lauren Perry: Ahhhh thank you for finding Ben and Hannah! Your photos are the reason this book isn't a standalone. Your art inspired me to make this story so much more than I planned. Thank you!

Rinny, Melanie, Krissy: We've been friends since we were babies it seems like. We've had bad boyfriends, weddings, love, hate, friendship, sisterhood, and babies. Through it all, we've kept our friendship strong and it doesn't matter that we go months without uttering a word. If I called tomorrow, I know you'd be here. It's a friendship many will never be fortunate to experience. I love you so much.

Crystal: Even when we bring out the most hostile parts of each other, we are able to find our friendship. I think it's something special and unique that, no matter how ugly it gets, we see the beauty. Thank you for loaning me your husband to kill off. It was fun and we should totalllllly do it again!

Lucia Franco: Without your convo this book would've never happened. Thank you for cheering me on and being as excited as I was.

Tammi Ahmed: You are a graphic queen! Thank you for making me such beautiful art! I love every creation you come up with.

My children: You two have no idea the depths of my love for you. Thank you for my great big hugs, my fun snuggles, and making me remember there's more to life than books. You are my world.

My husband: I met you when I wasn't sure who I was. You loved me and helped me become the woman I am today. I may want to smack you but there's no one else I'd rather build snowmen with.

about the author

CORINNE MICHAELS IS an emotional, witty, sarcastic, and fun loving mom of two beautiful children. She's happily married to the man of her dreams and is a former Navy wife. After spending months away from her husband while he was deployed, reading and writing was her escape from the loneliness.

Both her maternal and paternal grandmothers were librarians, which only intensified her love of reading. After years of writing short stories, she couldn't ignore the call to finish her debut novel, Beloved. Her alpha Navy SEALs are broken, beautiful, and will steal your heart.

connect with corinne

www.corinnemichaels.com

Connect on Facebook
www.facebook.com/CorinneMichaels

Connect on Twitter
https://twitter.com/AuthorCMichaels

Connect on Goodreads

Connect on Instagram
http://instagram.com/authorcorinnemichaels